Room 706

Room 706

ELLIE LEVENSON

Copyright © Ellie Levenson 2026

The right of Ellie Levenson to be identified as the
Author of the Work has been asserted by her in accordance
with the Copyright, Designs and Patents Act 1988.

First published in 2026 by Headline Publishing Group Limited

3

Apart from any use permitted under UK copyright law, this publication may
only be reproduced, stored, or transmitted, in any form, or by any means, with prior
permission in writing of the publishers or, in the case of reprographic production, in
accordance with the terms of licences issued by the Copyright Licensing Agency.

All characters in this publication are fictitious and any resemblance
to real persons, living or dead, is purely coincidental.

Cataloguing in Publication Data is available from the British Library

Hardback ISBN 978 1 0354 2369 9
Trade Paperback ISBN 978 1 0354 2365 1

Typeset in Sabon by CC Book Production

Printed and bound in Great Britain by Clays Ltd, Elcograf S.p.A.

Headline's policy is to use papers that are natural, renewable and
recyclable products and made from wood grown in sustainable forests.
The logging and manufacturing processes are expected to conform to
the environmental regulations of the country of origin.

Headline Publishing Group Limited
An Hachette UK Company
Carmelite House
50 Victoria Embankment
London EC4Y 0DZ

The authorised representative in the EEA is Hachette Ireland,
8 Castlecourt Centre, Dublin 15, D15 XTP3, Ireland
(email: info@hbgi.ie)

www.headline.co.uk
www.hachette.co.uk

*This is the way the world ends
Not with a bang but a whimper.*

'The Hollow Men' by T. S. Eliot

Sonder: *n.* the realization that each random passerby is living a life as vivid and complex as your own – populated with their own ambitions, friends, routines, worries and inherited craziness – an epic story that continues invisibly around you like an anthill sprawling deep underground, with elaborate passageways to thousands of other lives that you'll never know existed, in which you might appear only once, as an extra sipping coffee in the background, as a blur of traffic passing on the highway, as a lighted window at dusk.

The Dictionary of Obscure Sorrows by John Koenig

Chapter 1

1.05pm
Room 706

Kate sat back in the hotel armchair. The clock on the built-in bedside shelf showed it was just after 1pm, which meant she had about an hour until she had to leave. In front of the chair was a small footstool in the same fabric, the room-service menu on top. She kicked the menu onto the floor and stretched out her legs, feeling the pull in her calves as she extended her toes back towards her body, their chipped burgundy polish shining with the reflection from the wall lights, her bare thighs pressed together by the narrow width of the chair. Her cheeks felt flushed. She could hear the shower in the bathroom and knew that James would be carefully washing any hint of her away. He'd have brought his own shower gel in a small leather washbag, something masculine. She imagined he'd be easy to buy presents for. He'd like gentlemanly things – wooden boxes, leather folders, cufflinks.

Kate didn't bring her own shower gel when they met. She liked to use the hotel toiletries. She had grown to love hotels over the past few years, with their touches of corporate thoughtfulness. She even enjoyed the three-star anonymous places they mostly used, with signs in the lobby for corporate away days and seminars such as 'Authentic management: Eden Suite'. Today though, they were in a nicer hotel, just one block back from the River Thames.

James was the one who always booked the hotel. Kate knew that he usually did this through a website that specialised in day rates for otherwise unoccupied rooms. She didn't know what it was called, though she always thought of it as fuck.com. Occasionally the site threw up good deals on slightly fancier well-located hotels like this one, the kind that attracted tourists and couples in London for a mini break from other parts of the country, as well as business visitors with expense accounts.

Other than the sex, the complimentary toiletries were the best part. Had Kate been on a business trip she'd have felt obligated to sweep the small bottles into her bag to take home for Annie, whose collection, mostly courtesy of Vic, rarely made it to the bathroom but were key in her daughter's favourite game of 'science lab', being lined up in size or colour order again and again and mixed into various potions.

But as Kate was not on a business trip and could not take anything home to show that she had been in a hotel, she'd have the pleasure of using every last drop of the body wash

Room 706

and shampoo and lotion in the mini bottles herself, taking her time, maybe even washing her hair twice to use it all.

It's why she didn't mind that James always showered first and then left. His diary rarely gave him more than a couple of hours free. When he was gone, she'd take time to enjoy the peace. She'd have her bath, or shower if there wasn't one, then a short lie down on the bed to lazily relive all they had just done, sometimes even bringing herself to climax again, with an alarm set to ensure she was awake to get back in time to pick up the kids from school. Not that she ever did more than doze after sex with James. He left her exhausted, but wide awake at the same time.

Kate felt a bit exposed sitting naked on the armchair. She was, after six years of doing this every few months, physically relaxed with James, uninhibited during sex and comfortable with her body. But afterwards, once he was dressed and had snapped back into formal mode, she started to become self-conscious about her nudity.

She grabbed a big cushion from the floor. There were so many of them. They'd thrown them all from the bed shortly after she'd arrived in the room. The cushion covers were designed especially for the hotel chain, the logo printed onto the front of each one in a font made to look like embroidery. She hugged it to her body, and it did the job of mostly covering her. Now that they were not focused on each other's pleasure, Kate could hear the sounds of the city through the thick hotel windows, the constant whirrs and buzzes of helicopters and sirens.

James poked his head round the bathroom door. He was vigorously towelling himself, his body practically dry but water glinting on his dark grey cropped hair. She wanted to reach out and touch him again, but touching after he had washed was not what they did. When they left the room they left every trace of each other behind.

'Everything okay?' he asked. Kate smiled and nodded, and he disappeared back into the bathroom.

On the desk next to the armchair was a remote control and, in front of an old-fashioned telephone, a small box with a Union Jack design. Next to that was a hotel-branded notepad and a pen. She picked up the box and opened it. Inside was a handwritten note purporting to be from the manager. *To our valued guests – a thank you for staying with us.* Underneath the note were two chocolate truffles. She picked one up and bit into it then reached for the remote control and pointed it at the television mounted on the wall above the desk.

It had been on for a couple of minutes, sound low, showing a twenty-four-hour news channel, but she'd mostly been ignoring it, enjoying the post orgasm buzz. Later, on the way home, she might start to feel a little guilty and have to work on appearing normal when she picked up the kids and re-entered family life, but right now she couldn't keep her smile in. She finished the chocolate she had started, stretched out her legs again and settled back in the chair. She could hear James in the bathroom brushing his teeth.

A couple of words from the news report grabbed her attention. 'London' and 'hotel' she thought she'd heard them say. Whatever the words were, they were enough to make her get up and focus on the screen.

'Oh fuck!'

Chapter 2

Earlier that morning

If this morning had been ten years ago, before she had children to get to places in the right clothes at the right time with the right lunch, Kate may have taken far longer getting dressed and preparing herself for the day to come. But she had no time for that today. There was time to get her nice shower gel from the bathroom cabinet and use that instead of the sweet watermelon and pineapple smelling gunk that came out of a mermaid shaped bottle in a slick of pale pink, and that was all. She kept her hair dry with a shower cap that looked as if it belonged to a character in a Victorian book of illustrated tales. She knew she'd be washing it that afternoon anyway.

'We need more rolls,' Vic said as Kate came into the kitchen, handing her a mug of tea that said *World's Best*

Papa on it. 'There were enough for today's lunches, but none for tomorrow.' Kate nodded at him in acknowledgement. She didn't know why her kids had a pathological hatred of sandwiches yet were happy to eat rolls.

'What's on your agenda today?' Vic asked.

'I'm interviewing a psychologist for a piece I am writing for the magazine. An article about sleep and mental health.'

'Where are you meeting, somewhere fancy?'

'I need to look up where exactly,' Kate said lightly. 'But nowhere special. A coffee place near Waterloo, I think.'

The lies came easily.

'You didn't want to do it virtually?' Vic asked. He knew how much she liked working from home when she could, relishing the luxury of a quiet house.

Kate shrugged in reply. She liked to stay as near as possible to the truth.

'They're in London for the day so I thought I'd do it in person. This is yours by the way.' Kate held up the mug. The kids had bought it for Father's Day a couple of years ago. Well, Kate had. She'd been thrilled to see it in a gift shop at London Bridge, a Papa amongst the Dads and Fathers and Daddies.

'I love you enough to let you use it,' Vic said over his shoulder as he headed upstairs for his own shower.

Kate grabbed the kids' lunch bags and loaded them with the cheese rolls Vic had made. He'd put out crisps and a yoghurt for each kid too, though he'd forgotten that Annie only liked raspberry ones. Making the substitution, she added them, along with an apple each, and filled their water bottles.

Then she quickly chopped some carrots and potatoes, got

Room 706

the pouch of ready-made stock and the chicken thighs from the fridge, and threw them all in the slow cooker. She added a handful of pearl barley. It was the last of it. She opened the shopping list on her phone and added pearl barley and bread rolls, underneath toilet roll and ketchup. The chicken was meant to be fried over first, but there was no time for that and she really didn't want to smell of oil. Besides, this dinner was just for them – it didn't have to be perfect.

It took more time to find matching socks for each kid in the clean washing pile than it did to do anything else that morning. She felt hot and bothered by the time she had found some, let alone coaxed them on to wriggling feet.

'Nearly time to go,' Kate shouted from the kitchen, where she tweezed a stray eyebrow hair that had appeared overnight, using the mirror stuck to the inside of the plate cupboard and tweezers from the medical kit. She let the words go ahead of her to the living room where the kids were at either end of the sofa, sitting with their feet flat against each other and watching a video of a family in the American Midwest getting ready for their own school day.

'Teeth. Shoes.'

'We can't, Mummy. Ashleigh hasn't finished eating her golden nuggets,' Annie said.

'Which one is Ashleigh?' Kate asked.

'The girl.'

On the screen a redheaded girl, aged about ten and wearing a baseball cap and dungarees, spooned cereal into her mouth. Kate moved the kids' legs and sat in between them, pulling each foot towards her to push on their shoes.

'Ashleigh is going to be late for school then, isn't she?'

'Oh Mummy, this one is from months ago.' Annie looked at her with pity.

The kids loved this family, watching their videos religiously. Five sons and a daughter, all perfectly behaved, all putting their own shoes on and with parents who had a weekly date night and wore matching pyjamas.

'Anyway, Ashleigh doesn't go to school.'

'She doesn't?'

'No, her Mummy and Papa teach her at home and every afternoon they go to the woods for outside school. Can we do that?'

'No. There are no woods near here. And I have already taught you everything I know.'

'Everything?' Annie looked doubtful.

'Yes.'

'But I am only seven.'

'I know.'

Annie was quiet for a few moments before speaking again. 'Mummy, I miss Fluffy.'

'I know, darling. But you'll see him again this evening. We're going to walk home from school via the surgery and pick him up.'

Fluffy was Annie's rabbit, named by her when he was a small ball of fluff. He'd arrived on Annie's fifth birthday, even though he very much was not a birthday present. 'Pets are not meant to be gifts for birthdays or Christmas,' Kate and Vic had stressed to her. 'Pets are big commitments, not just a temporary plaything. It's entirely a coincidence that

Room 706

the rabbit we have been thinking about getting, and that you so desperately wanted, has come to live with us on your birthday.' Rabbit accessories were appropriate birthday presents however, and they'd wrapped the hutch and feeding bowls alongside Annie's other gifts.

He was at the vet for investigations into recurrent urine infections. Given Fluffy had been mostly ignored by Annie since he'd nipped her finger some months ago, Kate was a little surprised that she had even noticed he wasn't there.

It was a good morning. No one shouted. No one had a breakdown over wanting a jumper when they had been given a cardigan. No one refused breakfast, although not much of Lenny's cereal had been eaten, Kate noticed, as she spooned the cement-like leftovers into the bin and opened the dishwasher. Nine-year-old Lenny seemed to go through stages when it came to food. Some days he would practically eat them out of house and home, polishing off two bowls of cereal and some toast, then sneaking in some biscuits before leaving the house. Other days he ate practically nothing. Kate didn't want breakfast herself today either. Her stomach was too jittery for that.

The dishwasher was full of clean items. Kate shut it again and put the bowl in the sink, giving it a cursory rinse before yelling up the stairs to Vic that she'd see him later.

Vic worked for a literature charity that linked up businesses who had money to buy books with schools that needed them. It was a long way from his former life in financial services, but he liked the calm office environment and the feeling of doing good in the world. They got free children's books too – the kids' shelves were overflowing with them. He usually went to work earlier than this, but today he had the dentist at 10am.

The walk to school was easy enough. Although it was November, it was not particularly cold. Lenny and Annie skipped ahead, leaving Kate to walk ten metres behind them. She occasionally shouted 'Wait at the road' to the backs of their heads, though they knew that and waited anyway before racing ahead again once they got to the other side.

And then kisses, on top of his head for Lenny, who had started to reject public displays of his mother's affection, and on the lips for Annie, who still demanded them. Then 'I love you' to each, and a wave, and they ran through the gate.

Kate walked purposefully away from the school. If she slowed down, even a little, someone would try to engage her in conversation with an enquiry about whether she had volunteered for a forthcoming school trip or questions about what they were up to on the weekend or moans about teachers' errors on the kids' homework sheets. She wrapped her scarf tight, nodded at the other parents walking towards the gate with their own kids, and strode off. Only then did she realise that Vic's appointment was late enough that he could have taken them. She swallowed down her irritation at the thought of him having a leisurely morning, perhaps taking the time to trim his beard and then have a quiet coffee while he listened to a podcast. She had no right to be annoyed, given what she was on her way to do, but still it rankled.

Room 706

It was a ten-minute brisk walk to get from school to the station and a further half an hour on the train for Kate to get into central London from their unfashionable suburb. She usually liked to read on the train, but today she didn't feel able to concentrate enough to do anything. Once at Waterloo she had forty-five minutes until she was due to meet James.

She popped into the mini supermarket in the station to look for rolls, but they had none left except ones with seeds on top, and no way would Annie eat those. Kate took out her phone and messaged Vic. *Can only see rolls Annie would deem yuk. Can you buy some?* He gave the message a thumbs up, but she knew he'd probably just pick up a pack at the corner shop near their house on his way home. They weren't fresh and Kate shuddered at the list of additives on the back of the packet. Surely there shouldn't be food colouring in bread rolls. She set an alarm to remind her to pick up some nice ones later.

She bought a chicken wrap to keep for her lunch. She was always starving after sex. Lenny had a playdate with his friend Henry arranged for after school, but she should get something as a snack for Annie. She eyed a box of flapjacks and some grapes, but didn't buy them. Turning up to the hotel room with lots of shopping felt too much like her domestic life encroaching on this other area. She'd get them on the way home.

Kate headed to the high-street chemist that was also on the concourse. This bit always made her feel nervous. She tried to walk in as if she was just buying some shampoo or make-up remover, found the aisle still quaintly called 'family planning', and picked up a packet of condoms and a tube of lubricant. Kate didn't think it was possible to buy condoms and not feel like a teenage girl. To her relief there was one three-pack of condoms left among the larger packets – she hated spending money on something she'd just throw away in the hotel. All the condom packets were in plastic cases with security tags, which meant she had to go up to the cashier to buy them rather than use the self-serve till.

I am a grown woman, she said internally, on repeat, until the transaction was over. I am a grown woman. I am a grown woman.

Away from the station and sitting in a coffee shop on the ground floor of an office block opposite the hotel, Kate nursed her cappuccino. She could see the doors to the hotel foyer from her table by the window, mini palm trees in giant plant pots either side of the revolving doors, a doorman dressed, rather improbably, in a red waist-length jacket with gold braiding, a luggage trolley by his side. Two youngish people with large backpacks were about to try the revolving doors and Kate watched as the doorman gestured at them to use the outwards opening door to the hotel's Martini bar, a few metres to the right, as they waved away his offer of help with their bags.

She'd been to this hotel once before, attending a conference for women in the media, and knew the first and second floors were meeting rooms. She'd never been to the bedrooms though.

James was going to get there at 10.30am and then he'd message her the room number and she would go up and join him, that was how they usually did it. Her phone pinged exactly on time. Kate stood up, drained her coffee cup, popped a mint from her bag into her mouth, took her coat from the back of her chair and then looked at the message. *Running late, there by 11.* She sighed then sat back down and pulled out her laptop.

She tried to use the extra time to do some background reading for her interview with the psychologist. She really was interviewing her, that bit had not been a lie. It was going to be tomorrow though, by phone, and she still had prep to do. It was such a luxury to dive deeply into fascinating subjects. It's why she had leapt at the chance to work as a contributing editor for *Hidden Depths*, shortly after she returned to work from her maternity leave with Annie. Somewhere between a glossy magazine and an academic journal, the tagline was *For women who are clever but tired*. In this role Kate mentored some of the younger journalists, represented the magazine at various industry conferences and wrote one long piece every second issue. It fitted perfectly around school drop-offs and pick-ups, allowing her to mostly work from home.

It was hard to concentrate on the paper about sleep meditation apps while also feeling tight with expectation, half an eye on the hotel entrance. James must have slipped in while she was distracted, because she was taken by surprise when her phone pinged again. *Room 706.*

Chapter 3

1.07pm
Room 706

James must have heard Kate exclaim from the bathroom. He walked into the bedroom holding a towel around his torso with one hand and his toothbrush in the other. 'I'm running you a bath.' He followed Kate's eyes to the television and dropped both.

'Fuck!' she said again.

They both stared at the screen.

She felt as if she was on the descent of a huge rollercoaster, her internal organs all rising up ready to be vomited out. Kate breathed deeply. This must be some kind of joke. An emergency planning exercise or something.

'Is that definitely us?' James moved closer to the television, looking closely at the screen.

Room 706

'I think so,' she said, dropping the cushion and walking naked over to her bag, discarded by the door. She reached inside for her phone. The news alert on the lock screen said *Major incident in London hotel*. Kate felt sick. She could taste the chocolate she'd just eaten. It took two attempts to unlock her phone, her shaking hands touching the wrong buttons the first time. A breaking news story was topped with a photo of their hotel, clearly showing the entrance with giant plant pots and the pink lights of the martini bar. She'd spent long enough looking at it while waiting for James that morning to know without any doubt. And, in front of the building, a cordon and dozens of flashing blue lights.

Kate read rapidly. *A major incident has been declared at a hotel in central London after reports come in that gunmen have taken over the building. More to follow on this breaking story.* Her stomach flipped. This was real.

She showed her phone to James, who was using his own to look at a different news site that was using the same picture.

'It might not be here,' James said. 'It could be any hotel, they all look the same. It could just be a stock photo. We'd have heard noises if something like this happened here.'

'Would we? We're seven floors up.'

Kate looked at the television again. The live footage zoomed in for a moment on the hotel's exterior and again she saw the mini palm trees.

'It's here,' she said. 'I'm certain.'

Along the bottom of the screen a ticker-tape caption

appeared: *Gunmen take over central London hotel. Hundreds trapped inside. Casualties reported.*

Kate was pacing, moving her attention from her phone to the television and back again. She could feel her heart hammering. Breathe, she told herself, just breathe.

'Fuck, James, fuck. What are we going to do? This can't be happening. Maybe journalists are just exaggerating the whole thing because it's a slow news day. It's probably one small incident in the lobby or in front of the hotel and it's been made into something big.' She sounded unconvincing, even to herself. 'Maybe we should just get out of here now. It'll take ages to get home if they've closed off streets and stations. Do you think we can just leave, find the back door or something?' Kate finished, her voice tailing off even before she had finished speaking.

She caught a glimpse of her naked body in the mirror. Her dress was in a heap on the floor next to the bed and she picked it up. She was sticky with sweat, bodily fluids and lubricant, but pulled it on over her head regardless.

The ticker tape on the television continued: *Major incident declared. More information as we have it.*

James was looking at a diagram in a frame by the door, the fire-escape plan. It showed the rooms on their floor and the nearest exits. Kate went to stand next to him, studying it too. The hotel was rectangular with a corridor along each side, the building wrapping around a central courtyard which housed the garden and terrace bar. Rooms such as theirs had windows facing the streets around the hotel. Rooms on the other side of the corridor looked over the outside space and across to the rooms opposite.

The lifts and stairs formed lobby areas in the middle of both the front and back corridors, with service lifts and another flight of stairs in each of the back corners.

James pointed to them on the plan. 'We'd have to get to one of these,' he said, 'then I guess it's down to the lobby or up to the roof.'

'That relies on there being no people with guns guarding the exits,' said Kate. 'Shit, James, that's not really a risk I want to take right now.'

'No, quite.'

'Is that really it?' said Kate. 'Are they the only options?' Her arms and legs felt tingly, spreading to her head. She thought she might faint. She moved to the main part of the room and steadied herself on the desk, looking again at the television where they were filling time with a map of central London. The location of their hotel was circled on the screen.

'I'm not moving. They could be in the corridor outside,' Kate said. 'We don't have enough information yet.'

'Then turn the bloody sound down,' James snapped, joining her.

Of course. She hadn't thought of that. She hadn't had a chance to think at all yet. The noise of a television would be a giveaway to anyone looking for occupied rooms. She found the remote control on the desk and pressed the mute button.

'Sorry.'

'Me too.' James took a deep breath and ran his fingers

through his hair. 'Shit, Kate, this is . . .' He left the sentence hanging.

'Yeah,' Kate said.

They said nothing more for a moment. The whirr of the helicopters seemed closer than before. It wasn't helicopters, Kate realised, but bath water running. She went into the bathroom, picking up James's toothbrush and towel as she went, and turned off the taps.

James was staring at the silent television when she returned.

'It is here,' James said. Kate followed his glance to the television, where the name of the hotel was now being shown in the caption on the screen.

She sank onto the bed. 'Fuck, a terrorist attack. This can't be happening. I have kids.'

'We don't know they are terrorists,' James said after a long pause.

'Well who else takes over a hotel with guns?' Kate said.

James was rubbing the sides of his head. 'Maybe it's some kind of robbery gone wrong. Everyone just assumes terrorism don't they, these days. But probability-wise you're much more likely to be caught up in a robbery.'

'Robbery? Of what, cushions?' Kate kicked one of the smaller ones near her feet.

She looked at the silent television again, and took a sharp intake of breath. They had the small caption *Live* on the top left of the screen and now, clearly visible, hanging in the window of one of the second-floor conference rooms of the hotel, was a huge flag, one they both recognised from previous incidents around the world.

Room 706

James rubbed his hand over his forehead and closed his eyes. 'Shit.' Then, 'What floor are we on again?'

'Seven.'

Kate gasped as she remembered something. 'I put the "Do not disturb" sign on the door as I came in.'

James nodded, immediately understanding the implication. Nothing would say room occupied like a 'Do not disturb' sign.

'I'll get it,' he said.

'I don't know. What if there really are people with guns out there?' Kate replied.

'The sign will let them know we're in here anyway,' James said as he walked towards the door, still naked. He listened, then cautiously opened it.

Kate watched him look down the corridor in both directions, then reach to pluck the sign from the door and close it again, holding the handle the whole time, ensuring it did not make a bang. It clicked shut. In any other circumstances his nudity while doing so might be comical.

James turned the lock and hooked the chain across the door, coming back in to sit on the bed. He wiped his forehead with his hand and took a few deliberate slow breaths.

'Did you see anything?' Kate asked.

'No.'

James was focused now, walking around the room, touching the furniture. The desk was built into the wall, as were the shelves that did the job of bedside tables. The bed was too high and wide to be anywhere else in the room. There was nothing that could be used as a barrier except for the chair Kate had been sitting on, and the small footstool. He moved both of these to be against the door. They didn't look as though they'd stop anyone getting in.

Kate did a calculation. According to the fire-escape plan there were eight rooms on each of the shorter corridors and sixteen along the front and back corridors. The hotel had nine floors, with bedrooms from floor three upwards. She did the sum in her head – 336 rooms, each of which may or may not have people in them.

She was brought back to the present when James headed towards the window. Of course that would be an easier way to check things, it should have been the first thing they did. He started to pull back the net curtain covering the window.

'Don't!'

The urgency in her voice stopped him.

'Why not? I doubt they have snipers aimed at every room.'

'No, but we're facing the front. And there will be news cameras covering the whole building. Do you want your cock to be leading the hourly news?'

He nodded at her and started to dress. He put on his pants, his trousers and his shirt. Usually Kate loved the way James wore clothes. They were good clothes, well made. A navy suit with a grey silk lining, a pale blue shirt, a silk tie just the right side of gold to be tasteful. Now they seemed too fine for this situation, an outfit for someone who liked to appear in control, not pacing around a hotel room, unsure what to do.

'Now?'

'Okay.'

Room 706

James carefully pulled the net curtain aside at its edge, and a sword of bright light fell across the room.

Kate peeped over his shoulder. Blue lights were flashing in the reflection of the windows of the building opposite and reflected back from their hotel's windows, backwards and forwards to infinity, millions of blue flashing lights.

Both of her kids had gone through nee-naw phases, like all toddlers, waving at firefighters and mimicking police cars and ambulances. Even now, years after they had moved on to other interests, it was hard not to point them out in the street, not to say, 'Look kids, a nee-naw.' Now there were nee-naws beyond their wildest toddler imaginations. She desperately wanted to be at home cuddling them. Would she ever even get that chance again?

Don't think like that, Kate, she told herself.

She closed her eyes for a few moments and pictured Lenny and Annie, then opened them again and peered at the blue lights.

When Lenny was learning to count he used to say 'One, two, loads'. That's what it felt like now – one, two, loads. Oh, Lenny. Nine years old and exactly how a nine-year-old boy, drawn for a comic, would look. Grubby and messy and smiling and sporty and probably smelling of mud and chocolate, never quite sure whether to grunt or cuddle.

She realised she was holding her breath. Breathe, she told herself. Breathe in, breathe out. She turned away from the blue lights and the net curtains and James. The television was showing the same scene she had just been watching through the window, but from a different angle. She was trying to think, but her brain was not working as well as she would hope. Fuck. This was not good. She stood on the spot trying to keep herself steady. Breathe in, breathe out.

A loud high-pitched beep suddenly started.

'My phone alarm. Bugger. Shit. Sorry.'

'Christ, Kate, turn that thing off,' James hissed. He looked both terrified and furious, as if he'd just been mugged in the street and made the split-second decision to chase his attackers.

'Sorry. I'm sorry. Nearly got it.' The beep was loud and incessant.

She found her phone on the bed and pressed stop. 'Sorry. Sorry.'

The phone was silent now but flashing at her. She'd given the alarm a label: *Leave in one hour*. There was another set to go off in fifty minutes, a ten-minute warning. Kate cancelled that one, switching her phone to silent.

'Shot because you forgot to turn your phone alarm off. Bloody hell.'

'Stop it. You're being a twat.' He looked at her, surprised, as if no one had ever spoken to him like that before.

Maybe they hadn't, Kate thought.

She softened a little. 'I set an alarm so I don't forget to leave. I have to be at the school gate by 3.15pm.'

'You're right, sorry. I'm snapping. This is just . . .' James faltered.

'Just . . .?'

'Not ideal.'

'Uh-huh.'

They both listened. They could hear nothing outside the room.

'It's okay,' James said. 'I can't hear anything.' Kate couldn't either. 'I don't know if that's a good thing or a bad thing,' James said.

'Let's interpret it as a good thing,' Kate replied. If James was going to lose his cool then she'd have to be the calm one.

Think about the things you can change and ignore those you can't. That was the kind of thing her mum used to say. She couldn't change being trapped here in the room with James. But she could sort out the practical things. 3.15pm. That was less than two hours away. She was going to have to tell Vic she couldn't make it to pick up the kids, even if she didn't tell him why. Or perhaps she could just ask another parent to get Annie as Lenny had his playdate with Henry arranged already. Then she wouldn't need to be home until about 6pm. Vic would be home after that, as he'd work late to make up for his dentist visit, so he'd never even need to know anything about today. Surely the police would sort it soon and she'd be home for dinner even if not for school pick-up. The thought of Vic made her breathing ragged again. What would Vic say if he knew where she was, who she was with? She pictured his face and her eyes prickled with tears. She couldn't bear for him to think of her like this. Kate closed her eyes and counted to ten in her head, trying to get her breathing under control, then opened them again.

Right on cue, as if Vic could sense her thinking his name, her phone silently flashed with a message from him. *Seems to be a huge incident in central London. You ok?*

Kate stared at the screen. She didn't reply.

Chapter 4

Sixteen years earlier
Italy

Kate and Vic stepped through the doors onto a narrow street and then stopped, shyly looking at each other, slowly breathing in the warm air. Rome was hot, even for Rome. They had been strangers just a few hours ago, until Vic had sat next to her in the otherwise empty cinema, and they had talked the whole way through the film.

After what seemed like an eternity, Vic opened his mouth as if to speak, then shut it. Kate held her breath, willing him to suggest a drink. He was the first person she'd had a conversation with in days and she wasn't ready to go back alone to her stifling room in a residence where she knew no one.

He opened his mouth again and spoke this time. 'Can I buy you an ice cream?'

She breathed out. Hopefully she didn't seem too desperate. Kate could see the shape of him now that they were standing, and in the light of the street she took him in properly. He was tall but not imposing, broad-shouldered and open. He was wearing a patterned shirt that was casual without being too loud, the top buttons undone so that the hairs on his chest were visible. He looked like a man, when all she had known before were boys.

'But you're a stranger,' she said. It had sounded flirtatious in her head. Now it sounded accusatory.

'Not technically,' he replied. 'I was, a few hours ago, but we've been speaking since then. We're practically old friends now.'

That was true. She knew more about him than she knew about most people, and more about him than she knew about anyone else in Italy.

They had been the only two in the cinema but the ticketing system had given them seats next to each other. Ten minutes into the film, which was arty and beautiful with a story that seemed impenetrable in any language, Vic had turned to her. 'Can you explain to me what is going on?' he said in English.

'I have no idea' she had replied in Italian, before laughing and repeating it in English.

'How did you know I'm English?' she'd asked, a moment later.

Vic looked at her with a cheeky grin. 'Because you flinched at the nudity.'

'I did not! Besides, there hasn't been any nudity, has there?'

Room 706

Kate turned in her seat to look at this man who had struck up conversation.

'No, you're right. Truthfully, when I bought my ticket, the guy at the front said to me that the only people who are coming to see this film are foreign students, so I took a punt. I was going to try French next.'

They'd spent the entire film after that talking to each other, enjoying the air-conditioned room, comparing favourite films and books and walks around the city. It had felt easy. They only paused on the two occasions an usher came in to check everything was fine. 'It's okay, it's just us in here,' Kate said quietly when Vic paused mid-sentence at the sight of the usher's torch.

'I'm having a nice time. I don't want to be thrown out,' he said.

Now outside, Kate wanted their time together to last longer. His offer of an ice cream hung in the air as she considered how to respond.

'Do you make a habit of picking up young women in cinemas?'

His face fell. Shit, it was the wrong tone again. Why couldn't she have just said yes, like a normal person?

'Who said that's what I am doing? It's just ice cream. But there's no pressure.' He stuck out his hand for her to shake. 'If it's a no we can just say goodbye and thank you for the chat.'

Kate studied Vic's face. He had a neat beard, a balding head that had been closely shaved and deep eyes that looked thoughtful.

'I'm sorry. That came out wrong.'

They stood there a bit awkwardly for a while longer. 'Would it be possible,' Kate said eventually, 'instead of an ice cream, for it to be a glass of wine?'

Seated outside a small bar Vic knew, Kate studied him again. This was a kind man, she decided, with a kind face. He had told her during the film that he was living with his *nonna* and implied he'd left a job in London that had gone wrong.

Now he told her more. He'd hated his job designing systems for others to use to make money. He'd studied maths because he was good at it, and because numbers felt similar to poetry, and had been sucked into financial services by recruitment rounds at university and the lure of a big salary. Without even noticing, he'd been doing it for almost a decade, and one day woke up and realised how unhappy he was. After this, he couldn't stop hating it more and more, until he was no longer able to get out of bed in the morning. His older brother Tom was the one who had scooped him up, bringing him to live with his own family in their house in the London suburbs.

Tom had looked after him for three months, Vic said, and then, as he got stronger, suggested he come to stay with Nonna.

Vic's voice stayed steady as he told Kate all of this. She liked that he could be so matter of fact about what others might perceive as weakness.

'I've made my peace with it now,' he said, as if reading her mind. 'What's the point of shame? It happened. It is what it is. I see it as an opportunity to reassess and start again.'

Nonna was his dad's mum, and although she spoke no

English, and Vic's Italian, he said, was barely passable, they were incredibly close.

'How do you communicate?' Kate asked.

'Food. Hugs. Eyes. I talk and she smiles. She talks and I smile. Ever since I was a little boy, when we came to Italy, to Nonna's apartment, I felt safe.'

'That's very special,' Kate said, feeling a wave of sadness wash across her as she thought of her gran's house, and then immediately of her mum.

'Yes, it is. Do you have that, a safe space?'

They'd been drinking quickly and were nearly through the carafe of wine. Kate had to concentrate to hold on to her thoughts. She had always felt incredibly safe with her mum, in their flat on a small housing estate in north London. Although the estate was busy, other people rarely came into the flat. Their home was just for the two of them.

She opened her mouth to say that, but something else came instead. 'My mum's dead. She died. This summer.' And before she could swallow them back, tears slid down her cheeks as she poured out the whole story. How at the end of her second year at university, at the hall of residence where she paid cheap rent in return for being the senior student, keeping an eye on the freshers alone in the world for the first time, she'd been called to the porters' lodge to meet the police. They told her that her mother had been in a car crash, that she was in a critical condition, that they would drive her now on a blue light to the hospital, that no, they couldn't say everything was going to be okay, and did she need some help to get things – her wallet, her keys, some spare clothes? And could they call anyone to accompany her, and was she sure that there was no one?

'I'm so sorry,' Vic said. 'What a loss that must be.'

'Yeah.'

'Did you get there in time?'

Kate couldn't speak for a moment. She nodded, looking around at the other tables of couples and friends, wiping her tears with her hands.

'I'm so embarrassed. Everyone must be wondering why I'm crying.'

Vic smiled so kindly that she started to cry again. 'Don't worry about it,' he said. 'They're all caught up in their own worlds. I bet they haven't even noticed.'

'I did get there in time. Depending what you mean by that. In time would have been before she got in the car to wherever she was going that day. I fantasise about that, about how if I'd gone home that weekend maybe her plans would have changed, or maybe she'd have been in the car a minute earlier or a minute later, and not swerved to avoid another car that changed lanes without signalling. I think about it all the time, in fact. If I hadn't gone to university. Or if I'd gone to one close to home and not moved out. Even if I'd just phoned her that day and delayed her journey. It's silly. But any of those actions might have changed things, might have meant she wasn't doing that journey on that day at that moment. So no, I didn't get there in time. But yeah, I did get there in time to say goodbye.'

She took a deep breath. Something about Vic made her want to tell him this, perhaps because he'd been so open about his own vulnerability. 'She wasn't awake, but she was alive. I like to think she could hear me when I said thank you for being my mum, that I loved her so much. That I would try to make her proud. All the clichés you know, but they're not, not when it's you that's saying them.'

'Oh Kate.' He reached across the table and covered her hand with his. 'I'm so sorry.'

A pigeon pecked at some crumbs on the pavement near their table and they watched it in silence for a bit.

Vic spoke first. 'Were you there, when she died?'

'Yeah.' She pulled her hands away from his and cupped her glass.

'And was there anyone to help you, when it happened?'

'No. It had just been us for a long time. Both of my grandparents are dead. My mum had no siblings. I have no siblings. There are no aunts and uncles. No close friends of the family. My best friend, Eve, she was abroad. And there was no one else to call.'

Vic's attention was wholly on Kate. She couldn't stop herself from continuing.

'My degree is in languages, Spanish and Italian, that's why I'm here. It's a four-year course and you have to spend the third year abroad. I've been to Spain – I spent the summer there last year – but I'd never been to Italy. I was going to come early, get my bearings before my courses started, search for a shared house, that kind of thing.'

She was waffling, she knew she was. But also, she needed to get it all out. And this man, Vic, he was looking at her with kind eyes, just letting her speak.

'I pushed my flight back and spent the next three months sorting out my mum's life instead. I had to get the death certificate and carry out her funeral plans and empty the house and decide what to put in storage, then return the keys to the housing association because I couldn't take it on and still be a student somewhere else. And now I'm here and I'm all alone and,' she tried to pretend to laugh but it didn't disguise the sob, 'and I am crying to a stranger in public, drunkenly telling my life story over too much, or maybe not enough, wine.'

Vic took her hand and pressed a napkin into it. Kate tried to smile.

'It's okay,' he said. 'It's okay. I'm here.' He didn't ask any more questions and Kate was glad of it.

'I'm so embarrassed. I didn't mean to tell you any of that,' she said, blowing her nose.

Vic looked gently into Kate's eyes. 'There's no need to be sorry. It sounds like maybe you needed to tell someone.'

'I'm a bit drunk. I haven't spoken to anyone for days, not properly. I shouldn't have landed all that on you. I should go.'

'You're very brave to come here knowing no one,' Vic said.

'I don't know anyone at home either.'

Kate stood up to leave and Vic stood up too.

'You don't have to go.'

'I want to. I need –' she gestured around herself – 'space, sleep, carbs, I don't know. Something.'

Vic nodded. 'Okay.' Then, a moment later, 'Will you be okay?'

'Yeah. I mean it's horrible, the residence. The room has a tiny window higher than my head so I can't see out. It's

Room 706

super-hot, totally soulless, no one speaks to each other. The kitchen isn't really a kitchen at all, there are no cupboards and no fridge. I don't really know why I thought it was a good idea. I might look for somewhere else, find someone looking for a lodger or something. But yeah, I'll be okay. It's just somewhere to sleep really. Being here, being in Italy, immersing myself in the language, taking the classes I've chosen at the university, that's the point isn't it?'

She tried to smile and shrug at the same time as if it didn't really matter, though her head was too fuzzy to coordinate such a move and a small grunt escaped through her nose.

'It was great to meet you,' Vic said.

'It was great to meet you too.' Kate gestured at the soggy screwed-up napkin on the table. 'Sorry about all that.'

They stood there for a few moments in silence. He'd not offered his phone number, or asked for hers, and she could feel her now swollen face start to redden in embarrassment at her own unmet expectations. Kate was just about to walk away when Vic spoke.

'Will you come and meet my *nonna*?'

'Sorry?'

'Come and have dinner with us. She loves having visitors. And, well, I would really like to see you again.'

Kate nodded and attempted a smile.

'Tomorrow?' Vic asked.

'Yeah, why not.'

He fished in his bag for a pen and notebook and scribbled the name of a metro station on a page that he ripped out and gave to her. 'I'll meet you here at 8pm.'

'You could just give me your phone number you know.' Kate had a slight ringing in her ears from the wine and the sobs.

Vic shrugged. 'I'm not using my phone very much at the moment. I stopped altogether for a bit as part of my recovery and I guess I'm out of the habit now. Besides, it's exciting isn't it?'

'What is?'

'Not knowing whether you'll come.'

She genuinely laughed at that. She would like to meet this man again, who knew how to talk and how to listen.

She'd just started walking away when she heard his voice again.

'I hope you do.'

And, as she continued walking, he called out again. 'Bye then.'

'See you tomorrow,' she said, under her breath.

Chapter 5

1.11pm
Room 706

'I think we should call the police, let them know we are here,' Kate said.

'I think they already know there's a hostage situation going on.'

How could she be a hostage when no one, not the police, not the hostage takers, knew she was here? 'If a tree falls in a forest,' she murmured.

'What?'

'If a tree falls in the forest and there is no one there to hear it fall, does it make a sound? That's the philosophy question.'

James looked blank.

She wished it was Vic here, not James. He'd get her references. He'd know what to do to make her feel calmer.

On the other hand, thank goodness it wasn't Vic. She would never want to take him away from Lenny and Annie, and if she wasn't going to make it home they would need him.

'What if they ask questions?' James said.

'Who?'

'The police. They will want to know why you are here.'

'The police don't care who's fucking who,' Kate said.

'No. But they might tell your husband. Or my wife.'

'So I won't give your name.'

She regretted her tone as soon as she said it. But James didn't seem to notice. What would the police do if she did give both their names? Would they tell Vic that she wasn't there alone? She imagined the conversation. 'Good evening sir. We regret to tell you that your wife is caught up in the incident in central London, the one in a hotel. You may have seen it on the news sir. That's right sir, she's there in a room, hiding. Don't worry though, she won't be lonely, she has company. That's right sir, a man. We believe they have been fucking each other for some years now. But don't worry sir, we're doing our best to get her home.'

'James?'

He looked at her again. The shape of the word in her mouth was weird. They rarely used each other's actual names.

'Does anyone know you are here?' Kate asked quietly.

'No.'

'What does it say in your diary? Where does your PA think you are?'

'I always just put our meetings in as "private appointment". I imagine he thinks it's some kind of medical thing.'

Room 706

Kate sat on the edge of the bed, turning to face the wall. She didn't want to look at James while she made the call, knowing that he thought she shouldn't. Vic's message was still on her screen, unanswered.

As soon as she'd got through and said that she was hiding in a room in the hotel that was currently under attack, the emergency operator put Kate through to a special incident room. She was greeted by a woman whose no-nonsense tone made her sound like a secondary-school teacher.

'Can I have your name please?'

'Kate Bright.' Kate spoke as quietly as possible.

'Is that your full name, madam?'

'Er no. Catherine Rachel Bright. Catherine with a C.'

Kate could hear the operator typing as she answered and pictured her details on a computer screen: *Catherine Rachel Bright – hiding in room*. It just seemed so unreal.

'And what room are you in?'

'706.'

'What is your home address?' The woman spoke with studied indifference, as if she did this all the time and was no more interested in the specifics of Kate's situation than a doctor's receptionist wants to know whether your appointment is about a life-changing lump or a repeat prescription.

'Can you tell me what's going on, please?'

'Yes madam, let me just get some details. We need to know exactly who is in the building.'

'Oh, the thing is, it's kind of a secret. I'm not meant to be here.'

There was a brief pause before the woman spoke again.

'Madam, are you armed?'

'You think I'm with the gunmen. God no. I . . . I . . .'

She struggled to know what to say. Was she going to admit to an emergency operator that she was having an affair, the first person she had ever told? She turned to look around the room. James was standing in the corner, as if by being as far away from her as possible he really wasn't there.

'I am not here,' he mouthed, shaking his head.

'I, er, my husband thinks I am somewhere else.'

It sounded so ridiculous she almost laughed, though the serious tone on the other end of the line snapped her back into focus.

'We are just compiling a list of who is in the building,' the operator repeated.

Kate gave them her date of birth and home address.

'Thank you. Are you alone?'

'Am I alone?' Kate looked over at James again.

'Yes madam, are you alone?'

James was still shaking his head.

'Yes, I'm alone. I, er, just needed an afternoon to myself. I have children . . .'

The operator interrupted.

'I need to give you some important information Ms Bright. Please pay complete attention.' The operator paused. Kate didn't say anything. 'Ms Bright?'

'Yes?' Kate whispered.

'The hotel you are in is currently being controlled by a number of armed gunmen.'

Room 706

'I've seen the flag. On television, I mean. And online – there are pictures.'

'Please just listen, Ms Bright.' It was the teacher tone again. Whether she replied or said nothing, each time Kate felt as if she'd done the wrong thing. 'We do not know how many attackers there are or where they are located, so you should not leave the room for any reason. Do you understand that?'

That was a direct question.

'Yes,' she whispered again.

'We are still trying to piece everything together, but we do know that a number of hostages are being held in the meeting rooms and that the lobby and the first two floors are controlled by the attackers. This situation is very, very serious.'

Kate took a deep breath.

'We need anyone who is in the hotel to be absolutely quiet and unknown. Right now the best way to remain safe is to remain hidden. Can you do that Ms Bright?'

Kate only realised that she had nodded rather than said yes when the operator carried on talking anyway.

'Please turn off all the lights in the room. Do you have a phone charger with you?'

'Yes.'

'Keep your phone charged if possible. Do not flush the toilet or run water. Do not make phone calls after this one. And please make sure your phone is on silent. Turn off the vibrate function if you have it on. No TV, even on mute, because the flicker could show from under the door. I am going to send you a number you can use to message us. Please do this if you move position or find out any information you think we should know, if it is safe to do so.'

'Do you need my number?'

'I have it on my screen already Ms Bright.'

'Oh.'

'And stay away from the door in case of bullets.'

'Bullets, right.' Kate swallowed hard. 'How long . . . how long do you think it'll be? I have children, I need to pick them up,' she said weakly, her voice cracking. She sat down on the bed.

'Ms Bright?'

'Yes.'

'We know it is a lot to take in. We're doing our absolute best to keep you safe. If anyone at all knocks on your door, whether they are male or female, calm or commanding, speaking English or any other language, ignore it. Do not let anyone know you are there. If the fire alarm goes off, ignore it. Ignore absolutely everything. Just stay silent and stay in your room.

'How will I know if it's the police coming to rescue me?' Kate was sure she sounded ridiculous.

'Don't worry about that for now.'

Shit, they didn't know either. Maybe they wouldn't be saved at all.

'Ms Bright, I just need to tell you a bit more information and ask you a couple more questions. Are you on any medication?'

'No.'

'Do you need us to call anyone for you?'

Kate hurriedly thought. She couldn't keep this from Vic.

Room 706

She knew now that this wasn't a minor incident, that there was no way she'd be home in time to get the kids, even at 6pm, and even if she was, what would she do, serve up the slow-cooked chicken and pretend it had just been an ordinary day? And if the worst happened? She shuddered and pushed it from her mind.

'Yes please. My husband.' She couldn't look at James, though she could feel his presence on the other side of the room.

She gave them Vic's name and number. It was cowardly, but it might sound better coming from the police than from her, and she couldn't bear the thought of hearing Vic's voice right now, of speaking to him. Not with James listening.

'Ms Bright, we are going to disconnect the call now. Please do not post anything on social media about your situation. The fewer people who know you are there the less likely you are to be found by the wrong people.'

'Okay.'

The line went dead. Kate had expected something more before they hung up. A 'good luck' at least.

She sat for a moment and then turned to face James. He was looking at her. White noise rushed in her ears.

'What did they say?' he said quietly, walking back into the centre of the room and sitting on the bed.

'It's real. They said it's real. They said no television, no lights, no running water, no noise, keep phones charged and avoid the door in case of bullets. It's serious, they said so.'

Her throat had a lump in it and she swallowed hard before she spoke. 'Fuck!'

Chapter 6

Sixteen years earlier
Italy

Kate recognised Vic by his shape before she could even make out the features of his face. She arrived at the metro station ten minutes early and he was already there, leaning against the wall, reading a book.

He looked up as she approached, stuffing the paperback into his bag and smiling widely. She thought, as she had the day before, what a kind face he had. He pulled her in for a hug.

His enthusiasm took her by surprise, though it felt nice to be greeted so warmly.

'You came.'

'Did you think I wouldn't?' she asked, once he had released her.

Room 706

'I wasn't sure,' Vic replied. 'What about you, were you certain I would be here to meet you?'

'Oh wow. Genuinely it didn't actually cross my mind that you wouldn't be.' It was the truth. She instinctively trusted him already.

'Good. I am indeed a man of my word.'

Kate imagined how anyone watching them might interpret their meeting, and Vic's hug. They'd think they were two old friends seeing each other for the first time in a while.

'You got home okay last night then?'

'Sorry?' Kate hadn't been paying attention.

'Yesterday? I felt bad all night for letting you walk back alone, you know, after a bit too much wine and all that.'

'Oh. No, don't worry. I was fine.'

Kate held up a small posy of yellow flowers. 'Are these okay do you think?' and then, a moment later, to clarify, 'For your *nonna*, not for you.'

'They're perfect. She'll love you.'

'And she didn't mind not knowing whether there would be a guest or not?'

'She's my *nonna*. She cannot conceive of the idea that someone would not come to dinner if invited by her handsome grandson.' Vic lowered his voice into a conspiratorial tone. 'I'd have had to ask a random passer-by if you hadn't come, so as not to disappoint her.'

He was as sweet and as funny as Kate had remembered from the day before. All around it felt as if Rome was bursting into life, or perhaps it had been like that all along but she hadn't noticed.

'It's amazing here. This, this is exactly what I thought it would be like. Piazzas and cobbles and colourful buildings, mopeds and, and, I don't know . . . Italians.'

'There are definitely Italians,' said Vic. 'It's full of them.'

Kate laughed.

'And mopeds,' he said, pulling her out of the way as one sped past. His hand was still on her arm a moment later, and Kate, realising it, suddenly felt awkward.

Vic broke the awkwardness easily. 'Let's not get run over. At least not before dinner. And he moved his hand down to hers and pulled her towards a bright orange apartment building.

Any worries Kate had about meeting Nonna dissipated the second she walked into the apartment. Nonna greeted her with kisses and exclamations, compliments about her style, thanks for the flowers, delight at Kate's Italian despite Kate having only uttered a few words, insistence that Kate call her Nonna. She was thrilled to meet a friend of Vic's, and any friend of his was always welcome in her home.

Despite Vic's protestations, his Italian was far better than he had suggested. The conversation flowed about everything and nothing, with Nonna telling them about the changing neighbourhood and her views on local and national politicians. Nonna had clearly been briefed not to mention Kate's mum and, for the first time since she had died, Kate felt her body relax a little.

After the meal, Nonna showed Kate around the apartment. It had three bedrooms, and the third was a simple room with a single bed, a wardrobe, a small desk, a chair and a window onto the internal courtyard over which many lines of laundry were strung. An intricate quilt in reds and oranges was folded over the bottom of the bed. An electric fan was on the desk, and a small vase of dried flowers.

'This is your room,' Nonna said in Italian, squeezing Kate's arm.

'My room?' Kate wondered if she had misunderstood the Italian. She struggled to keep up as Nonna continued. 'My grandson says you are not happy in your residence. Why not come and stay with us? Vic needs a friend here. You need a friend here. I like you. I think . . .' Nonna paused for dramatic effect. 'I think you like me.'

Kate laughed. She did like Nonna. And Vic.

Vic appeared at their side. 'All okay?'

Kate wasn't sure whether Vic had been in on the idea. 'I think Nonna has just suggested I come and live here,' she said in English. She saw from his face, which she was learning never hid his emotions, that this was as much a surprise for him as it had been for her, but surprise quickly turned to delight.

'Oh yes, that's a genius idea. You said you were going to look for somewhere else to live. Here would be perfect. Nonna loves company.'

'Really?'

'Yes, really.'

It felt too good to be true, to make a new friend and to find somewhere new to live in one go.

'I can't afford much rent,' Kate said.

'I don't think she wants your money,' Vic replied.

Kate considered his face for a moment. He looked genuinely pleased with the idea.

'What about you, do you love company?' Kate asked.

'Of the right sort, absolutely,' he answered.

Her head was nodding before she even realised she was accepting the offer.

'Then yes please. Oh my God, yes please.'

Chapter 7

Eight years earlier

Returning to work a year after Lenny was born was, in many ways, glorious. It was a relief to be able to have drinks while they were still hot and uninterrupted conversations, to go to the toilet without hearing cries for her from the next room and to wear smart clothes and dangly jewellery without fear of it being yanked by chubby baby hands. Kate hadn't realised how much she had missed the kind of work that needed thought and planning. Before Lenny was born she'd worked her way up quickly to deputy news editor on a weekly newspaper about the housing sector, and now she'd negotiated a four-day week for her return. To do this she had moved sideways into the role of opinion editor, commissioning and editing other people's columns and deciding what the publication's own line would be on key issues.

'Summer is always slow. Use it to take key people for lunch,' she'd been told by her editor. 'See who would be good to write a guest column, maybe come up with some ideas for long-term projects we can follow.' Kate didn't love making small talk with strangers, preferring to find stories hidden in annual reports and Freedom of Information requests, but she did as her editor suggested, making a list of people in the sector that she should get to know and inviting them to lunch.

Top of her list were the CEOs of the major housebuilding companies in the country. Most were hard to pin down, and she had to arrange via their PAs a date several months into the future. So it took Kate by surprise when one of them personally replied to her emailed invitation, suggesting they meet the next week.

The eighth-floor restaurant her colleague had recommended was in an office block overlooking the river, and was full of people who looked like they were having working lunches, jackets on the backs of chairs, phones on the table.

Kate was there first and had just ordered a bottle of sparkling water when she saw a man being directed towards her. He was tall, slim, clean shaven and angular. He didn't look as if he had ever constructed anything himself, not even a flatpack, though the company he ran was responsible for some of the largest housing developments in the country.

'Hello, I'm James,' he said, holding out his hand to shake as she stood up to greet him.

'Kate,' she said as she shook it.

'You were surprisingly easy to book for a lunch date,' she said, by way of a first line, once they had sat down. James laughed. 'Am I supposed to pretend that I am in great demand and have nothing free until autumn?'

'Everyone else has done just that.'

'The way I see it,' said James, 'when your sector's most important publication asks you for lunch, they have either uncovered a huge scandal and are trying to find out more, or they have no dirt on you but need some column inches filling and want you to fill them. It's in my interests to find out which.' His tone was friendly, almost teasing.

'Which of those do you think it is?' Kate asked, trying to match his tone.

'Well,' James said, peering into her eyes. 'We have no scandals to uncover, I think.'

'You would say that.'

'I would. But nevertheless it's true.'

'I'm pleased to hear it.'

They made small talk about summer plans until a waiter came for their order. James told Kate he preferred to avoid being away in August. They usually went to the south of France in September, he said, once schools were back and the resorts weren't full of children, but while the sea was still warm.

They skipped starters and went straight to the main course, gnocchi with a blue cheese sauce for her, steak tartare for him. The thought of steak tartare turned her stomach – raw meat topped with a raw egg. His was a bold choice for a work lunch, she thought. She looked around the restaurant at the other diners and felt the urge to laugh at the absurdity of it, that she might be here in smart clothes, playing at being a professional, when tomorrow she'd be having the day just her and Lenny, on the floor with toy dinosaurs or singing nursery rhymes.

Concentrate Kate, she told herself, snapping back to her conversation with James.

They spoke a bit about the housing sector while they ate, discussing James's company's plans and how it was responding to changes in the availability of particular materials and calls for greener developments. Kate wondered whether to take out her notebook but somehow, even though it was a work lunch, it didn't feel appropriate. No, she'd see this as a background chat and follow up anything interesting afterwards.

Finishing his meal, James folded his napkin before putting it on the table. He leaned back slightly and gazed at Kate. She wondered if she had sauce on her chin, but decided he seemed too polite to be looking if that was the case. She wiped her face just in case before putting her own napkin on the table.

'So how do you become a journalist specialising in housing?' he asked. She could have just spoken about how it was the first job she was offered, and that it had proved surprisingly interesting so she had stayed, but for some reason she found herself telling James instead about her year in Italy. 'There aren't that many obvious careers for linguists, other than teaching, which I didn't fancy. But also in Europe the newsstands are much more obvious than the UK. Here you have to go into a shop if you want to buy a publication, it's almost clandestine. There, people do it on the street at those little kiosks that look so cosmopolitan with their displays of magazines and newspapers. I think that started it, people-watching as I walked around the city, guessing who was going to buy what. I mean, I didn't do anything about it, not even when I got back here. I didn't join the student newspaper or anything. But it planted the seed, so when I graduated I did a course and . . .' She shrugged.

'The rest is history?' he suggested.

'Yes, something like that.'

She'd been trying to impress him by mentioning Italy, she thought later, when going over their meeting in her head. She wanted him to know that she spoke other languages, to think of her as European, as cultured and adventurous. And it had worked.

'A year in Italy sounds pretty amazing.'

'I met my husband. At the end of my third week there.'

She wasn't sure why she blurted that out either. She also wanted him to know she had a husband, she supposed. She was out of practice at networking after a year of maternity leave, too excited by someone being interested in her rather than cooing over the baby.

The waiter appeared to take their plates and she stopped talking. James returned to the subject as soon as the waiter left.

'So you got to Italy and pretty much straight away met the man you would go on to marry?'

She smiled at the memory of Vic in the cinema. 'Yes.'

'Why was he in Italy? Is he Italian?' James asked.

Kate paused. Vic's story was not hers to tell. Under the table she dug the fingernail of her ring finger into the pad of her thumb, the sharp pain reminding her to slow down, to think about what she was saying. 'His dad is Italian, but he is English. He was having a career break. He's a bit older than me.'

'Love at first sight?'

She searched his face to see whether he was mocking her in some way, but he looked genuinely interested.

'Maybe not first sight. Not love anyhow. But he was staying with his grandmother, his *nonna*, and within a week of meeting him I moved into her spare bedroom and she wooed me for him through the medium of pasta. Each night she would cook us dinner and then leave us to wash up and finish the wine while she went to call on friends, and, well, we fell for each other.'

James smiled widely then. 'It sounds like a dating show. One where Italian grandmothers choose a wife for their grandson.'

Kate smiled too. He didn't seem like a person who would watch much reality television. 'I'd definitely watch that,' she said.

He was looking intently at her, seeming to be genuinely interested. 'So you are fluent in Italian?'

'Yes. That was my degree.'

'That's impressive. I can't speak any other languages. What else can you speak?

'Just Spanish and French.'

She said it as nonchalantly as she could, trying not to make it look like she was boasting.'

'Ah, all Romance languages.'

He said it teasingly, slightly rolling the R. Was he flirting? It sounded like it. She bit back her instinct to tell him Romance

Room 706

languages had nothing to do with the schmaltzy kind of romance.

The waiter came to their table again to take their dessert order and, feeling emboldened by having been the centre of attention, Kate ordered the lemon mousse. She felt pleased when James signalled that he would have the same. It arrived quickly.

'You have asked me a lot of questions,' Kate said. 'But I haven't really asked you anything. And the reason I invited you here was to get some stories.' She picked up her dessert spoon and for the first time felt self-conscious about eating in front of this man.

Amusement played at the corners of James's mouth. 'So I was right, you haven't uncovered a scandal. What a relief.' He picked up his own spoon and dug straight into the mousse, taking a large mouthful.

'Sorry, no,' Kate said. 'Lunch with CEOs is one of my KPIs. You're meant to feel flattered that my publication is interested in you . . .'

'I am very flattered,' James interrupted.

'. . . and I am meant to come away with some stories about developments and the promise from you that you'll write us a column on why the government is wrong and housebuilders are right.'

'Right about what?'

'Anything,' Kate said. She was enjoying herself now, the witty backwards and forwards, the gentle teasing, the joy of talking to a new adult. She ate a mouthful of mousse herself, and had just swallowed it when James spoke again.

'I'll give you all that if we can have lunch again.'

The way he said it was so normal, as if doing so would be the most natural thing in the world, that it took Kate a moment to realise this was out of the ordinary.

'Okay. I mean, why?'

He shrugged. 'Why not? This is fun. You're interesting and easy to talk to. I am enjoying your company. My PA is on holiday so I can do anything I want within reason. Let's meet next week and by then I will have thought of some stories for you.'

Kate looked at James again. Everything about him felt very controlled and she found this intriguing. She'd watched him fold his napkin with precision earlier and now she couldn't imagine him eating even a bowl of cornflakes in the morning without a napkin to hand.

But this hour had been the most fun she'd had at work since returning from maternity leave, and the idea of doing it again was nice.

'Okay.'

'Good. Same time, same place?'

Kate nodded. She wasn't sure what to say next. Was this a normal thing to do, to meet up twice? Why not? She hadn't been lying about these lunches being part of her work objectives. On the other hand, no one else had yet met her once, let alone twice. Just go with it Kate, she thought. It's just lunch.

'So, now that you know you will get some things to write about next week, let's carry on getting to know each other. Go on, ask me anything.'

Room 706

Having agreed to another lunch, James now seemed a bit like an old friend. She felt much more comfortable in her responses, as if she had just been given permission to be herself.

Kate scrutinised his face. He absorbed it, not seeming to squirm.

'What do you want to know?' he asked again.

She rolled her tongue into the side of her cheek, tasting the bitterness of the lemon. He clearly wanted to be questioned about his life.

'Are you in therapy?'

'Anything but that.'

She blushed. Had she gone too far? That was pretty personal after all. But then James laughed and she joined in.

'Not really. I am happy to answer. I don't know that I see the point of therapy,' James said.

She raised an eyebrow.

'You can do it on yourself, can't you? *Tell me about your childhood, James.* My childhood was fine. *Really, James, was it fine?* Yes, it was fine. *You went to boarding school didn't you, James?* I did. *How did that make you feel?* It stopped me being able to feel. *Shall we talk about that?* No, no need.'

'It sounds to me,' said Kate, 'like you need therapy more than most people.'

Her words hung in the air for a little longer than she would have liked before James's eyes crinkled and he smiled.

'Maybe. But I think there's a lot to be said for keeping things buried,' he said. 'You know,' he added, 'that therapists all have their own therapists?'

Kate nodded. She was feeling a bit uncomfortable now, like her question had opened up a conversation they didn't know each other well enough to have.

'It's just a fancy form of pyramid selling,' he said.

He ate some more mousse then rested the spoon against the ramekin. 'I have no need for pyramids,' he added quietly.

For a moment Kate thought she could see in him the shadow of a small boy being left at boarding school, but if it was there at all it disappeared very quickly.

They both reached for the small leather folder containing the bill when it arrived, their hands grazing each other as they did so. Her publication had a strict policy against accepting gifts, and she was meant to put it on her corporate credit card, but James's pull on the folder was stronger.

'It's on me,' he said, not even looking at the paper inside as he waved the waiter to them and handed over his card. Kate let him, slightly rattled by the intimacy of their conversation, the agreement she had made to meet again the next week.

She replayed the lunch in her head as she walked back to her office. Had she been too unprofessional? She didn't usually tell her work contacts anything about her personal life. It was as if he was the journalist, not her. Still, it had been nice meeting someone new, believing that their interest in her was genuine, having lunch in a restaurant with no high chairs and a menu aimed squarely at adults. She couldn't remember the last time she and Vic had done that.

She was still on a high from lunch when she left the office to head home, though this faded pretty quickly as she walked to the station. Although Kate enjoyed the journey to work each day, unencumbered by a child, the journey home was invariably awful. As her train got nearer to Lenny's nursery, feelings of impending doom would creep in. By the time she reached her stop she'd be sure that she would be punished for her feelings of freedom in the worst possible way, not so much for daring to leave her child but for daring to enjoy the time away from him.

Her primary fear was that Lenny's nursery would for some reason catch fire. She'd approach the building expecting to see a wall of flames, children banging on windows trying to get out. And then, as she rounded the corner from the station and saw the nursery still standing, with no flames or smoke or fire engines, she'd have to calm herself down before walking in and spotting Lenny through the glass panels of the inner door as he took his key worker's hand, retrieving his coat and any artwork he had done that day, before breaking into a smile, and then a run, when he saw his mummy.

That afternoon the niggling feeling that the nursery might be on fire started the moment she stepped onto her train. By the time she got to her stop she could barely remember lunch. Kate was sure that when she arrived to get Lenny she'd be confronted by the sorrowful face of a firefighter holding back tears.

When she arrived at nursery, everything was normal.

Chapter 8

1.30pm
Room 706

Kate was sitting on the bed. The television and lights were off, following the advice of the emergency operator. She still hadn't replied to Vic's message. How could she tell him that actually no she wasn't okay, that she wasn't just caught up in the ripples of chaos caused by any attack, but was right there in the centre of it. Would the police ring him immediately? How would he take it?

She scrolled through her phone again. Posts about the hotel now made up the majority of her social-media timelines. She scanned every news website one after the other, trying to spot new information about her own predicament. One newspaper had already set up a live blog, though the information on it was sparse. She looked at a new photograph of the hotel that

Room 706

they were all using, one that showed the flag that now hung from the façade. Kate looked for the window to their room in the photo. Seven floors up, three across from the wider windows that were the lift lobby. She zoomed in. The image was blurry up close with nothing to suggest the room was occupied. She zoomed out again.

It's strange, she thought, looking at the flag, that one piece of material can strike such fear into people, when used differently it could be a curtain or a sarong or a tablecloth.

People were asking each other in open messages online if they were okay. It was virtue signalling of the most public kind. No one actually in the hotel was going to say that they were there, especially if they were there for the reason that she was. She wanted to reply to each and every one of them, caps lock on. *I AM NOT FINE.*

Breathe, Kate, she reminded herself again. Put your phone down and just breathe.

James was looking at his phone too. She knew she had pissed him off with the 999 call, that he hadn't wanted her to do it. Would he make a thing of it, she wondered, or let it drop?

'What are you looking at?' Kate asked quietly.

He showed her his screen. He was looking up accounts of previous attacks by this group.

'Oh God.'

'Yes. It's not great reading to be honest.' He ran his fingers through his hair, leaving his hand on top of his head for several moments.

'Tell me.'

'You really want to know?' he asked her.

Kate nodded, though she wasn't actually sure that she did. She moved closer so she could hear him more easily.

'Worldwide they claimed eight attacks last year. Two of those were bombs – one in a marketplace and one at an election rally. Three involved driving vehicles into crowded groups of people including one where they then got out of the car and shot passers-by. Another involved attempting to take over an oil refinery.'

'Attempting?'

'They got through the perimeter fence and shot some of the guards, but it seems security forces were waiting for them inside.'

'They all sound different?' She counted them on her fingers, saying them in her head. Marketplace. Election rally. Three cars. Oil refinery. That was six.

'Right. There's a security expert quoted here who says this group has no real central command but urges its followers to plan attacks in their own communities.'

'Oh God,' Kate said again. 'Okay, the other two?'

'It's not good. They also claimed responsibility for a circus siege in the Caucasus where they seem to have bought two dozen seats dotted around the big top and then took it over in the interval.'

She had seven fingers held in front of her now. 'Do I want to know how that ended?'

'Probably not.'

'Tell me anyway.' She put her hands down, making fists

around her thumbs, trying to concentrate on what he was saying and not her urge to jump out of the window.

Not that hotel windows on the seventh floor usually open, she thought.

James read from his phone. 'After fifteen hours, during which the performers, including exotic animals, and audience were held together in the main tent, the terrorists allowed a group of women and children to leave, conveying the message with them that they would shoot five of the remaining hostages every hour until their demands were met.'

'What were their demands?' Kate wanted to know everything he knew.

'It doesn't say.'

He carried on reading. 'When shots were heard from within the tent, government forces stormed the venue. In the ensuing shootout, seventeen of the hostages lost their lives, with five of these thought to be the result of friendly fire from rescuing forces. No animals were hurt.'

Kate snorted then laughed, a shrill weird sound, higher pitched than her normal laugh. James shushed her, quietly at first then more aggressively.

'Sorry, sorry. It's awful. But the line about the animals.' She snorted again, laughing through her nose, then began to cry. 'Fuck. Fuck fuck fuck fuck fuck.'

Once she regained control she spoke again.

'That's seven. What was the other?'

There was a long pause. Without meeting her eyes James eventually answered.

'A hotel.'

There was nothing to say to that. She could see James scrolling on his phone and following links. He was calm and methodical. Was this how he was at work, why he was so successful in his career?

She picked up her own phone to look up more about the previous hotel attack, but she couldn't bring any of the words into focus. She clicked instead into her photo archive. The most recent photo appeared first. It was Lenny and Annie earlier this week, in school uniform, balancing on a low wall they passed each morning.

'Take a picture of me, Mummy, standing on one leg,' Lenny had said.

'I want to be in it too,' Annie had insisted, standing next to him, also on one leg but with one hand on the fence next to it. Annie had a gap in her mouth where a tooth had recently fallen out and a plaster on her leg visible between the bottom of her dress and the top of her socks. Kate loved them so much. Had she told them that today? Had she shown them enough love throughout their short lives that if she didn't make it home they'd feel her love forever anyway? She was fairly sure she had said 'I love you' to them both at the school gate that morning.

'Where was it?' she asked.

'What?'

'The hotel.'

Kate could feel her heart pounding, and counted the beats for as long as James was silent, trying to keep them steady.

'South America. The good news is everyone got out alive.'

'The bad news?'

Room 706

'It lasted forty-eight hours, and there were bombs, except they failed and didn't go off.'

'Forty-eight hours?'

'Yes.'

She couldn't be here in this room for forty-eight hours. The kids needed her. She needed them. And nothing James said made sense anyway. Why would the same terrorist group attack a hotel, an oil refinery and a circus? She didn't get it. What did they want? And how could whatever they wanted possibly have anything to do with her, with James, with anyone else who just happened to be in this hotel on this day?

She was going to have to reply to Vic at some point. If she didn't, he'd worry. She almost snorted again at this. He'd be more worried once he knew she was here. She felt a stab of pain in her chest and her fingers tingled. Was she having a heart attack? She concentrated on breathing and the pain and tingly feeling receded.

Stop it Kate, she told herself. You can't have a panic attack, not now.

She picked up her phone. As she did it flashed at her. Vic had messaged again.

Police called. What's happening?

And straight away, a second one.

I love you. It'll be okay.

Chapter 9

Sixteen years earlier
Italy

'What's that?' Vic asked when Kate first used the phrase 'dead prostitute friend'. Nonna had left the apartment after dinner to play cards with friends, and they were washing the dishes. It was six weeks since Kate had met Vic, five weeks since she'd moved in, and a month since their first kiss, though they continued to mostly pretend to sleep in their own rooms out of deference to Nonna, and she pretended to believe them.

'It's the person that you call to help dispose of the body when you wake up hungover in a hotel, surrounded by the detritus of the night's hard partying, and on the floor is a dead prostitute,' Kate explained. She had been telling him about Eve.

'That's pretty dark.'

Room 706

'Yeah.'

'Do you often wake up in hotels with dead prostitutes on the floor?' he asked.

'Hasn't happened yet.'

'Live ones?'

'Never. You?'

'No.' Vic looked horrified. 'I'm a nice man. I don't do drugs. I don't pay for sex. I love my *nonna*. I do the washing up.'

She laughed at this and he pulled her in for a kiss, his hand tender on the top of her back, the hairs of his beard soft against her face.

'Tell me more about Eve,' Vic said.

'She's my best friend. My only friend really. I mean I have people at university if I want to socialise, or swap lecture notes, but it's all just surface level. Really it has just been me and Eve since our first day at primary school.'

'That sounds intense,' Vic said.

She shrugged. 'Yeah, I suppose it is. But not in a bad way. I've always loved having just one best friend. I never felt I needed anyone other than her and my mum. I tell Eve everything; she tells me everything. Even now, even though we went to different cities to study. We spent the whole of last summer together in Spain, two and a half months, and it was like we'd never spent a day apart.'

'Oh wow. Where did you go? What was that like?' Vic always wanted to know more. He loved hearing about her life and her experiences.

'All over. Spanish trains are easy to navigate. Mostly I used money I had saved from my student jobs. And we picked up a bit of cash-in-hand work every so often, giving out flyers for clubs, that sort of thing. It's totally different to here. Italy is romantic. It's busy, but it's not rushed. Spain though, Spain is sexy. Bullfights and flamenco and tempers. It felt like at any moment my life was about to begin.'

'And did it?'

She wasn't sure how to interpret his look, half inquisitive, half expectant.

She gave him what he wanted. 'No. That's happening now.'

He grinned at her. Kate felt powerful being able to make him so happy with just a few words. She'd never felt that before. She meant it too. Being with Vic did feel like the beginning of a new phase. She put some suds on her hand and blew them gently in his direction. He caught one and clutched it to his heart and they both laughed.

'It'll sound crazy, but we had this thing.' Kate turned back to the water. It was easier to talk about herself if she wasn't looking at him. 'We each made a list of people in our lives, the same number of people as we had nights away. And every day we each spoke about one of the people on our list. The rules were that we could speak about them for as long as we wanted without interruptions. We always went somewhere beautiful to do it. A beach, a town square, at the top of a hill we'd hiked up, that kind of thing. And some people took five minutes to talk about, some took over an hour. Only when we were finished could the other ask questions. It meant we always had things to discuss. And at the end of the trip, well, no one knew me better than Eve

Room 706

before we went, but afterwards, I don't know that it would be possible to.'

Vic nodded. 'That's . . . that's . . . I don't know the word. It's not something I've ever experienced, a friendship like that. Where is Eve now?'

'She studies in Scotland. She was in America this summer when everything happened.' Kate swallowed. She had not brought up her mum with Vic since the first day they met, and Vic seemed to know that she was not ready to talk more about her, did not want to be asked questions. 'She went early. Her term finished before mine. She was a lifeguard on a kids' summer camp. When my mum died she was the only person I wanted and I couldn't get hold of her. They weren't allowed phones, or email, it was a kind of off-grid eco camp, I don't know, something like that. She likes experiences and adventures. The only way to reach her was by actual mail.'

'Did you write to her?'

'Not straight away. I wanted her to enjoy the camp. I wrote to her after the funeral had been arranged. I told her not to come back for me, that I definitely did not want her to change her plans. Post takes ages in America anyway so she wouldn't have got back in time.'

It was hard to talk about this. She didn't want to cry, not now, not while she and Vic were having such a nice time. She bit the inside of her lip to steady herself and counted the bubbles in the water until she felt in control of her emotions.

Vic must have sensed how she was feeling. He didn't say anything more for a few moments, and when he did she was ready to carry on.

'How did she take that, when she found out?'

'Found out what?' Kate had forgotten to listen for a moment then realised he had asked another question.

'That you didn't tell her straight away,' he said tentatively. 'About the funeral.'

'Oh. Yeah. I think she was shocked. But maybe also relieved. She'd had this amazing summer, and if she'd known she'd have come back for me. So she was cross, but kind of grateful too I think. Besides, you can't show someone you're annoyed when their mum has just died, so she didn't really say anything.'

'It's true isn't it, that female friendship is so complicated,' Vic said.

'Not really. But the world doesn't just revolve around me does it? I didn't want her to come back on my behalf. If you love someone you let them go, don't you? And I wanted her to have a good summer – it felt like we were becoming adults, learning to make plans without each other.'

'I'm very close to my brother. But beyond that I don't think I've ever had the kind of friendship you've just described. I don't think many men do. It's quite sad really.' Vic was looking at her intently. 'Maybe this is the nearest thing I've ever had to it, to what you describe with Eve.'

'I'm your best friend?' Kate asked.

Vic nodded. 'Well, more than that, I hope?'

He looked at her expectantly. She beckoned him to her and they kissed again, his face in her hands. She pulled away and looked at him.

'More than that,' Kate confirmed.

Room 706

'Does that mean you are officially my girlfriend?'

She really laughed then, at the idea that he might have to ask. 'Yes,' she said. 'I am officially your girlfriend.'

He nodded and puffed out his chest, swaggered to the sink and nudged her aside.

'My turn to wash,' he said, plunging his hands into the water, pulling out a serving dish and handing it to Kate to dry, still covered in tiny bubbles. She watched him as he turned his attention to another dish. Girlfriend. She'd not been a girlfriend before. It felt silly and lovely at the same time. It meant, she realised, that he was her boyfriend. She couldn't stop herself smiling at the idea.

'You must have other friends though, at university?' Vic asked, returning to their conversation.

'Yeah, I suppose. No one who knows my middle name though.'

'Is that your mark of closeness?' Vic asked, glancing at her sideways.

'Uh-huh.'

'Then you'd better tell me yours.'

Kate put down the dish and leaned in close to whisper in his ear. 'Rachel.' She stayed in that position for a few extra moments, her nose in his neck, his smell already familiar to her. He put his soapy arms around her waist and pulled her even closer to him.

'It's nice to meet you, Catherine Rachel,' he whispered. 'I am Victor Antonio.'

'I've never actually stayed in a hotel,' she said a few minutes later. 'Let alone found a dead prostitute in one.'

Vic looked at her. 'Never?'

'No, never.'

Admitting this made Kate feel very young and inexperienced. It was the first time the ten years between them felt like a barrier. She was quiet for a few moments, watching Vic scrub tomato sauce from a stainless-steel saucepan, before she elaborated.

'My mum and I, we used to go to campsites for our holidays. We didn't have that much spare money but, even so, I think she was just a tent kind of person. We hired a campervan once and I loved it, but she liked doing it properly. Under canvas. With Eve in Spain, we stayed in hostels, haggling over pennies here and there you know, the kind where you take your own sleeping bag and have bunk beds in dorm rooms. Occasionally we'd get a private room in a hostel, but not in a hotel. I've never had maid service or a chocolate on my pillow or a breakfast buffet.'

Kate watched as Vic wiped down the kitchen surfaces and then hung out the tea towels to dry, trailing drops of water across the floor as he did so.

He turned to her when he'd finished. 'I like talking to you.'

'I think I was talking at you really. I didn't speak to anyone all summer and now I can't stop.'

'I hope you never stop,' he said. 'I want to know everything about you.'

Kate smiled at him, but felt slightly funny about that. She didn't even know that much about herself yet.

The next evening when Kate went to bed, there was a blue foil-wrapped chocolate on the pillow and the sheets were turned down for her. A handwritten note said *Courtesy of Hotel Victor Antonio.*

Later that night, when Vic softly knocked on her door, she showed him the foil, opened out and pressed flat between the pages of a book.

'I'll keep it as a souvenir of my stay,' Kate said.

'If it's memories you are looking for, I think I can do better than that,' he said, sliding under the sheet of her single bed with her, kissing first her mouth, then her neck, then everywhere else.

A week later, Vic took Kate to Florence by high-speed train for the weekend. It was chilly, but the city felt cosy as they wandered the Uffizi and ate a plate of meats in a small dark restaurant. They looked at gold on the Ponte Vecchio and after a pizza slice from the counter at a place nearby, they headed to the cocktail bar in their hotel, all crushed velvet and low lighting.

'I wanted to take you to your first proper hotel,' Vic said. 'I didn't mean for it to look like an opium den.'

'It would be my first opium den too,' Kate said. 'And thank you.'

'Nonna loves Florence,' Vic said. 'It was her idea I bring you here. Her papa was from this region. He went to Rome to look for work, met her mama, and never left.

'It's beautiful.'

'Where's your dad from?'

'Sorry?'

'You never mention your dad.'

'No.'

'Why not?'

'I don't know him.'

'Not at all?' He looked surprised, like he was struggling to suppress saying something he shouldn't.

'No.' Kate shrugged. Talk of her dad brought up no feelings of emotion in her at all.

'You've never met him?'

'Nope.'

'Do you know who he is?' Vic wasn't going to let this go. She understood his interest. Most people knew who their dad was even if they didn't have a relationship with them.

'Kind of. Not really.'

Her mum had barely known him either. He had been a short fling on holiday, she'd said. A German boy on a French campsite. Teenage fumblings. Cheap beer. A bit of fun.

Her mum was honest with her. She only knew his first name and the vague part of Germany he was from. He was good-looking in a kooky way. He was going to study engineering. He did perfect dives into the campsite pool. He spoke English with an American accent. 'There was no internet then. No mobile phones. I couldn't have found him if I'd wanted to,' Kate's mum told her.

'And did you want to?' Kate had asked her.

'Truthfully, I barely thought about it. You were mine, all mine.' Kate's mum had smiled when she said that, like she was in possession of a wonderful secret.

Kate had never missed him. There wasn't a dad-shaped hole in her life. There was nothing.

Room 706

'You can do DNA tests nowadays and find people online,' Vic said. It's kind of new, but in a couple of years enough people will have done it to create a worldwide database, and everyone will know everything about where they come from.'

'I know.'

There was silence between the two of them. Sometimes she found Vic's desire to know everything about her endearing, basking in the glow of his attention. Other times it was too much, oppressive even, the weight of his interest bearing down on her.

He must have felt this. He broke the silence by changing the subject. 'Do you know what facilitated the invention of the skyscraper?'

'No.'

'Lifts.'

'Lifts?'

'Yes lifts, elevators. If you didn't have lifts then people working on the top floors would have to walk up all the flights of stairs each morning. You couldn't have skyscrapers until you had lifts.'

'Yeah, that makes sense. Why?'

'I was wondering about hotels.'

'Oh.' Kate found the way his brain worked fascinating.

'I was thinking about what led to their invention.'

'There have always been hotels,' Kate said. 'No room at the inn for Mary and Joseph and all that.'

'Yeah, places for travellers to stay. But not hotels as a destination. That's a more modern thing I think.'

'I guess holidays then. Workers' rights, annual leave.'

'And modes of transport,' Vic said.

'Maybe condoms,' Kate suggested.

'Ha, yes. Maybe so.'

Their drinks arrived.

Vic played with the orange peel garnish on the edge of his glass.

'I think you're right. Definitely condoms.'

He looked sexy, lit up in the soft glow of the bar.

'I like to imagine who else is in the hotel rooms,' he said. 'In room 316 an elderly couple are celebrating their golden wedding anniversary. And next door to them in 315 a couple are about to do it for the first time.'

'Who else?' Kate asked.

'Directly below them in room 215, a very glamourous older woman, a cougar if you will, is about to give a young man the very best night of his life. She spotted him from her moped and beckoned for him to follow her, and he will never ever even know her name.'

'What about the room above the old couple?'

'Room 416?'

'Yeah.'

Vic thought for a moment.

'A baby is about to be conceived. They've been having no luck in that department, but the papa-to-be has been to pray to his creator at the basilica this afternoon and tonight he's going to be a creator himself.'

Kate laughed. He reminded her of Eve with his capacity to come up with ways to make entertainment out of nothing. 'You want me to believe all this?'

Room 706

'No. But it will be something won't it? Every room will have a story. No one ends up in a hotel by chance. Maybe you've been kicked out of home. Maybe you left voluntarily. Maybe it's just a holiday. Maybe it's a special night. Maybe you're celebrating. Maybe you're escaping. Perhaps –' he staged a cough, looked at her cheesily, pretended to slick back his eyebrows – 'perhaps you are trying to impress a beautiful young lady.'

'Perhaps,' Kate said. 'Perhaps the lady . . .'

'The beautiful lady,' Vic interrupted.

She nodded slightly, accepting the compliment. 'Perhaps the beautiful lady does not need impressing.'

Vic met her eyes.

'Or perhaps,' she continued, 'perhaps she is hoping to have some help in the morning when she wakes to find a dead prostitute in the room.'

'If that happens,' said Vic, 'and I really hope it does not, then I'm your man.'

Chapter 10

Eight years earlier

Kate was standing in front of her wardrobe, trying to choose an outfit for her second lunch with James. She couldn't even remember what she had worn the week before. She'd been doing her best not to think about this lunch and had mostly succeeded. She had plenty to think about at work, and at home she had a child who still always wanted to be in the same room as her, preferably with his hand resting somewhere on her at all times, checking she was still there.

Now that the lunch was tomorrow however, she felt nervous. She wanted to look both professional and sexy, like a woman for whom lunch with the same CEO two weeks in a row was a normal part of networking.

'Are you okay?' Vic said, looking at her appraise her clothes.

Room 706

'Uh-huh, work lunch with an important contact tomorrow,' she said.

'Wear this.' Vic pulled out a bottle-green dress. 'You look amazing in it. They'll spill all the company secrets.' He kissed her neck, running his fingers down from her ear to her shoulder and she relaxed back against his body. They had sex that night and afterwards she held him close to her.

'*Ti amo*,' she said, speaking Italian.

'*Ti amo*,' he replied.

She wore the green dress to lunch, getting there in good time and hoping to be calmly seated before James arrived. But as she entered the building she saw him come out of the bathroom in the lobby and they reached the lift doors at the same time.

He smiled when he saw her. 'We're both early!'

Kate smiled back. 'Yes.' She noticed how nicely tailored his suit was and wondered whether it was made to measure. No men in her office wore ties and she was surprised by how sexy it looked. His face appeared freshly shaved. He'd had his hair cut since last week.

'I'm excited to see you.' James did not look like he ever got excited, but she accepted his claim with another smile as she felt her cheeks redden. What did he mean by that anyway? They were just two people working in adjacent sectors, who'd enjoyed each other's company while having a professional lunch. The lift door pinged open and they stepped in. To Kate's relief, they were quickly followed by an older woman, meaning they did not have to speak. To avoid returning to her previous train of thought, Kate spent the short ascent to the eighth floor consciously thinking about what it was that made the other person in the lift look American. It came to her as the lift doors opened. Perfect teeth. That's all it took to make the difference.

'Y'all have a nice day,' the woman said as she left the lift.

Kate nodded to herself. She'd been right.

They were on the other side of the restaurant this time, by a window. The sun bounced off the river and onto the buildings on the other embankment. Only now did Kate think to wonder why neither of them had suggested trying a different restaurant this time.

Once they were seated it took an inordinately long time for James to say anything. To stop herself from speaking first she ran through US state capitals in her head. Lists always calmed her down and she still had the woman from the lift in mind. Alabama – Montgomery. Alaska – Juneau. Arizona – Phoenix. Arkansas – Little Rock. California – Sacramento. Colorado – Denver. Connecticut – Hartford. Delaware – Dover. She got as far as Kentucky – Frankfort before he said something.

'If I give you a story first, then perhaps there will be no limitation on the more interesting conversation this time,' he said finally, a little stiffly.

Kate smiled at him. 'Sure, if it's a good one.' His awkwardness made her nerves disappear, and she relaxed in her seat.

James started to brief Kate on a story about the government failing to hold housebuilders responsible for implementing fire-safety measures. It was a good tip, and she remembered what it was like to feel the thrill of finding a story no one else had. She'd pass it on to the news editor and it would probably make the front page if it stood up. The national papers would likely be interested too. Kate took out her notepad and made some rapid notes.

After she had asked James all her follow-up questions, she hit him with the question she asked everyone when she was working on a story: 'What should I have asked you?'

'That is an excellent question. Let me think.'

Kate met his gaze. She had the urge to touch him and see what his skin felt like, how smooth his face was. As she thought this, she felt her cheeks redden. She looked away first.

James spoke eventually. 'What you should have asked me, is why I wanted to meet for lunch again.'

Witty answers about that not fitting into their 300-word front-page slot came to mind, but Kate kept them in. She fancied him, she realised, like a teenage girl might fancy a sixth former who had spoken to her in the corridor once, and now she wasn't sure how to act normally.

Stop it Kate, she told herself. This is a work lunch. It's what grown-ups do. They have lunch. They discuss business. They flirt a little. Then they go back to the office and know there will be a friendly face next time they bump into them at a conference or reception.

She wondered if he was attracted to her too. Probably not, she thought. He probably just got off on flattering younger women, flirting and seeing if he could make them flirt back. She had a jittery feeling in her tummy, nervousness mixed with attraction.

The awkward silence got the better of her first this time. 'Why did you want to meet again?'

The waiter appeared to take their food order before James could reply. They'd not looked at the menu until that point, and each ordered the same as they had last week.

'And to drink?' the waiter asked. Kate hated drinking during the day. It just made her want to sleep all afternoon. But if the conversation so far was an indicator of how the lunch was going to go, she could do with some help relaxing.

'A glass of house white please,' she said.

'Small or large, madam?'

'Large.' James ordered water and she suddenly felt embarrassed by her request for wine. It's not strange to have a glass of wine with a work lunch, she told herself. In fact, it showed that she was confident enough to order what she wanted. She tried not to play with her pen, which was resting on her notebook.

Ordering had broken the tension of the moment and Kate wasn't sure whether or not to be relieved. James gave a small shrug. 'So, you've got a story for your editor?'

Kate nodded.

'Then we can talk about other things,' he said, looking directly at her.

She knew that something had just happened between them, even if the question, the one he had told her to ask, remained unanswered.

Fucksake Kate, she said to herself, is that all it takes? One man to show a bit of interest and the next moment you are thinking about having sex with them? Not that she met many men anyway. Her life was Lenny and Vic and work, nursery runs and quick-to-cook dinners, nappy changes and evenings with an ear constantly listening out for a child waking up. Even when they were awake enough to have quiet sex, as they had last night, she was listening the whole time for the creak of Lenny's bedroom door and the call of 'Mummy'.

Her wine arrived. She drank a mouthful and willed it to work quickly, scrolling through her head for something to say.

'Last week I told you about meeting my husband. So how did you meet your wife?'

He widened his eyes at that. 'Which one?'

'You're a bigamist?'

He gave a broad smile. 'It did sound like I was saying that didn't it? No, I have been married twice. My first wife was what I believe you call a starter marriage.'

Kate hadn't heard the term before, although she could work out what it meant.

'We had a mortgage, but our finances were pretty simple. We didn't have kids. We didn't even have a pet together. We met in our first term at university and we were together for seven perfectly nice years, then we split up and she went her own way and I went mine.'

'That sounds very neat and tidy. Why did you split up?'

James paused. He drank some water and dabbed his mouth with the napkin from his lap.

'Well, at the time I thought it was a case of being too young. We met as students and got married as soon as we graduated. I was very career focused whereas she wasn't really. There were no arguments, but maybe that was the problem. There was nothing. We just co-existed, having a perfectly nice but retrospectively quite boring time. And one day she said she didn't want to co-exist any more and I realised I didn't really care and we saw a lawyer and that was it. If we had not been married it would have just been the kind of break-up on which no one even commented.'

Kate wasn't so sure. She and Vic had been together for nearly eight years and she'd never experienced adult life without him. If they split up she wouldn't just be picking up the pieces, she'd be building them from scratch.

'Do you know what she is doing now?' Kate asked.

'Actually, I do. Kind of. Well, not now, but I have heard from her since. About ten years ago I received a letter from her at work asking me to take a paternity test to see whether her child, then a teenager, was mine.'

'Oh.' This was not going how Kate expected. She tried to keep her face relatively expressionless. The way he spoke was very controlled, as if he had just said that it was nice weather today rather than told her about the possibility of having a secret child. Well, he knew how the story ended already, Kate thought. None of this was a surprise to him, not now.

'That's when I realised I had probably been a bit naïve thinking the break-up was just because we had grown apart. I didn't know whether I wanted a child I had never seen before to be mine. Or whether I should be furious that this meant she had both slept with someone else and hidden a pregnancy from me. That she'd have been pregnant when we split up. That actually this was probably the reason she wanted to split up.'

Room 706

'That sounds like a lot,' Kate said.

'Yes. It was a lot. And it went from being a lot to not being a lot as soon as the test showed that the child was not mine. I hadn't told my wife – my current wife – what was happening, and I never had to.'

Kate looked at him. She couldn't imagine Vic ever being able to keep such a secret from her, thank goodness. If an ex wrote to him and said he might be the father of her child, Kate would be the first person he'd tell, she was sure of it. Putting aside the fact he wore his heart on his sleeve, he'd need her reassurances that she would be there whatever the outcome.

After a few moments James spoke again. 'There is something about you that makes me happy to speak at length, to speak about myself even. That's not something I have ever told anyone else before.'

Kate smiled at him. She liked the feeling of being the only person to know these things.

'It's nice,' he said. 'I feel like I've known you a long time.'

'Me too.' Did she? Or was it the wine making her feel this way? It was just one glass but with pregnancy and then breastfeeding even that was rare for her.

James raised his glass of water. 'To intimate conversation.'

Kate lifted her glass to meet his, though she raised an eyebrow in what she hoped was a quizzical manner. The word intimate made her blush.

He noticed. 'Oh, yes, that may be the wrong word. Not like that. Unless you want to speak dirty to me of course.'

Kate's stomach was churning. She hadn't met men like

this before, so self-assured and confident. Perhaps she should make an excuse and leave now. Yet she wanted to know more about this man and his relationships, and to see how far their conversation might go. She tried to think of a pun about talking dirty, but gave up.

'Tell me about your current wife,' Kate said instead.

She felt stupid immediately after saying the word 'current', as if it was temporary, even though he had used the word first.

'Bea.'

'Bea.' Kate didn't know why she'd repeated it.

'We . . .' James was struggling. Kate decided to help him.

'How long have you been married?'

'Twenty-two years.'

Kate did a quick calculation. Twenty-two years married, a starter marriage, the CEO of a huge company. Must be over fifty.

As if he could read her mind, James told her. 'Fifty-one. You?'

'Twenty-eight.'

'Isn't that young to be settled down these days, to have a child?'

Kate shrugged. 'Is it? I don't know. Maybe it is for women with careers. But inside I've always felt older than I am. My husband is ten years older than me. I was twenty when I met him in Italy, nearly twenty-four when we got married, twenty-seven last year when I had my son. None of it is that unusual . . .' She trailed off.

Kate wanted to bring the conversation back to James, to his life. 'How did you meet your wife?'

Room 706

'Bea? At a dinner party. My friend's wife set us up. She's also a little older than me and she walked into the room and was just so . . .'

What was he going to say? She guessed beautiful.

'Together,' James said.

Fifteen minutes later Kate knew all about Bea, her work as a food stylist for photoshoots, her rich but emotionally distant family who lived in the countryside and her son by her first marriage, whose father had insisted be sent to the boarding school where generations of his family had studied.

'His father is a good man. It's not the school I went to, but it is very similar, with the same values,' he said. Kate didn't want to ask what those values were. Were they different to her values, she wondered, or those her children were being taught? She couldn't think of anyone she knew who had gone to boarding school.

'Do you get on with your stepson?' she asked.

'Oh yes. When he was younger we bonded over rugby and I would take him to games. Now he comes for Sunday lunch every few months and we have a drink after work occasionally, when our schedules allow.'

When the waiter had cleared their plates, James asked her whether she had time to stay for coffee. She said yes. No one kept tabs on where she was in this new role, as long as the work was done.

Kate learned that James had no children of his own, was thrilled his stepson had gone away to school as it meant he could be a step-parent without having to do any actual parenting, had an actual wine cellar in his house and, completely unexpectedly, liked barge holidays, taking a week every spring to slowly wind across the English countryside, exploring the canal network.

'What do you like about them?'

'Locks and ducks.'

'Locks and ducks?' That was an unexpected answer from a man wearing a silk tie.

'Yes. I like ducks. Not just when I am on holiday actually. Every morning on the way to the station, I buy a coffee and a bag of duck food in the park café. It's next to a big pond. They recognise me now, the ducks, and swim to the edge before I even throw any in. I'm the first, I think, before any toddlers have got there yet.'

Kate smiled at the thought of James in his expensive suit, feeding ducks in the park on the way to work.

'So your wife, does she know you are having lunch with me?'

God, why did she say that? Why wouldn't his wife know? She felt stupid the moment the words left her mouth.

'Why would she? Do you know where your husband is?'

Kate thought about it. She was fairly sure she knew where Vic was. He'd be at work, eating lunch at his desk or with colleagues in a meeting room.

'Now you know about the ducks, and about my ex-wife, you know more about me than anyone else,' James said, before she could answer his previous question.

He caught her eye and held it. The feeling he'd given her earlier, of nervousness and expectation, was back.

Room 706

She took a sip of coffee and ran her tongue over her teeth.

'Are you a happily married woman, Kate?'

Shit, he'd read her mind. She thought of Vic. Were they happily married? She'd never really asked herself the question. They shared a language of in-jokes and a child they loved more than anything else in the world. Vic was the person with whom she wanted to share all the observations about her day. But what did happily married even mean? Sometimes she was bored by their lives. Sometimes she just wanted the days or weeks to be a little more varied. Occasionally she thought she should have had a few more adventures before committing to a job, a husband, a career, a family. Mostly she tried not to think about this kind of thing.

'Yes. Very.'

James lowered his voice. 'Kate, I've not stopped thinking of you since last week. I felt something, and I felt that you felt it too.'

Did she feel something then? She didn't know. But he was right that something was happening now. She nodded. She couldn't speak.

He hadn't finished. 'But Kate, I will never leave Bea.'

Kate found her voice. 'Oh James,' she said. 'Don't be silly. I am very capable of liking someone, maybe even sleeping with someone, and not falling in love with them. I love my life. I love my family.'

She wasn't even sure where that came from, let alone whether she was capable of it. She'd married her first real boyfriend after all. Was this her signing up for some kind of arrangement? Had she just suggested they sleep together?

She felt excited at the idea and also embarrassed that he now knew she was even thinking about it, but James caught her eye and smiled, and she felt strangely calm again.

'Well, we could drink to that,' he said, neatly placing his now folded napkin back on the table and raising his coffee cup to meet hers. 'To not falling in love.'

Chapter 11

2.02pm
Room 706

Vic's message needed a response. But what could she possibly send him that would explain things? What did he even know?

What did the police say? she typed and sent.

He replied straight away. *That you are in the siege hotel. Are you okay? Are you hurt? I love you.*

I'm fine. Hiding in a room. I love you too.

Kate put her phone face down before she could see any reply. She didn't think she could say anything more right now. All she could think about was how sticky she felt, how much she needed to wash.

Her bra and knickers were on the floor by the side of the bed. She scooped them up before heading into the bathroom. She took off her dress and, ignoring her thumping heartbeat, dipped a flannel into the bath James had run for her nearly an hour ago. She used the tepid water to clean every inch of her body, before rinsing the flannel and hanging it over the shower screen. She took a clean towel from the rail to dry herself. When she was finished she got dressed again, with underwear this time.

James was looking at his phone when she returned to the bedroom.

'Security services claim they have foiled sixteen major terrorist attacks in the UK alone this year,' he said.

'Where are you reading that?'

'It's a recent paper from some security think tank.'

'Are you finding it helpful?'

He gave her a wry smile. 'No.'

'It's a shame they didn't foil this one.' Kate felt a bit clearer now that she was clean and properly dressed. The white noise in her head had stopped and she felt able to think.

'I keep trying to remember who was in the lobby when I came in,' said Kate. Talking very quietly felt normal now and everything she said was a low whisper.

'And can you?'

'Kind of.'

How could she tell James that when she walked into hotels to meet him she tried to focus on nothing other than the present, that to cheat on her husband meant taking herself to a different plane, one where only she and her lover existed. That to do this she would walk, staring straight ahead, trying to convey a sense of purpose, making eye contact with no one.

She racked her brains now. There had been a group of

Room 706

what looked like young media professionals, all in identical dark-rimmed glasses. Their scarves were still on, all three of them, despite being inside and having taken their coats off. Were they men or women? She wasn't sure. Two men and a woman she thought, or maybe one man and two women.

There was a couple speaking English with Indian accents. The woman in a sari and trainers. She had noticed the incongruity, the pink-and-gold material brushing against a pair of white running shoes. And there was a woman dressed as if she was in the English countryside, waiting by the lifts.

Kate thought about the lift. There was nothing out of the ordinary about it. This one didn't need a room key to operate it. On its walls were A4 frames in which adverts for offers had been placed. *Book your Christmas office party here now* one said. Kate remembered thinking it should be the other way round – *Book your office Christmas party here now*. The letters were made to look like tinsel, wrapping around a Christmas tree. And in the background, strangely, the silhouette of hills with the Hollywood sign, as if that was where Christmas belonged, not the North Pole, or, she supposed, Bethlehem, if you wanted to be technical.

What had the countryside lady been wearing? She'd had a blouse with a collar, maybe light blue. She'd had a green jumper with a cable-knit pattern running up it. Hair that had definitely been blow-dried. Pale pink lipstick. And what her mother would have called 'a bosom', one that made the woman look larger than she was.

She told all this to James. 'Do you think I should let the police know?' she said.

James shrugged. 'Did any of them look like terrorists?'

'I don't know what a terrorist looks like. Do you?' she snapped.

She knew what he meant of course. He meant did any of them look foreign. Of course some people looked foreign – it was a hotel. And what did foreign look like in London anyway? Families in her kids' school spoke more than forty languages between them; she'd read that in the school newsletter on 'culture day'.

'I meant did you see anyone out of place. Anyone who didn't look like they had a reason to be here, anyone not checking in or out?'

'No. Did you?'

If James noticed her tone, he ignored it.

'No.'

She picked up her phone to see what Vic had said in response to her last message. He hadn't replied.

Chapter 12

Sixteen years earlier
Italy

'What did you make of your first night in a hotel?' Vic asked over breakfast in Florence. Kate didn't know what to say. It was everything – lovely and corporate and overrated and comfortable and strange all at once. Knowing that so many other people had probably had sex on the same bed made her feel slightly weird, as did towels that were not her own, though their plump fullness made up for the fact that she wasn't the first person to have used them.

She had to say something, Vic was waiting for an answer.

She took a sip of her coffee and looked him in the eye. 'I love you.'

'I meant to say I loved it,' she confessed to Eve some weeks later, when her friend came to Rome for a visit, a few days into the new year. Eve was staying in a cheap hotel near the main station and Kate joined her, sharing the double bed in the small room.

'You wait your whole life to stay in a hotel then two in two months,' Eve said.

'Yeah, this one's a bit less salubrious though.'

'Still, handy for drugs and paid-for sex.'

'Great.' She threw a pillow at Eve. 'Come on, let's go and explore. We can save the drugs and sex for later.'

Usually the chattier of the two, Eve was quiet as they walked around the city. It was odd to be out with Eve and not have a steady flow of observations in her ear. *Look at that woman's coat, isn't it wonderful? Oh wow, the colour of that car is cool. Did you see that puppy? I wonder how many cobbles there are on this street alone?* But Eve seemed lost in her thoughts and without her chatter they were silent.

'What is it, Eve? You're so quiet.'

Eve shook her head.

That's when Kate noticed she was crying. 'Oh sweetheart, what is it?'

'I'm so sorry. Just, every time I look at you, I think it.'

'Think what?'

'That your mum died and I wasn't there for you.'

Kate pulled Eve to her, hugging her friend tight. 'There was nothing you could do,' she told her. 'You were in America. You didn't know.'

Room 706

'No, but when your letter came I could have left and come straight to you.'

'I wouldn't have wanted that,' said Kate. 'You were having the time of your life – you said so in your letters. I deliberately didn't write sooner.'

'I should have come, though,' said Eve, 'as soon as I did find out.'

'Eve, I saw you before I came here. You came straight to see me from the airport when you got back to Europe. Before you went to see your own mum or anything. You did come.'

'Yeah, but you were coming here the next day. I didn't help with the funeral, the packing up the house, any of it. I'll never forgive myself for not being there.'

Kate handed her a tissue from her bag and Eve noisily blew her nose.

'I don't think there's anything to forgive,' Kate said.

Eve didn't seem to hear her. She carried on speaking. 'Not just for you. I mean mostly for you. But for your mum too. I liked her a lot. I knew her almost my whole life you know. I would have liked the chance to say goodbye.'

They broke apart and walked the city together in silence, Kate trying to think of a way to absolve her friend. She didn't like seeing Eve upset like this. She was usually so upbeat, so excited about life and its possibilities.

'I think,' Kate said eventually, 'that the death of your mother may just be the kind of thing you have to face alone.'

Eve stopped walking and faced her. 'You're the grown-up now.'

'Yeah, I suppose I am.'

They were in front of a large church taking up the whole side of the piazza where they had stopped.

'Shall we light a candle for your mum?' Eve said.

'I thought you didn't believe in God.'

'What's that got to do with it?' said Eve. 'I believe in candles, and light, and hope and . . .'

'Fairies?' Kate offered.

'No, in love and in ritual.'

Kate half shrugged and half nodded. 'Will it make you feel better?'

'Probably. I like all of those things and I like . . .' Eve pulled the small guidebook from her pocket and read about the church in front of them for a moment. 'I like thirteenth-century religious mosaics.'

Kate lightly punched her arm. 'Thirteenth-century religious mosaics? Is that a specialist subject of yours?'

'Absolutely,' Eve said, pulling Kate towards the door. They put their coins into a metal box and each took a candle.

Kate looked sideways at her friend as Eve lit her candle and gently placed it onto the spiked holder. She was silently mouthing some words, her head bowed. Kate reached over and held her hand. 'Thank you Eve,' she said. Eve looked at her, her eyes glistening. 'I love you Kate. I'm sorry.'

Kate lit her own candle and placed it next to Eve's. 'I love you too.'

'I thought Italy was meant to be hot,' Eve said, pulling her coat tight as they left the building.

'Not in January.' Kate laughed. 'Did you not do any research?'

Room 706

'Nope.'

Kate removed her scarf and wrapped it around Eve. 'Wear this,' she said, giving her a hug.

The next day they spent the morning tailing a family of tourists across Rome, into the Vatican City and out again, across piazzas and around the remains of ancient buildings, trying to get into the background of their photos without the family noticing.

'How long do you think it will take?' Eve giggled, 'when they look at their holiday snaps, for them to realise we are in them all?'

As they walked, Kate heard about Eve's exploits with her fellow camp counsellors in America, and with her fellow students now she was back at university. In return Eve listened to Kate talking about Vic.

'So you were at the hotel breakfast and you told him you loved him and then what?' Eve asked, as they left the family of tourists to it and headed for a bar Eve had found in her guidebook, where a variety of *aperitivo* dishes came free with a glass of wine.

What had happened? Kate thought back. She'd said it and Vic had said nothing in reply, just stared at her. She was just about to retract it, to apologise for going too far, for fucking things up when they were lovely just as they were, when she realised that Vic wasn't not speaking because he didn't want to, but because he couldn't. That silent tears were falling down his cheeks. Eventually he seemed able to speak.

'I love you too. Since the moment I met you.'

She felt kind of embarrassed by this. She had liked Vic straight away, but love, she'd not even thought about that until she'd said it by accident.

'Well, he said I love you back and then I realised I do love this man. I love him and his *nonna* and Italy and his head full of facts and his eagerness to please and his beard and his laugh and his vulnerability.'

'You big softie,' Eve said, smiling. They sat silently for a few minutes before Eve spoke again.

'What about fun?' Eve asked.

'Fun?'

'Yeah. Is he fun? Are you silly together? Do you go out dancing all night? I don't know, has he made you take a pedalo on a lake somewhere and then pretended to fall in?'

Kate laughed at that. 'We haven't been on a pedalo,' she confirmed.

She thought a little more about the word fun. 'He's not fun in the silly sense. But I'm not either, you know that. I mean he's not one who would start the dancing at a party, or be the centre of attention. But I would hate that. Do we have fun? I don't know. We walk, we talk, we cook. We eat. We sit next to each other and read. We people-watch and make up stories about them. We're –' she looked for the word – 'comfortable together. And with my mum, he gets it. He doesn't ask a gazillion questions, but he doesn't pretend she's not dead either.'

'He sounds great. I can't wait to meet him.'

'Tomorrow,' Kate said. 'He wanted to give us some time

the two of us first. But tomorrow he's going to meet us. We've saved the Colosseum especially.'

'Friends, Romans, countrymen?'

'Yep, that's the one. Kind of. Mark Antony says it in the play. But actually Julius Caesar died about a hundred years before the Colosseum was built,' Kate said.

'Oh.' Eve made a face. 'I should probably actually read the guidebook.'

'I've been doing a module on it.'

'On Julius Caesar?'

'No. On Rome's architecture.'

Kate was nervous about the two most important living people in her life meeting each other. She felt a bit like she was cheating on Eve by being the first of them to fall in love. And these three nights away from Vic had made her question what she felt anyway. It was the first time since meeting him that they hadn't seen each other every day. What if he wasn't how she remembered him, if time apart had broken the spell?

But he was gloriously himself when he arrived at their hotel the next morning, clutching a tray of takeaway coffees and a bag of cannoli. 'The best cannoli outside of Sicily,' he announced with triumph, kissing Kate on the lips before saying in a stage whisper, 'I've never been to Sicily.' He then turned to Eve and gave her a hug. 'You must be Eve. I'm Vic.'

'He's great, a real keeper,' Eve said to Kate later as they queued for the women's toilets in a nearby café. Kate had left Eve and Vic to chat most of the time, standing slightly apart, taking in the magnificence of the ruined amphitheatre by herself. She could see Vic checking she was okay every so often, asking with his eyes whether he should bring her into the conversation, but she had been happy to let them talk. She realised how much she needed the two of them to like each other.

'Really?'

'Oh yes. He's clever and funny and interesting. And he adores you.'

'Do you think he does? Sometimes I feel like I'm just a silly little girl playing at being an adult and he likes the idea of being the older one, of teaching me things.'

'And the rest of the time?'

'The rest of the time he just adores me.'

Eve laughed. 'I like him a lot. Hold on to him.'

Chapter 13

2.28pm
Room 706

All that Kate could think of was Lenny and Annie. She chewed her inner lip and pictured the two of them, feet against each other on the sofa that morning. She thought of how Lenny's nose crinkled when he concentrated and how Annie still sucked her thumb when she was tired, and about how until recently their idea of a big treat had been to share her bath, limbs everywhere, no regard for the water splashing over the edge or the number of towels being soaked through. Her being here today was nothing to do with them, nothing at all. They didn't deserve this kind of mother, who got herself into this kind of situation. She rubbed her fingers hard against the top of her nose and over her eyebrows, giving slight relief to an ache that had developed at the front of her head.

It would be time to pick them up from school in less than an hour. She should arrange something. She wouldn't get there in time, even if the police burst in and saved the day right now. She'd been ridiculous to think that was even a possibility. Then she remembered. She was only meant to pick up Annie. It was okay, she thought. She could get another mum to pick her up. She could ask Suzy, mother of Daisy in her class.

Kate's head was spinning. She wished Vic had replied to her last message. What had she said to him? That she was hiding in a room. She imagined his brain trying to work out why she was in a room at all. Surely he'd come to the logical conclusion, the correct one, that she was there with someone she shouldn't be. She felt sick. She'd have to put it out of her mind for a moment while she sorted arrangements for the kids.

Kate scrolled through her phone for Suzy's number. Suzy was the kind of mum who sent round reminders when school had a dress-up day or was closed for another bloody inset day. She was organised and good at being the parent of school-age children. Kate was about to send her a message when she remembered that Daisy had a swimming lesson, that's why they never had playdates on Thursdays. She could ask Suzy to take Annie along to watch she supposed. Poor Annie, she hated the pool with its overheated viewing area and smell of chlorine. And Suzy didn't believe in snacks. Annie would be hungry and bored and uncomfortable.

How would Vic react if she sent him a message about practicalities without addressing the huge question of why

Room 706

she was caught up in all of this? She'd just have to do it and see what he said.

I am arranging alternative pick up for Annie. Will ask Daisy's mum. Lenny is at Henry's house. So you'll need to pick them both up around 6.

She was still composing her message to Suzy when one from Vic came through.

Getting on tube. No signal for 20 mins. It must have only sent once he'd got off and exited the station. She felt a huge relief that Vic hadn't just decided not to reply at all.

A second message came through quickly, in response to hers. *Don't worry. En route to pick them both up now. Rearranged playdate for Lenny – thought better to have them home.*

Kate didn't even know Vic had Henry's mum's number.

And then a third message: *I love you. Let's just concentrate on getting you home safely.*

She couldn't think of a more perfect response, short of a message telling her the whole thing had been some kind of elaborate hoax. She willed his message into being – she just wanted to get home safe and hug her babies and be with Vic.

Kate messaged him again. *Are they saying what the terrorists want? How do they think it will end?*

She wasn't sure who she meant by 'they'. The government probably, maybe the media.

She could see the ellipses showing that Vic was typing and then the flash of a message received notification.

There doesn't seem to be a specific ask yet. Not one that is being reported anyway though some experts are saying they are expecting them to demand a prisoner release. Main aim is to instil fear I guess.

Kate quickly typed one back. *Well it's working. Terrified.*

Vic replied straight away. *I love you Kate. It's going to be okay.*

Kate suddenly remembered Fluffy. The rabbit, the sodding rabbit. It felt too much to ask Vic to get Fluffy too. It would be okay – what were they going to do with him at the vet if she didn't turn up, put him down at 6pm? No, they'd have a spare lettuce leaf and a cage overnight surely, and a hefty extra charge on the bill.

Kate saw James notice her messaging. 'What are you doing?' he asked.

'Sorting out my life.'

'Oh. What's so important?'

Of course James would think that she meant she was writing an addendum to her will or sending Vic the code to a safety-deposit box at the bank or something life-or-death. He was a man. He wouldn't be thinking about who would be getting the rabbit from the vet or making dinner. She looked at him but didn't reply.

It's not just that life goes on when you're not there, she thought, it's that the shit bits of life go on too. Everything still needs doing.

She refreshed the news pages on her phone. Hundreds of hostages, they were now saying. Guests and staff from many different countries, numbers unknown. She read the analysis section of the live blog she'd spotted earlier. Their home affairs correspondent must be working incredibly hard

Room 706

to have written a piece so quickly. The intro was stark: *In many ways a hotel is the perfect place for an attack of this kind, impacting visitors from across the globe and striking fear into the heart of every major city.*

She scanned all the coverage trying to find out what the terrorists wanted. Far down an analysis piece on the website of a financial newspaper, she found something. *Some experts have suggested that this specific location may have been chosen due to the connections of the hotel owners to a weapons manufacturer that has been the target of protests in the past. However, most security experts we spoke to think it is more likely a random attack based on proximity to a major transport hub, thus impacting travel across the South East and causing maximum disruption. Demands from this group in the past have often included the release of political prisoners, but if that is the case in today's attack, details have not yet been made public. Western governments rarely admit to negotiating with terrorists, and therefore any demands must be, publicly at least, presented as neither relevant nor achievable.*

Which would be better, outcome wise, she wondered. For the terrorists to really hate the hotel owners, or to have taken over somewhere random to cause chaos?

Oh God, Vic. Poor Vic. What had she done to him? Kate closed her eyes and tilted her head back. At some point, Kate knew, Vic was going to ask why she was there, in the middle of one of the biggest terrorist attacks London had ever seen. Maybe she should just confess all now. Maybe he'd understand that it was nothing to do with him as a person.

That she would no more want to have the kind of sex with him that she had been having in this hotel than she wanted to sit at home on the sofa and watch a TV drama with James. That this was just an escape from the mundane everyday, something to make herself feel good. Could he understand that and also know that he was the only one she loved, that she needed him and never intended for him to find out or get hurt?

Or perhaps he knew everything already. Was that a possibility, that he knew but chose not to know? In some ways it was a comforting thought, though it also made her feel sick, that he might have known all along. But what if he genuinely had no idea? That was most likely. After all, she had been meticulous in leaving no trace, in never writing anything down, in never bringing the toiletries home.

No, she couldn't risk the likely scenario that he had no suspicions, and it all being too much for him to take in if she told him now. This could not be the moment he found himself unable to cope with life again. The kids needed him. She needed him.

What could she tell him instead? When Lenny was a baby she had been so tired that all she ever wanted was a night alone in a hotel where she could shut the door and have no one at all know she was there. Maybe she could tell him she had been doing that today.

Vic just couldn't ever get his head around what it was like to be alone with a baby all day. The constant attentiveness, the interruptibility of everything. The checking – is he breathing? Is he wet? Is he hungry? What kind of cry is that? Am I leaking?

Room 706

Who will hold him while I pee? Do I have spare clothes for him? For me? What about extra nappies, muslins, wipes, dummies, teething gel, barrier cream, nipple pads, energy?

'Tell me how I can help,' Vic asked as they ate a late dinner in their kitchen one night, Kate having spent an hour stroking Lenny's head until he finally slept.

'I just want to go to a hotel alone and sink into a bed that someone else has made and order room service and not leave for twenty-four hours,' she told him.

'Wouldn't you rather go with me?' Vic had asked.

'No.'

He'd been offended. Kate had known he would be. He'd rubbed his beard and wouldn't meet her eyes. She'd resented this, how her hotel fantasy born out of utter exhaustion led to him needing to be comforted.

He'd brought it up again later. 'You want to go with a lover?'

'What?'

'Your hotel. You want to be there with someone else?'

He'd thought she wanted to take a lover. She'd wanted to laugh then, at the very idea of it, that she'd even have the energy or the space in her head for someone else.

'No. I just want to be somewhere entirely alone. Just for a short while.'

He'd looked sad again. 'If that's what you really want we can arrange it,' he said.

'But we can't, can we? He only takes the boob. He only settles for me.'

'He's four months old.'

'I know.'

The next day she'd cried the whole afternoon, holding Lenny on the sofa.

Now she tried to compose a message to Vic in her head. *Do you remember that hotel fantasy of me alone, sleeping? I was doing it today.*

Why today? It wouldn't make sense to be in a hotel today, when she was picking the kids up. He wouldn't believe it. Or that she still felt that she needed this, years later, with children who mostly slept through the night and when she had whole days working from home, both kids at school.

What if she was with the psychologist, not with James? Where had she said she was meeting her? Somewhere near Waterloo, that was what she had told Vic, as close to the truth as possible.

Maybe the psychologist was staying in this hotel. Maybe they were meeting here. Yes, that was it. Had she told him their name? No, she didn't think she had. But it wouldn't take long to do an internet search for psychologists specialising in sleep – there couldn't be that many. Best not to say she was here with someone specific. What if he tried to contact their office and it turned out they were not actually in London today?

Telling more lies to cover up her big lie felt pretty grim. Shouldn't the lies just stop at some point? Kate pressed her eyes with her fingertips and wondered what to say to Vic. No, the lies were to protect him. To protect her, but also to protect him. Okay, she'd say she got the wrong day, that was a good one. She'd messed up, had forgotten it was rearranged to be tomorrow, came in, realised, thought 'Fuck it I'll get a cup of tea in that hotel over there.'

No, no one gets a cup of tea in a hotel, not in an area surrounded by coffee shops. Why would she come into a hotel if not to book a room? To use the toilet maybe? But wouldn't she have gone to the toilet in a coffee shop, not a hotel? She didn't know now. Maybe the one in the coffee shop had been out of order.

When had she ever just happened to be in a hotel if not as a guest? For meetings, seminars, the very occasional afternoon tea for a baby shower or celebration of some kind.

She took some deep breaths. Just passing was a good idea. Maybe she had seen an offer on a poster. Yes, that was perfect. She'd come in to enquire about booking a room for a meeting, or maybe to enquire about rates for the conference rooms. That's it, she was going to arrange a round-table event in February for *Hidden Depths*, a discussion between scientists and philosophers on the ethics of reproductive science. That much was true, she was doing that. They needed a conference room in a hotel where they could also put up the participants, and as she was passing – why was she passing? Because she fucked up on the interview dates – she thought, 'Oh that might be a good place, I'll pop in and check rates and see if they can show me the meeting rooms available.' It was a bit beneath her paygrade, usually the features assistant would do that kind of thing, but she was passing, and she would be chairing the event, which would be written up verbatim, symposium style, so she wanted to check the room was fit for purpose.

So what happened? She went to the front desk, she stood in the queue behind a person checking in, and while waiting to speak to someone she heard a commotion. There were shots. She picked up her bag and she ran. The front door was blocked. There was screaming. She went through a door marked 'stairs' and just climbed and climbed until she was tired. She exited the stairs on the seventh floor and there was a cleaning trolley in the corridor with a master keycard on it. She grabbed it, ran down the corridor, used it to enter a room and shut the door.

No, that was shit, what about the cleaner? Where would they hide without their key? She thought again. She exited the stairs on the seventh floor and there was a cleaning trolley propping open the door to a newly serviced room. The cleaner was nowhere to be seen. Kate entered the room, thrust the trolley into the corridor and locked herself in.

Yes, that all made sense. Okay, now that she knew her story she could pre-empt Vic asking, she could tell him herself.

Kate picked up her phone to tap this all out, and immediately forgot what she was going to say. Did the details matter anyway? What mattered was that she was here, now.

I love you, she wrote. *I'm so sorry.*

Chapter 14

Fifteen years earlier
Italy

'Tom's coming today.'

Kate was curled up in a chair by the window in Nonna's living room, reading in her favourite spot, when Vic walked in with the news.

'He's been at a conference in Turin. He's going to get the train down and spend the afternoon with us, then fly home from here tonight.'

The idea of meeting a brother was fazing. She didn't have any experience of siblings. And she knew how important Tom was to Vic.

'How long is the journey?'

'About four and a half hours.'

'Wow.'

'He wants to see me.' Vic shrugged.

'And Nonna,' he added a moment later.

'Is she excited?'

'I'm going to tell her now,' he said.

A scream of delight from the kitchen confirmed that Nonna was very excited. Vic was anxious though, flitting from room to room, constantly pulling down his shirt and unable to sit for more than a moment. Kate hadn't seen Vic like this before. He'd always talked about his breakdown, and Tom's intervention, with a lightness that made it sound distant, as if it was a funny anecdote from the past rather than something that still affected his present. Now she wondered if there was more to it than she'd realised.

'I'm going to meet him at the station later,' Vic said as he walked around the room again.

'Do you want me to come with you?'

'Yes please.'

Seeing Vic vulnerable was different to him telling her that he was vulnerable. Not that he had ever used that word. Knowing that Tom was on his way, Vic almost became a little boy in front of her. His shoulders became a bit less square. He twisted the bottom of his shirt around his fingers, pulling it tight until his fingers went white, then releasing it to a rush of colour as blood filled them again. He forgot to smile.

Vic gripped Kate tightly as they made their way to the station. She let him squeeze her hand as they walked and tried to match his pace, hoping her presence was enough to let him know how much she cared for him, how protective she felt.

Room 706

She knew there was no point trying to make conversation. Opposite the station entrance, they stopped.

'I'll go in alone. Can we meet you there?' he said, gesturing across the main road to a café with tables outside.

'Of course. I have some reading to do anyway.'

She wanted to reach out and give him a big hug, but it felt wrong, as if she'd be patronising him. She smiled instead. 'Are you okay?'

'Of course I am. It's my brother.' He shrugged off her concern, took a breath and strode towards the entrance, crossing the many lanes of the bus station in front of the modernist building. A moment later she picked her own way across the bus lanes, carefully keeping him in sight. She saw Vic check the board for the correct platform and position himself where it met the concourse. He looked small from a distance. She knew that introducing her to his big brother was a big deal, bigger even than her introducing him to Eve. What if Tom didn't like her? Would Vic listen to him and call things off? And, if he did, would she have to leave Nonna's house too?

Kate stood about thirty metres away, pressed against a wall. They'd timed it just right and Tom's train was approaching. She watched Vic wipe his hands on his trousers and stand up a little straighter. She knew immediately which one was Tom amongst the disembarking passengers. He had exactly the same shape and gait as his brother. He saw Vic and walked towards him, stopping about half a metre away, the way a father might inspect his son. Then a pause and a tight hug, far tighter than Kate expected siblings to do. She could see Vic tensing, trying slightly to pull away, and Tom holding on, and then releasing him just enough so he could stare into his face. She suddenly felt full of concern for Vic. Things must have been even worse than he'd told her, to be hugged like that. Tom said something. Vic nodded, and they started to move apart.

Kate rushed back out of the terminus, back to the café. There was an empty outside table, thank goodness. She was seated and pretending to read a book before Tom and Vic had exited the building. Hopefully they wouldn't notice that there was no coffee cup in front of her.

'This is Kate.' Vic sounded very stiff and formal.

Kate stood up to greet them.

'Kate, Tom. Tom, Kate.'

It took slightly longer than it should have for Tom to smile.

'I'm so pleased to meet you. Sorry it's going to be such a brief trip.'

Kate smiled too. She didn't know what to say. She was still thinking of an appropriate response when he spoke again.

'It's warm for April. Shall we have a picnic?'

Tom and Vic had clearly discussed what they would do in advance. The three of them walked the twenty-five minutes to the Villa Borghese Gardens, the spring sunshine warm on Kate's skin. No one spoke but it didn't feel quiet – there was always so much to look at in Rome that you had a constant conversation between your head and what was going on around you anyway. She wanted to hold Vic's hand, but it felt silly, walking three abreast, to claim possession like that.

Once they were sitting down under a tree, Vic announced

that he would go and get some food for them, bounding off before anyone could protest. Kate and Tom looked at each other. Only then did she realise she hadn't yet said a word since he'd arrived.

Who's going to speak first? Kate wondered.

It was Tom.

'It's great to meet you,' he said.

Kate smiled again.

'Vic's really fallen for you.'

'It's mutual.' It came out a little spikily. She couldn't help but feel scrutinised.

Tom looked at her, not unkindly. 'I'm glad.'

She picked at the grass. Tom broke the silence again.

'I hear Nonna adores you too.'

Kate's smile felt easier this time. 'I adore her.' Her nerves at being observed so closely made her carry on, speaking a bit too fast. 'She's made me feel so welcome. I've never met anyone so warm, so genuine and so generous. I don't mean in terms of having a stranger come and live in her home, though that too, but in terms of the company. Just sitting with her feels good, you know. And . . .' She was going to say 'and she gave me Vic' but stopped herself. It was too much. 'And I'm really grateful,' she finished.

Tom nodded. 'I know. Vic feels the same. I do too. It's why we thought Italy was the best place for him after, you know, when he needed a reset.'

'I can't wait to see her later,' he continued. 'But Vic was adamant that I should meet you first, have a chance to get to know you.'

'Oh. Well what do you want to know?' She was less nervous now that they were actually talking.

'What are you studying?' he asked.

'Languages. Some poetry. A bit of art and history and architecture. I can pick and choose my courses as long as I get enough credits.'

'That sounds fun. Do you like Rome?'

She paused before answering. 'I do. It's always crowded, but there's so much to see just by walking around. I'm on a bit of a shoestring budget, just using my student loan and savings from my job last year. But my student card gets me cheap admission to loads of things so I'm trying to make the most of it and, well, really I just like reading in beautiful places, or people-watching, so it's perfect for that.'

She watched Tom watching her. Perhaps she shouldn't have said so much. Like his brother, he seemed to have a way of giving her space to say things.

'You're more than ten years younger than Vic.'

'Yeah. That's not going to change.'

Tom laughed. 'Sorry, I have so many questions. Vic, well, he's more than a brother. It's like . . .' Tom paused. 'Well, it's more than that. It's like he's part of me.'

Kate nodded. She didn't know whether this made her wish for siblings or be pleased she had none.

'What about your parents? Do they mind about the older boyfriend?'

Kate looked at Tom. 'Vic hasn't briefed you?'

'No.'

Room 706

'My mum died. Quite recently. I never knew my dad.'

Tom nodded. 'I'm sorry.'

'Yeah.' She clicked the fingernails on each hand against her thumbnails. 'Vic's been great,' she offered.

'I'm pleased.'

'What about your parents?' she asked back.

'Vic hasn't briefed you?'

'No.' They both laughed this time. 'Well, yes actually, a little bit. But he hasn't gone into much detail.'

'There's not much to say. They are there. But they are –' he paused – 'distant. Reserved. A different generation.'

This was exactly what Vic had told her, though she had thought there must be more to it than that.

'But Nonna . . .' Kate started.

'I know, she's the total opposite.' He shrugged. 'It must have skipped a generation.'

Neither of them said anything for a few moments.

'How old is your daughter?' Kate asked, for the sake of saying something, though she already knew this from Vic, and from Nonna who regularly showed Kate photographs of her.

'Six, nearly seven. She's called Clara.'

It was a moment before Tom spoke again. She liked him, Kate thought. She could see them becoming friends. He was direct and honest and, like Vic, he seemed genuinely interested in people.

'If it's excitement you are looking for, you're not going to get it.'

'Excuse me?' She thought she had misheard him, but one look at his face showed she had not.

'Vic's not going to be exciting,' Tom said.

'What makes you think I want exciting?'

'Nothing. I am just saying.'

Kate shrugged. 'No one is ever just saying.' She met his eyes. Tom had the good grace to look away.

'I'm not trying to scare you off. I am just saying. Vic, he's very loyal, very loving. Whatever he's told you about wanting adventure, I know my brother. He wants someone to love and someone to love him. He'll give you solid and stable and boring. In a good way.' He met her eyes again. 'Definitely in a good way. I am just trying to tell you, if you want excitement, well, what Vic wants, what he needs, is the opposite of that.'

Kate took her time to work out what she wanted to say. It was hard to be cross, when Tom was so obviously looking out for his brother, but it felt like with this comment he had overstepped the mark.

'It's very sweet that you look out for him. But he's a grown-up. And so am I.' Was she a grown-up? She wondered if even feeling the need to say it meant it wasn't really true. Like a toddler proclaiming their 'big girl' status.

'Yes, of course. Sorry.'

She could see Vic in the distance, coming back, a thin plastic bag in his hand. She could guess what would be in it. Cheese, salami, grapes, bread, maybe some orange-flavoured fizzy water too. Vic had stopped and seemed to be crumbling some of the bread he'd bought into crumbs for the pigeons. She saw Tom see Vic too.

Room 706

'He's still healing.'
Kate nodded.
'Don't hurt him.' Tom looked into her eyes.
'I'll try.'

Chapter 15

Eight years earlier

Kate kept her lunch hour free, thinking that perhaps James might want to meet her for the third week running. Their second lunch had ended oddly, straight after their promises not to fall in love with each other, when a waiter walking past their table had lost control of the tray they were carrying and knocked a glass of water straight into Kate's lap.

Desperate not to make a fuss in front of James, Kate had hastily wrapped things up. The spillage had broken the moment anyway, and immediately made Kate wonder whether she had imagined it. She paid the bill this time, despite James's protestations, then made her excuses. It took ten minutes using the hand dryer in the restaurant toilets before her skirt was dry enough to wear back to the office. It was probably for the best that this had happened, things

Room 706

had got a bit weird. Plus she appreciated the symbolism, cold water being poured on their sexual feelings. She'd have loved to be able to tell Vic. He'd have laughed at that.

A week later, sitting behind her desk at 11.45am, Kate was waiting for an invitation that had not come. She'd just assumed he'd ask her again, same time, same place. She had let herself believe she was desirable when he was probably just flattering her, enjoying the power of making her feel wanted. Now, refreshing her inbox, she felt silly, like a child with a raffle ticket not understanding why their number hadn't been called. She didn't even want the prize.

With no lunch plans and no pressing deadlines, Kate pondered what she might do. She felt a bit sick and tried to remember what she had eaten for breakfast that morning. She was probably just hungry. She'd go for a walk and buy a sandwich on the way back to the office. As she pulled on her jacket, her work mobile rang. No one ever rang it, so the ringtone came as a surprise. Her stomach lurched. Was one of the kids hurt? But the number showing on her screen was not the school's.

'Hello?'

It was him. He didn't even need to say his name. She could tell from the intake of breath before he even returned her greeting. Of course, her work mobile was on the company website somewhere. He must have got it that way.

James skipped the pleasantries. 'How about we lunch *al fresco*?'

From anyone else the use of this phrase would make her cringe, but the way he said it sounded exciting, sexy even. He gave her the address of a small park, just a courtyard really, tucked away in an area just outside the financial district, where old houses and cobbled streets had not yet given way to high-rise offices.

'Just bring yourself,' he said. 'I've got lunch covered.'

It felt kind of thrilling to be told what to do like this, to just follow instructions and not have to think about anything else.

James had bought a ready-made hamper from a high-end deli. They sat on a bench and he took out the contents. Stuffed olives, thick baked dough sticks, a pasta and salmon salad, white wine in a chiller.

He poured her some wine into a plastic glass, then some for himself.

The way he looked at her made Kate feel self-conscious. She felt heat creeping across her chest in a full body blush.

'I am just going to say it,' he said.

Kate waited.

'I needed to see you because . . .' He faltered. 'I'm not good with words,' he said. 'Or feelings.'

Kate found herself enjoying his nervousness. It was good to know it was not just her feeling this way. For a moment she felt powerful, before it gave way to guilt.

'I love my husband,' Kate blurted. Was that presumptuous, even saying it? It was surely just repeating what they had already said at their lunch anyway. She could feel sweat on the back of her neck, prickly and damp.

Kate meant it. She and Vic had rescued each other and Kate couldn't bear to know what would happen if they let each other go.

Room 706

'I love my wife,' James replied.

She swallowed. It was fuzzy between her ears and she felt nauseous, not just because she had, without really noticing, already drunk almost all her glass of wine.

'What is it you want then?' she said.

James leaned across and kissed her. His lips were firm against hers, as if they belonged there. She couldn't help but respond. He moved his mouth to her cheek and she took a deep sniff of him. He smelled woody and spicy and expensive. The fuzziness covered her whole body now. She had never tried drugs but surely it must feel like this. Every part of her felt alive. She didn't think she'd ever felt quite like this before, not in her teenage fumblings, not with Vic, not ever. Maybe she had got married too young.

James pulled away. 'Do you want it too?'

Kate couldn't do anything but nod. So this was what they meant when people spoke about chemistry.

An image of Vic flashed before her eyes. She felt a bit like she had been punched in the stomach, all of the air sucked out of her.

'I have to go,' she said, abruptly getting up from the bench, heading away from James, from this.

'Can I call you?' James shouted after her. She didn't answer, quickly walking the rest of the way out of the park. She managed to get through the gate and out of sight before throwing up the wine.

There was a church around the corner from the park's entrance, a big imposing building with a white tower and brown brick walls. She needed somewhere she could just sit for a while, and spotting its open door she quickly walked up the stairs and went inside. Although she was not religious, since her year in Italy she had loved old churches, the feeling of smallness in a huge universe that they invoked. They were everywhere in Rome, like mini wedding cakes, small sections of their big wooden doors open for you to go inside and just be. She sat in a wooden pew and leaned back, her face raised to the ceiling, the taste of thrown-up wine still in her mouth.

Shit shit shit, she thought. The inside of the church was mostly white and, despite the late summer sunshine outside, Kate shivered. It was like being inside a giant fridge. She wished she'd eaten some of the food before leaving the park. She wished that kissing James had not felt quite so good.

Was she really going to press the self-destruct button?

No. No I'm not. I love Vic. I love my child. I'm just a sad, under-appreciated and overtired mother, who has got excited that someone has shown her some attention.

It was like tossing a penny when you can't come to a decision. Her old editor had told her that. 'When you can't make up your mind, toss a coin or throw some dice, and if you get that sinking feeling in your stomach then overrule what they tell you.' Remember that, she told herself, you can overrule the coin.

And then she thought again of the kiss, the way it felt electric when his lips touched hers. She should have said no when he had asked if he could call. Rather than run away like a child, she should have taken control. She should have said that yes she was attracted to him, but that she

Room 706

had commitments and responsibilities and integrity and self-control. Why hadn't she?

Fuck, I am going to do this. No. No, I am not going to do this. I'm going to overrule the coin.

'You are,' the huge figurine of Jesus at the front of the church seemed to say to her.

'I thought I was meant to have free will,' Kate mouthed. She touched her cold fingers to her cheeks and waited for Jesus to say something back, but he didn't move.

After twenty minutes she managed to pull herself together. I'm going mad, she thought. Wine without food. Not enough sleep. Kate, she sternly told herself, you are not going to have sex with this man. You are not even going to see him again.

When her work phone rang a few days later, she pressed decline.

Chapter 16

3.03pm
Room 706

Kate sat on the bed and played with a loose thread on the duvet cover while looking at her phone. It was only two hours since they'd first found out their predicament. Nothing had happened. If she'd not turned on the television, not checked her phone, if the thick curtains were shut and she'd not tuned in to the helicopters and wondered why their whirr was constant, if she really had only been in the hotel to turn off and tune out, she'd be none the wiser as to her hostage status. Not until she tried to leave anyway.

'No one left and no one came.'
'Sorry?' said James.
'It's a poem. *Adlestrop.*'
James raised his eyebrows.

Room 706

'Nothing happens. That's the whole point of the poem. A train pulls into the station and no one gets off and no one gets on. That's what this is like. No one can leave and no one can come in. As far as anyone else is concerned, we are not here.' It had been one of her mum's favourite poems, quoted every time a train they were on stopped at a station anywhere in the countryside.

It was her mum who had introduced her to poetry, who insisted on reading her a new poem before bed every day. What would her mum have made of this situation? It was hard to know. They hadn't had time to develop a relationship of two adults. 'It's never as bad as you think.' That was her mum's response to most things, be it an argument at school or her own unplanned pregnancy. 'Take a breath, take another, get on with things.'

'And yet we are,' James said, breaking her train of thought.

'We are what?' Kate said.

'Here,' James said.

James did not seem like the kind of person who enjoyed poetry, let alone remembered any to quote. She wondered what he did read for pleasure.

She could ask him, she realised. It was as good a use of time as any. 'What do you like to read then, presuming it's not poetry?'

He considered the question for a moment before answering. 'I'm not really much of a reader other than the newspaper. Except on holiday, then I'll take something big. A history of the Roman Empire, that kind of thing.'

She could hear Vic in her head, somewhat scathing. 'I can't believe you are sleeping with such a cliché.'

A while ago she'd edited a piece on ageing for *Hidden Depths*. The journalist had spoken to women in their eighties and nineties. *What makes you sad about the thought of dying?* had been one of the questions. The team had debated whether to ask it. 'We're all dying,' one of the journalists had said. 'Isn't it unfair to suggest only the old are dying?' But they had posed the question and none of the interviewees had seemed to mind. She remembered the most poignant of the answers: 'There will always be unread books.'

Kate started to move around the room, looking at it in detail. She felt the need to know everything about her surroundings.

The mini fridge had a little sticker on the outside declaring that it had passed its electrical safety test just three weeks before. Well done fridge, she said in her head. She opened the door. It was empty.

She pulled out the desk drawers to see whether there was anything useful in them. They were empty other than a futuristic-looking hairdryer, conspicuous by its fanciness. Its cord disappeared into a hole at the back of the drawer, presumably plugged in behind the desk to make it less stealable. She felt almost insulted that the hotel would think she'd steal a hairdryer. If she had been with Vic they would have probably spent some time discussing whether it was better to have an unsecured cheap hairdryer, or a secured expensive one. He'd go for the cheaper one, definitely. He'd call it 'the honest option'. Then again, he didn't ever have the

Room 706

need for a hairdryer. She didn't think James would have an opinion on hairdryers. She briefly thought about asking him, but she didn't fancy his bewildered look at such a question.

A black glass ashtray was on the desk next to the notepad. She hadn't noticed it before. In it was a small piece of cardboard, folded so that it stood, a message printed on both sides. *Please be advised that this is a non-smoking room. A cleaning fee will be charged if smoking is found to have taken place in the room.*

Why have an ashtray then, Kate thought. Maybe they relied on the cleaning fee to make a profit. Vic would like this observation too, she knew it, the ashtray with the warning not to smoke. Another thing she couldn't tell him.

The second chocolate truffle was still in the open box on the desk, where she had left it. Just looking at it made her feel queasy. She picked it up and put it in the bin, on top of the condom wrapper.

On either side of the bed were light switches that she presumed controlled the whole room – she couldn't test them now. There were no plug sockets within reach of the bed, only by the skirting boards around the edges of the room. She started to write an imaginary review of the place in her head. *Poor socket positioning*, she mentally wrote. *Lots of cushions. Chocolate truffles. Dares you to smoke.*

In the wardrobe was a small ironing board and another cardboard note: *Please contact reception if you would like an iron.*

An ironing board but no iron, she added to her mental review.

At the back of the desk was a tray with tea-making things. The kettle was half sized. A wooden box contained a variety of tea bags, small pots of UHT milk and sachets of sugar. There was also a bowl of coffee-machine pods. Kate looked around for the coffee machine but couldn't see it. Perhaps it had been stolen. Perhaps the hotel was right to secure the hairdryer after all.

James stood up and started pacing the room, occasionally touching the net curtain as if to look outside, then thinking better of it, retreating until he did it again.

We're like lions at the zoo, Kate thought. Nothing to do but lie on the bed or pace in our cage.

She should use this time wisely, in case things ended badly. Kate picked up the branded notepad from the desk, and the pen next to it, and sat down on the bed.

'What are you doing?'

'Writing a note for Vic. Just in case.'

'What are you going to say?'

She shrugged. It was none of his business what she was going to say to her husband. Or had she made it his business by being here with him?

'I don't know. What would you want to know if it was your wife in this situation?'

James didn't answer that. Was he thinking that his wife would never be in this situation? Or that he wouldn't want a note from her if she was?

For just a moment, Kate felt sorry for his wife. She'd never really thought of her as a real person before. In as much as she had ever thought about her, it had been of them as two people bound together by some common sense of womanhood, not as a wronged woman to whom she was bringing pain and upset.

She couldn't start thinking about this, it was unhelpful. She'd always been good at compartmentalising and she did so now, pushing thoughts of his wife away and turning her attention back to the piece of paper.

Okay, think calmly, Kate told herself. What if it isn't terrorists? What if we aren't hostages? What if we are just trapped for another reason? A hungry dinosaur in the lobby perhaps. Lenny had loved dinosaurs when he was younger. They'd played all kinds of games together based on there being a rampaging dinosaur in the house. 'Quick, there's a T-Rex coming – hide!' Kate would shout, and they'd run up the stairs and into hers and Vic's bedroom, diving under the duvet and staying there until she snuck a hand round the edge of it, taking him by surprise with her tickle and shout of 'Roooooar'.

There's a dinosaur in the lobby. What do I need to tell my husband before it kills me? She pictured a dinosaur in her head. Why was this any less scary than a terrorist? Surely the point was that she was there with someone she shouldn't be, rather than the specific disaster that had led to them getting caught out. Terrorist or dinosaur, it didn't really matter.

She turned her attention back to her note. What did she really want for the kids? Make them brush their teeth twice a day. Encourage them to learn languages. Remember to tell them both about periods, not just Annie. Christmas stockings are important even when the kids say they are too old, and should always include bubble bath, chocolate, comedy stationery items and something that lights up or spins. Tell them you love them, every day, several times. Kate didn't know how to write any of this down.

Instead she wrote a collection of letters and numbers with an exclamation mark at the end.

'What's that?' James asked, coming to stand by her side.

She looked at him. 'The password for the online grocery app.'

Kate and James heard the noises in the hall at the same time. They sat stock-still and listened, practically sniffing the air. They heard the door to a room on their corridor open and two voices chatting.

'What are we doing again, Dad?' the voice of a boy said, clear despite being on the other side of the wall and door. He was shouting down the corridor. He didn't sound that old, maybe about Lenny's age, with a Geordie accent. Why wasn't he at school?

A man, less distinct but with the same accent, replied from further away. Something about a boat and the Tower of London. Then the boy's voice again: 'I'm going to press the button for the lift. Hurry up.'

Kate and James looked at each other in horror.

Then a third voice, a woman. 'I'm coming. Sorry.' And the room door banged shut. Then there were more footsteps and the softer banging of the fire door to the lift area.

'How can they not know?' Kate said.

'They must have one of the rooms facing the courtyard.'

Room 706

'Yeah, but the helicopters. Can't they hear them? Maybe they think it's normal for London. Haven't they checked their phones? Shit, James, we need to warn them.'

'How?' James said. 'There's no way. They'll have pressed the call button by now.'

'We have to. There's a child. They're just tourists.' She moved quickly to the door and started to move the footstool and the armchair James had put in front of it.

She was just about to unhook the chain when James placed his hand over hers.

'You can't, Kate. It's too late. You won't have time to warn them and save yourself.' His voice was a whisper but the tone was firm.

'There's a child, James. Get off of me.' She pulled her hand out from under his, but at the same time they heard the very faint ding of the lift about to open its doors and then, as it did, a scream.

There were raised voices now – too unclear to make out. And then a gunshot and another scream, and a moment later the very quiet sound of the lift doors closing.

James moved the armchair back into its place by the door and ushered Kate into the main part of the room. His face was drained of colour and he sat on the edge of the bed, leaning forward, his head in his hands. Kate stood in the middle of the room, watching him, unsure what to do with herself. Even just breathing felt like having to find some oxygen to extract from a jar of treacle. The bridge of her nose hurt.

Eventually she could bear the silence no more.

'Do you think they killed them?' she asked.

James looked up, then straightened his whole body. He spoke slowly when he answered.

'I don't know. Maybe it was just a warning shot? There was only one.'

'Yeah, let's believe that,' Kate said.

James put his finger to his lips. 'We need to be quiet. They are bound to check the rooms after that. They could be listening at our door now for all we know.'

'There was a fucking kid, James,' she hissed. How could he be so unmoved? She was starting to hate this man and his lack of emotion. How could she ever have found him attractive?

His lips were tightly pressed together, and he was breathing through his nose. He closed his eyes for a few seconds before opening them and speaking. 'I know, Kate. I am here too. But there was nothing we could do.'

She leaned against the wall and let it support her as she slid down to the floor. She breathed in hard as deeply as she could. She was being unfair. It wasn't his fault. And he was right to have stopped her opening the door. It wouldn't have saved that family from encountering the terrorists. They'd pressed the button to call the lift before Kate and James had even realised what they were doing, hadn't they? She replayed it in her head. When did they call the lift? Did they have time to let them know? Surely it hadn't been a choice of save them or not, but a choice of join them or not. Still, she hated him, and herself, for not trying.

Chapter 17

Fifteen years earlier
Italy

It was their favourite beach, just over half an hour by metro from the centre of Rome. All around them were couples who had paid a premium for a table and cocktails to drink while watching the sunset, and just metres away were Kate and Vic watching the same sunset, with bottles of beer from the minimart, in what had become a weekly ritual for them over the eight months they'd been together. The waves were gently crashing. They'd had the best afternoon watching other couples, making up their back stories.

'Which of these will have split up within five years?' Vic asked.

Kate looked around at them. 'Look at those two. She

made a face when he splashed her earlier. They're definitely not going to make it.'

'Yeah, and that couple over there, the two men, the taller one just wiped off the kiss from his boyfriend as soon as he turned away.'

'No, that didn't happen. You're making that up.'

'I'm not. He wiped it off.'

On the sea, a wave slightly bigger than the other waves rolled towards them.

'It's kind of mind-blowing isn't it?' Vic said. 'Every one of these people is at the centre of their own worlds. Every one of them has their own web of lies and loves and resentments, their own memories, their own grudges, their own hopes and dreams, their own arsehole exes and annoying best friends, their own grief, their own ambitions.'

Kate was silent.

'It's bonkers when you actually think about it,' Vic continued. 'We're all like tiny little planets, operating with our own laws of physics but sometimes colliding into each other's orbits.'

The grains of sand were still warm on the bottom of Kate's feet. She dug her toes into the warmth and lifted her feet up, letting it spill until there was just a small ridge of tiny particles along the top of each one. She found it hard to think about these big issues, about the point of life and what happens after. Sometimes Vic's thoughts, and his expectation that her brain was capable of engaging with them, felt overwhelming.

Maybe this was just his patter, said to all the women he met in order to sound like some kind of sexy philosopher.

Room 706

She desperately wanted this to be their beach, not the beach he came to with anyone else.

'Have you ever brought a girlfriend here before?' Kate asked.

'No.'

'But you must have had girlfriends?'

'I worked very hard. There was no time.'

'I don't believe you. You're a lot older than me. You've not been single your entire twenties.' She laughed a fake laugh.

He looked at her for a long moment. 'You're jealous?'

Kate chewed her lip for a moment before speaking. 'No. Yes.' She felt embarrassed now, unable to look him in the eye. 'Ignore me, I'm being silly,' Kate said.

Vic put his arm around her and pulled her closer to him. 'Yes, of course there were dates and things where we saw each other for a few months before it petered out. But there's never been anything serious. My fault probably, I was never very engaged. But also, really, I cannot get across quite how little time I had that I wasn't working. So yes, there were women. But nothing serious.'

He paused for a moment, then spoke again, quietly. 'You are the only woman I have ever introduced to Tom.'

'Sorry,' she whispered. 'I just wanted to know.'

She had known at the time that introducing her to Tom had been a big deal. It was good to hear it though. Vic was still speaking and she forced herself to listen.

'But also Kate, now that I have met you, I genuinely can't remember any of them.'

They sat there for a while, his arm still around her.

Remember this moment, she told herself. Remember it forever. The warmth, the weight of his arm, the sunset, the feeling of being loved. She timed her breathing to match his, wondering whether their combined exhalations would be enough to impact the world in any way. What was it they called it? That was it, the butterfly effect. She imagined their breath intermingling and moving across the Mediterranean Sea until it combined with the breaths of everyone else who exhaled at that precise moment in that precise direction, to cause a tornado on the other side of the world.

'What about you?' Vic asked.

'Sorry?' She was lost in her tornado imaginings.

'What about you? Have you had many boyfriends? Gentleman callers? Sexy older lovers?'

'Ha, barely. In fact not really, nothing serious at all. Nobody I ever took home to meet my mum.'

She looked at the sunset again. Despite his reassurances, and the feeling they gave her, it was impossible to let the subject go. 'I just don't want to be, like, one of many that you've brought here.'

What could she say to him? That if she was going to believe in this relationship, if she was going to give it everything even though she was too young to have experienced any other relationships, then she had to know that it was real, that he meant it.

Vic gently turned her face towards him. 'It's not a game, Kate. This is our lives. My life and your life. I've never brought anyone else here, but even if I had what matters is that we're here together now. Sometimes I feel as if you're just waiting for something to go wrong, like you're afraid to feel too comfortable in case the moment you relax into this relationship it's going to end.'

He was right; that was exactly how she felt. Nothing had felt permanent or stable since her mum had died.

'I'm not going anywhere Kate, not unless you want me to.'

She shook her head. 'I don't want you to,' she whispered.

'Good.' He moved his arm from around her and touched her cheek with his hand. 'I'm real, Kate. This is real. I don't say things I don't mean. I try to be honest. I like you. I love you. I'm happy.'

After a few minutes Vic opened two more beers with his keyring.

'Now you tell me something,' he said, passing her one.

Kate took the bottle and stared straight ahead at the sea. It was beautiful. She held the air in her lungs for as long as possible before speaking. 'Sometimes, when I am stressed, I hear voices.'

'What kind of voices?' He sounded interested, not judgemental.

'I don't know. Sometimes it's people who really exist. Sometimes it's like the other voice is just my own thoughts, but not my voice, and instead of thinking them, they are said to me.'

Vic said nothing. She dug her feet into the sand again letting new grains join the ones that were already there.

'I mean most people do. Not everyone, but most people can think things through using words. But it's more than that for me. I have whole conversations, as if I am actually there. They're as real to me as you are, as I am.'

She met Vic's eyes, which were focused on her face as she spoke.

'It's weird. I'm embarrassed. I am not as mad as I sound. But, you know, I've spent most of my life just me and my mum,' Kate said. 'People always used to say "Oh, you must be so lonely." But actually I've never been lonely, not until she died anyway. Growing up, if I wanted to talk to someone other than my mum, I just had to think a conversation into being. Does that sound incredibly weird?'

Vic took her hand and gave it a gentle squeeze. 'It doesn't sound any weirder than anyone else. And I'm pleased you've never been lonely. I've spent nearly my whole life feeling lonely.'

There were a few moments of silence between them. Vic broke it. 'I haven't felt lonely since I met you.'

Kate avoided having to speak by drinking some beer. Even though she worried it might disappear, sometimes the weight of Vic's love for her felt incredibly heavy. She swallowed her mouthful and smiled at him. 'Your turn to tell me something.'

'Okay.' He looked around them. 'See that wave,' he said, pointing at the sea. Kate nodded, tipping her feet from side to side to shake off the sand.

'That came from over there.' Vic pointed at the horizon. 'That's the end of the world, and right at the edge where the flat earth drops off there's a machine pumping out waves of different sizes.'

Kate looked at him and raised an eyebrow.

Vic laughed. 'You have absolutely no proof that is not the truth,' he said.

Room 706

'It's not even that hard to believe,' Kate replied. She felt lighter now.

'Do you know about the idea of the multiverse?' Vic asked.

Kate shook her head.

'It's the idea that every combination of everything exists somewhere. There's an infinite number of universes where every possibility of things has happened. There is a universe where you are called Vic and I am called Kate.' Kate laughed. 'There's one where I kiss you now.' He kissed her cheek. 'And one where I kiss you now instead.' He kissed her cheek again.

'There is one where you sat next to me in the cinema and one where you did not?' Kate said.

'That's right. And one where I have sat in every conceivable seat of every conceivable cinema next to every conceivable person.'

'My head hurts already.'

He kissed her forehead. 'Lucky we are in this universe then.'

The sun was sinking fast. Vic put his arm around Kate again and she moved closer into his embrace. It was a comfortable feeling, being hugged by Vic; their shapes fitted together easily. The couple they had seen earlier, one of whom had wiped off the other's kiss, walked past holding hands.

'What about us? Will we last?' Kate asked.

'Oh yes,' said Vic. 'For a start we've not paid silly money to watch a sunset that exists anyway. We'll last, as much as anything does, as much as tomorrow there will be another sunset, unless the wave machine malfunctions and pulls us over the edge.'

'I hope it's quick if it happens,' Kate said.

Vic pulled her close. 'I love you'.

'*Ti amo*,' she replied.

Chapter 18

Six years earlier

Kate wasn't really in a going-out mood. She'd been woken stupidly early by three-year-old Lenny declaring that it was morning. Having worked the whole day in the *Hidden Depths* office, she just wanted to go home and sit on the sofa. But Nicole had insisted they get together.

They'd met on Kate's first day as a reporter when Nicole swept into the communal kitchen as Kate tried to work out the politics of the mug cupboard. Nicole, who had already worked there for a year in the marketing department, complimented Kate's dress, handed her one of the unstained mugs from the back of the cupboard, and told her about who someone in the sales team was sleeping with, declaring that sharing this knowledge made the two of them friends as well as colleagues.

Now they worked in different places but, mostly due to Nicole's efforts, the friendship endured. Nicole's current role was in marketing at a publishing house, and the plan for the evening was to meet for a drink first and then go on to a book launch Nicole was meant to attend for work. Kate was just wondering whether she could get away with only going for the first part, when a message from her friend came through.

Really hope you're up for tonight, can't wait to see you. Meet at 6.30 in the usual place. N x

The usual place was a wine bar in Holborn. Kate tapped out her reply. *Might just come for one. Am knackered.*

A moment later her phone rang. Kate answered it reluctantly. Nicole skipped pleasantries and got straight to the point. 'I know you're tired, but you'll be more tired if you go home to your family. Come on, what'll happen if you do that? You'll have to do bedtime and clear up the dinner stuff even if you haven't made it. Vic is their dad, so let him do his job.'

'Okay, okay, I'm persuaded,' Kate said. She hated letting people down. Particularly Nicole who, Kate felt, saw her as a closer friend than she did. Kate enjoyed Nicole's company, but she never confided in her. She had never introduced her to Vic, or invited her to their house. But for occasional lunches or drinks after work, Nicole was perfect. Their friendship, and that they managed to maintain it, made Kate feel normal, as if she knew how to operate like everyone else. Nicole had one son, Finn, who she'd conceived during her first year at university and managed to look after alone while studying for her degree. Kate had never asked about his dad, and Nicole

Room 706

had never volunteered the information, although Kate knew Finn sometimes went to stay with him.

Nicole was already in the bar when Kate arrived, standing up so quickly to give her a hug that she nearly spilled her drink. 'You came! Brilliant. I was expecting you to wimp out. I'm so pleased you didn't.'

'Honestly, I thought about it, but you're right about what will happen if I go home. And also, I wanted to see you.'

Nicole beamed at that. 'Good! It's been ages. And it was your birthday recently, wasn't it?'

Kate nodded. 'Yeah. Well, a few weeks ago, mid-October.'

'That's close enough. Let's go and celebrate. We can drink the free champagne and forget about nappies and nursery places and being mum to a three-year-old and one-year-old for a bit, and you can tell me all about your swanky new job, at, what's it called, *Deep and Meaningful*?'

'*Hidden Depths*,' said Kate.

'Oh yeah, that's the one. For women who, how does it go, women who are clever but tired?'

'That's right.'

'Sounds like a bundle of laughs.'

'You should try it. It's for people like you and me, who would be changing the world if we weren't so knackered.'

'You maybe. I'm fine with the world the way it is thanks,' Nicole said, pushing a glass towards Kate. 'Here, I got you some wine.'

'So what's this event tonight?' Kate asked, nodding her thanks.

'Do you remember that case in the news a few years ago,

the woman jailed for killing her husband? The one where all the newspapers campaigned to get her out of jail because it was clear from the trial that she was the real victim? Coercive control and all that.'

'Of course I do, it was huge. Wasn't her conviction overturned in the end?' Kate asked.

'Yep, that's right. And she's written a book about it. It's the launch tonight. I didn't work on it but I have to make an appearance to be supportive. But also, I thought you might be interested. You know, deep and meaningful, hidden depths, nothing is ever as it seems.'

Kate dragged her fingers through her hair, feeling the pull on her forehead. 'I'm just worried I might let you down if I come. I don't know that I have it in me to make sparky conversation. I can barely do that at my own work events.'

'Well, what would you want to do instead?' Nicole asked.

'Sleep,' Kate said. 'Sleep anywhere. A bed, a gutter, the floor of the disabled loo. Lie in a hotel bed someone else has made and sink into it and sleep for a hundred years.'

'I mean that fantasy is fucked as soon as the 10am check-out comes round,' said Nicole, topping up their wine glasses from a bottle in an ice bucket next to their table that Kate hadn't noticed. 'Listen,' Nicole continued. 'Let other people do sparky. You can nod and smile and soak up their energy.'

Kate shrugged. 'Yeah, sorry. I'm such a fun sponge.'

'You're not. You're a mum. A working mum. But even when you're tired, you're one of the most interesting people I know.'

Room 706

'Really?'

'Yeah, really. You're well read and funny and you have views on things. I love hanging out with you. When I can convince you to actually come out rather than cancel,' Nicole said.

This was enough to give Kate a boost. 'You're so nice. I don't feel very interesting.'

'Well you are to me. Look, the launch isn't far and if it's awful we'll come back here and flirt with those men in ill-fitting suits over there.' Nicole nodded towards a group at a large corner table. Kate looked at them.

'It's the sales department of somewhere,' Kate said, smiling for the first time that evening. 'And you're incorrigible.'

'Undoubtedly,' Nicole said. 'What does that mean?' One of the men in suits looked their way and Nicole winked at him, before pulling on her coat. 'Come on, let's go.'

The threat that she might have to talk to them was enough to make Kate pull on her coat too.

The book launch was a short walk away in Bloomsbury, in an elegant townhouse, the second floor of which had been turned into an event space.

'Do you know why women like to read about true crime?' Nicole asked Kate as they walked to the venue.

'Nope.'

'Because every single woman in the world knows it is only their sense of doing the right thing that is holding them back. That socialisation has stopped them from hurting all the many people who have tried to damage or control them. So when they read about someone who has stepped outside of that box, that socialisation, they're not horrified, they're jealous.'

'I don't feel very socialised,' Kate said. 'I feel the opposite. My idea of a good time is just me in a darkened room, sitting quietly.'

'You are though. Think about it. Even just getting through the day smiling at people. Not reacting when someone walks in front of you or a stranger calls you "love". Not taking up space, not drawing attention to yourself, not antagonising any man who looks like he could be violent or aggressive. It's socialisation. And it's exhausting.'

Kate looked at her friend. She rarely saw her so animated about serious subjects. Nicole was more about fun and keeping it light.

'Is everything okay Nic?'

'Yeah. I'm just wondering what it'll be like to look at the face of a killer.'

The answer was disappointingly anodyne. The author greeted people as they arrived: 'Thank you for coming, I hope you like the book,' she said as they entered, not looking them in the eye, not inviting further questions.

'That was underwhelming,' Kate said to Nicole once they had made it to the drinks table.

'It was!' Nicole passed Kate a glass of wine.

'I thought you promised champagne,' Kate said, accepting it.

'Champagne. Warm white wine. What's the difference?' Nicole teased.

The book cover was glamourous, a heavily made-up eye

Room 706

with what seemed like little jewels around it, that were, on closer inspection, tears, like an arty print. There were copies of it hung all over the walls. Kate had been expecting the author to be similarly sexy. 'I wasn't expecting her to look so normal. But she could be me. She could be you,' Kate said.

'Like I said, I think that might be the point,' Nicole replied.

'Nicole!' An older woman dressed like a chandelier approached. Nicole gave Kate an apologetic look and turned to embrace her. Kate spied an open door onto a balcony and slipped through it with her drink.

Too late, she realised someone was there already.

'Are you escaping from the gaze of the killer?' they said.

The voice was familiar but their face was in shadow. It took her a moment to recall whose it was, but she remembered at the same moment he moved into the light.

Kate looked at James. 'Oh my God. I mean, hello.'

'Of all the murderer book launches in all the world,' he said.

She laughed though her stomach was lurching. 'Yeah. Though I think her conviction was overturned wasn't it. So not a murderer at all.'

James gazed at Kate, seeming to take in every bit of her. He was better looking than she remembered, tall and imposing.

'Would you like a cigarette?' he said finally, offering her the pack in his hand.

'You smoke?'

'No.'

'Me neither,' she said, leaning in to take one. He lit it for her, then lit his own from hers.

Kate had not smoked a cigarette for years, though she'd had the occasional one back in school, and as a student. Her mum had never minded. 'If it's the worst thing you do then we're doing okay,' she'd said when she found a pack in Kate's coat pocket, bought with money from her weekend job in a local coffee shop. But then she met Vic, who was adamantly anti-smoking, and she just pretended she'd never been a smoker. It was easy in a new country to reinvent yourself just like that.

Kate took a deep pull on the cigarette, trying to focus as she blew smoke out. The hit of the nicotine along with all the wine made her feel a little dizzy. She held on to the rail of the balcony. They stood next to each other in silence and looked out over the square, cigarette tips glowing in the darkening sky. A line of black taxis was at a rank, the drivers leaning against the front cab, chatting. A group of what looked like students sat with beers on the grassy square they overlooked. His arm brushed against hers. She wasn't sure whether this was deliberate or not.

It had been over two years since she had last seen James, since she had rejected his call. She'd managed to shift him from her head quickly enough. A toddler, a baby, a new job that was nothing to do with his sector. That whole time period had seemed a bit like a dream. And now it seemed as if it was yesterday.

'What are you doing here?' She hadn't meant to say anything.

She turned towards him in time to see his eyes crinkle as he smiled and prepared to speak. 'The author and I are on the parish council together. We often find ourselves on the same side, pushing for an extra park bench or new opening hours for the allotments.'

Kate didn't know what to say to that. It was a different world outside London, in so many ways. Locks and ducks, she remembered now.

'I didn't know it, but I was pregnant,' Kate said.

'Sorry?'

'When we last met. I was pregnant. My daughter, Annie, she's nearly eighteen months now.'

'Would you like me to disappear?' he whispered.

She wanted him to have never been there. But now that he was, she wanted him to stay. Kate shook her head.

'You are still incredibly sexy.'

She fought not to contradict him, to take the compliment. James thought she was sexy. Nicole thought she was interesting. Maybe she was both. Any thoughts of Vic and Lenny and Annie vanished from her head. She was Kate, sexy and interesting. She took a long pull on the cigarette. Even the smoke felt sexy as it curled out of her mouth.

It suddenly seemed like it was only days since she had run out of the park and left James with his posh picnic. A lot had happened since then. And yet, nothing had changed. The attraction was still there. She was still as tired, maybe more so. And he still had some kind of effect on her. Her whole body felt alive.

'Come?' James said. He tilted his head to the door, and she nodded. They'd said hardly anything but the pull was so strong. She stole a look at Nicole, who was holding court with her back to her, then got her bag and coat from the young man by the door and followed James into a rickety lift with diamond-shaped shutters that you closed once you were inside.

'Do you think we should check?' he said in the lift, as it moved between floors.

'Check what?'

'That the chemistry is still there,' James said.

He bent forward, held her shoulders and kissed her on the lips, pulling away almost as soon as hers parted, holding her close, breathing her in.

'Is it real?' he asked. Kate nodded. She couldn't have spoken if she'd wanted. She was there but not there. Almost completely vaporised.

'I am staying across the square,' he said.

His hotel felt like stepping into a gentlemen's club. The foyer walls were lined with old books and the furniture was heavy, made of dark wood. A smartly dressed older man behind a desk nodded at James as they entered and called him 'sir'. The lift was lined with leather.

'Is this where you stay when you are in London?' Kate asked.

'Sometimes. I usually commute daily, though tomorrow I have a breakfast meeting so there was no point. But yes, this is one of my favourites.'

The rooms continued the gentlemen's club vibe with a tartan bedspread, paintings of hunting scenes, heavy flocked wallpaper and a green and gold desk lamp looming over a blotter pad.

Room 706

From the window, Kate could see across the square to the balcony where they had been a few minutes ago, other people now occupying the space that had been theirs. James closed the curtains and gestured to an armchair. It was too low, too deep, too wide, impossible to sit in elegantly, but she sat anyway. She put her coat, bag and shoes in a heap beside it.

James looked at her while he removed his coat and folded it neatly over the desk chair, then unknotted his tie and placed it on top. He went to the mini fridge and removed two bottles of water. He handed one to Kate and opened one himself, drank half of it and put it back in the fridge, barely taking his eyes off her the whole time. She didn't think she could control her fingers well enough to open her bottle, so put it on the floor by her things.

Then James walked to Kate, crouched down, slid his hands up her legs until he found the edge of her knickers and in one seemingly practised movement pulled them down and over her feet. Kate gasped a little. Everything felt incredibly unreal.

He pulled her forward slightly in the seat and spread her legs, her dress sliding up now so that it was half under her bottom. Kate steadied herself with her hands on the wide arms of the chair. It was slow motion, but not because time had stood still. Everything James did was deliberate and neat. He put his face between her thighs and she closed her eyes, ready for the touch of his tongue. But there was just his breath.

And then he moved to the bed and sat on the corner, about two metres away. 'Touch yourself,' he said, 'show me what you like.'

Kate looked at him and laughed, a nervous laugh. James wasn't laughing.

'Please,' he said, and stood up and approached her, taking her right hand and placing it on herself. 'I want to watch.' And then he sat back down on the corner of the bed.

You don't have to do this Kate, she told herself. But she wanted to. She was sexy and interesting and no one had looked at her like this, not in this way, maybe ever. She wasn't sure that she could perform for him though. Not just like that.

'Just feel yourself with one finger,' he said. 'Feel how wet you are.' His voice was so hot that Kate did as he said, just one finger, just to feel. He was right; she was wet. She moved her finger onto her clitoris and started to move it the way she did when she was alone. No one had ever seen her do this before. Hell, she barely had time to do it at all any more. There was always a child in her bed, or a snoring husband. She watched James watching her before looking back to her fingers and, far quicker than expected, she made herself climax, letting out a small yelp then coming to and quickly pulling her skirt back over herself as far as she could.

'So sexy,' James murmured, and came towards her, dropping to his knees and putting his hands on her thighs, keeping her in that position even as her breathing started to return to normal. He put his head into the space between her legs, pushing her skirt back up, and this time he did touch her with his tongue, with broad insistent strokes, ensuring the pulsing she felt did not stop, continuing even as her thighs clasped around him, even as his hands moved to her wrists on the arms of the chair, keeping her as still as she could be, and

Room 706

this time the yelp could not be contained. He kept his head between her legs for some time, until he finally released his grip on her wrists, rising up to kiss her, the smell of her on his tongue and his chin and his cheeks. 'You taste so good,' he said. 'Taste it.' And she did, breathing in deeply, completely aroused by her own arousal. Then leaning back in the chair able to say just one thing. 'Fuck.'

After a while, Kate felt able to stand. 'I should go.' She looked at her phone. Not even that late, 10.27pm. There was a message from Nicole. *I think you left. Guess you were tired. Thanks for coming though. Let's have lunch asap xx*

And one from Vic. *Lenny is in bed, Annie is asleep on me. I am watching tv. All fine, no rush, enjoy yourself.*

Chapter 19

4.17pm
Room 706

'I don't understand why they haven't come to every room yet,' Kate whispered. She was sitting on the floor between the bed and the wall. James had put his phone down and taken his laptop from his leather briefcase. He was reading intently and didn't take his eyes away from the screen when he answered her.

'I am thinking that perhaps they don't have enough of them to do so. There are a lot of rooms. Or perhaps it just doesn't matter. It's not like we can do anything. Anyone who leaves their room will get caught on the way down, as we heard.'

That all made sense. She leaned her back against the wall and closed her eyes, keeping them closed while she spoke.

'We can't have been the only ones to hear what happened

though. Not the shot anyway. Or do you think us and . . . and that family, we're the only ones on this floor?' Kate gave an involuntary shudder. That's someone walking over your future grave, they used to say at school.

James shrugged. 'I don't know, Kate.' He spoke with a sense of finality, as if to say 'No more questions.'

She was clearly irritating him, and the fact of this made her irritated with him in return. But she didn't want to push it. They needed to remain on the same side, not battle each other.

'I know this sounds silly,' she said after a few minutes, 'but everyone I know, every post on all of my social media feeds, the whole world in fact, is talking about this one thing, and it feels like I'm the only person who can't mention it. Yet I'm the one here, actually living it.' She was speaking in an angry whisper. 'My colleagues are probably messaging each other saying, "That's weird. Doesn't she know London is being attacked? Why hasn't she posted a message of solidarity? Doesn't she care?" And now I have just let a kid walk straight into their arms, so they are probably right, maybe I don't care.' She was finding it hard to get enough air as she said this, her breathing ragged.

She forced herself to move her mind from the boy in the corridor to her own children. Kate closed her eyes and thought of Annie. Lovely, sweet, fierce Annie. Having a son was wonderful; she'd loved him instantly, the moment he was born. But having a daughter felt like you had cracked the secret of the universe, that you had managed to make a version of yourself, but better.

'What do you think about when you are bored, Mummy?' Annie had asked recently.

'Well sweetie, when I am in boring meetings, which happens sometimes, I play a version of the alphabet game in my head,' Kate had replied.

'The alphabet game?'

'Yes, you know the one. I choose a category and I try to find a word for each letter of the alphabet.'

'By yourself?'

'Yes. If I choose a hard one it can take loads of time.'

'What's a hard one?'

Kate had tried to think of one that was hard enough to satisfy Annie but not so hard it would take too long. 'Er, flowers.'

'Can we play it now?'

'Sure.'

'But Mummy,' said Annie, almost crying. 'I don't know any flowers beginning with A.'

'Agapanthus,' suggested Kate. 'I'll do A. I'll do any letter you can't get. I'll do A and B. Agapanthus, begonia. Can you do a C?'

Annie thought hard. 'I can. Crocus.' She beamed. 'And daffodil. And elderflower. Your turn Mummy.'

'Forget-me-not. Gardenia. Can you think of an H? No, okay I will. Hydrangea. Iris. Jasmine. I can't think of a K, darling.'

'I can't either Mummy, what shall we do?' Annie's eyes started to fill with tears at this.

'We'll skip it,' said Kate.

Room 706

'We can't.'

'Why not? It's our game.'

Annie thought for a while. 'Okay, but then we need two Ls. Do you know any, Mummy?'

'Yes. I know lots of Ls. Think of your friend at school.'

A frown. Then a look of delight.

'Lily!'

'Yes, that's right. You choose lily and I will add lupin and we have our two Ls.'

A hug, a grin, and then before the letter M, the sound of the key in the lock. Vic was back and Annie was flinging herself into his arms as if he had just returned home from war. And that was it. Poor marigold, poor magnolia, poor mayflower. No chance for their moment. Poor morning glory. Poor narcissus. Poor nasturtium.

I'll do it now, thought Kate, here in the room. Her chest felt tight and breathing felt heavy. What should she do? She heard Annie's voice in her head: 'Do cakes, Mummy.'

'Okay, darling, I will.' Her eyes still closed, Kate began to list cakes in her head.

Angel cake. Battenberg. Christmas cake. Danish pastry. That's not a cake. Okay, um, damn nice cake. Not a cake either. Er, dry crumbly cake. Ah, got one, digestive-biscuit fridge cake. She paused. Would she allow herself that one? Yes. Easter cake, hmmm, yes what else can you call a cake with chocolate eggs on top to make a nest? Easter cake it is. Fudge cake. Genoese cake. Hazelnut cake. Ice-cream cake. Jaffa cake. No, surely that's a biscuit, she told herself. Okay, Jamaican ginger cake. King cake. Lemon cake. Macaron. Also a biscuit. Madeira then. Nut cake. Really? Yes really. Opera cake. Pavlova. Queen cake. Red velvet. Sacher torte. Tea loaf. Upside-down pineapple cake. Victoria sponge. Welsh cakes. Not a cake. Kate agreed with her own thoughts on this one. Wedding cake. Not specific enough but she'd let it pass. Xtra slice of cake. Kate wondered if she was going mad. She might be, she decided, but it wasn't a bad kind of mad and it was helping her to calm down. Yule log. Zeppola. Kate thought of Nonna's version of these small delicious fried balls, always topped with the darkest of cherries. She listened for James. He was still breathing; he was still there. She wondered what he was thinking. Not this, for sure.

She felt a bit calmer now, having completed a list.

And then she heard it. The sound they had been expecting for the past hour, ever since hearing the family. Doors opening. Not loudly, but not quietly either. This wasn't a surprise attack, but she didn't think it was the police or Special Forces either, come to save them. It was too unhurried, too calm. She opened her eyes. James had heard it too. He sat upright, alert.

Another noise, clearer this time. James put his finger to his lips and she mirrored the gesture to confirm. He was afraid, she could see that in the tautness of his features. She was afraid too. Kate checked that her phone was on silent. The lights were off and so was the television. They just needed to stay quiet. She gestured for him to join her on the floor and he silently came to her. They sat next to each other, her right arm and leg pressed against his left arm and leg.

Kate heard a different noise now, the creak of the fire door between the lift lobby and their corridor, and then clear banging on the door of another room. The knocking was controlled, firm but not loud. If it woke you up, you wouldn't be unduly alarmed. You would probably call out to say 'Hang on' and then shuffle to the door to answer it. She caught James's eye again and he took her hand in his, the first time they'd deliberately touched, Kate realised, since finding out about the attack. He squeezed it before relaxing his grip and letting go.

Even though it was expected, the bang on their door took her by surprise. It was all she could do not to scream out loud. She bent her knees and put the soles of her feet flat on the floor, rooting herself, willing her body not to move a muscle, not to cough or give an involuntary squeak.

The voices were clear through the door, one male and one female. The male voice spoke first: 'Hello, is there anyone there?' The female voice followed up: 'There's been an incident and we need you to leave the room.'

Kate remembered the advice of the emergency operator – *Ignore absolutely everything. Stay silent and stay in your room.* She shook her head at James. He gave a quick nod in response.

'Hello, is there anyone there?' the male voice repeated. The tone was right, conveying a sense of importance without being emotional. Kate tried to detect an accent in either voice, to work out where they were from, but it was the kind of accent spoken by people who had been to international schools, or who had learned their English from the television. They were anonymous, unplaceable. 'Hello. Hello.' Knock. 'We are evacuating this corridor. Please open the door.'

Did they know which rooms were occupied? Were they consulting a list? And why, Kate wondered, didn't they have a master key? None of it made any sense.

It felt as if they were at their door for longer than the other rooms. What would happen if they answered it? She imagined what it might feel like to have a gun pointed at her. Would she go quietly? Would James? And then there was more banging but further away, the next-door room, the same script being followed. They had moved on. She hadn't realised how tightly she had been clenching her hands into tight fists until she unfurled them and realised her fingers were numb. Which room had the family who had called the lift been in? God, she hoped they were okay, that the shot wasn't actually at them, that they didn't kill the father in front of his son, or worse, the son in front of his father. She listened hard as the knocks and voices moved up the corridor. She didn't hear any doors open, certainly no screams. Were the other rooms empty, or were people hiding?

Eventually they heard the footsteps move back past their door and towards the lift lobby again. Neither of them moved or spoke for several minutes.

It was James who broke the silence, though he spoke so quietly Kate thought she had imagined it at first. 'Day bookings, or bookings through other sites, they must not register on the main lists. I think that's why they don't know which rooms are empty. That, and not knowing who has gone out for the day I suppose.'

'Yeah.' She kept her voice very quiet too.

'Maybe the front desk staff keep the money for themselves

Room 706

when you pay in cash,' James said. 'That's what I do. I make a reservation on a website and then I pay in cash when I get here so that there's nothing incriminating on my bank statements.'

For the first time in their entire relationship, Kate felt seedy. She pushed the feeling away. She chose to be here. It was her doing something for herself, not her being used.

'At least we know we can hear them if they're patrolling,' Kate said.

James nodded at that. 'Yes, I think you are right. They haven't seemed to bother being quiet with the doors. I mean we should probably continue being very quiet ourselves, just in case, but yes.'

I wasn't about to start shouting, Kate thought but didn't say.

'I don't understand why they don't have some kind of master key,' she said instead. 'Maybe the reception staff were heroes and refused to give it to them. But surely it wouldn't be hard to get one if they have guns or knives or whatever. That would surely be enough to persuade a member of staff to make them one, wouldn't it?'

'Maybe they killed the only person who knows how to program them.'

'James! That's an awful thing to say.'

'Sorry.' They hadn't moved from their place on the floor and she could feel the shape of him next to her.

'I've been reading about it. Information is surprisingly hard to find but there is some discussion on various websites. Mostly from people who have lost their keys on nights out and who are trying to get back into their hotel rooms when the reception desk is unstaffed. But some general systems stuff too.' He was talking quietly but quickly. 'Usually key cards are either programmed to stop working at a specific time, or when a new one is programmed that overrides the previous one so that it doesn't work any longer. But there is a way to deprogram the entire system so that no cards work. If that happened then there would be no way to get into the rooms, not without knowing how to disconnect the locking mechanism entirely.'

Kate nodded, trying to take this all in.

James spoke again. 'I don't know whether that would have been done by someone in the hotel though. Maybe a quick-thinking staff member did it. Or maybe it's something that can be done externally.'

A few moments of silence followed, broken again by James. 'I do think we have to be prepared for them to work it out eventually, for them to reprogram the system and check every room. Either that or kick all the doors in.'

'Yeah. But what happens if they do?'

She shouldn't have asked the question. She knew how he was going to answer it before he opened his mouth.

Don't say it, she thought. Please don't say it.

He said it.

'Then we're fucked.'

Chapter 20

Fifteen years earlier
Italy

Kate and Vic walked the few minutes from Nonna's apartment to the district's main square.

'Ice cream?' he asked.

'Yes please.'

'What flavour?'

'Surprise me.'

'I can't do that,' Vic said.

Kate shaded her eyes against the sun and looked at him. 'Why not?'

He reached out to her and brought her in close for a hug. He kissed her neck and moved his mouth to her ear.

'Because it's a test and you are setting me up to fail.'

Kate protested. 'It's not a test. I just don't know what to choose.'

'Okay. But don't blame me if I bring you back banana or peach and you wanted vanilla.'

Kate watched Vic walk away. Her classes had finished and her essays were all submitted. They'd spent the week playing cards with Nonna each evening, listening to stories about her childhood and bringing up her own children, and how she fell in love with Vic's *nonno* who was the most handsome man she had ever seen. Nonna seemed frailer than when Kate had met her, and keen to tell them her stories while she could.

Kate could see Vic on the other side of the square, buying the ice creams, and then turning to come back towards her.

'Chocolate!' he declared, triumphantly, as he reached her. 'Did I pass?'

Kate licked her ice cream. 'It wasn't a test.'

'But if it had been,' Vic persisted, 'would I have passed?'

She kissed him. 'Yes.'

They'd developed a game that week, on their afternoon walks while Nonna napped. Kate and Vic would give each other an age, either in the past or in the future, and they would have to tell each other either what they remembered or where they hoped they might be.

'Let's play our game,' Vic said.

'Okay, you first. You are eight and a half.'

Vic took a moment to remember.

'I'm in the garden with Tom and he's showing me how many keepy-uppies he can do, which is loads because he is

Room 706

five years older than me, and I am so impressed but trying not to show it. Then he offers me the ball and I have a go, but I am not as good as him. And he's being really nice about it but I want to cry, so I shout at him and then go and hide under this bush in our garden that had room to crawl inside, and you could sit in it like you had a massive green shell. And Tom spoke to me from outside the bush, telling me how he had practised and practised and how hard it was. And how one day it fell into place and he just woke up knowing how to do it, and how that would happen to me too, he knew it, and how about we go and get a snack from inside then try again. So I crawled out of the bush, but I didn't want to show emotion, so when he extended a hand to help me out we kind of got into a wrestle, but it was like a cuddle wrestle. And then it was okay.'

Kate slipped her hand into his.

'Your turn. Fourteen,' he said.

She took a moment to think. 'You're going to like this one,' Kate said. 'There was a boy at school, Craig, and once when Eve and I walked past him in the corridor he made a comment about our breasts, and when we'd got past him he turned around and touched my arse. So I stopped and faced him, and when he got all defensive I just raised my hand and slapped him across the face. We were put in isolation that afternoon, which was fine as they didn't think about it really and we were isolated together, me and Eve, so we just chatted. But my mum was called into school that same afternoon, and the headteacher gave us this big talk about how there was no room in the school for violence. And my mum just looked him in the eye and said: "I couldn't agree more. Now which of us is going to call the police about the sexual assault on my daughter?"'

'She sounds formidable,' Vic said.

'Oh she was, in her own way. I never once heard her shout. But I remember she kept eye contact with the head until he looked away and sent me back to class.'

'And what happened to Craig?'

'Ha yeah, that would be a neater ending wouldn't it, if he'd got into trouble himself. I don't think he had any punishment, but he never bothered us again.'

'Have you ever slapped anyone else?'

'Nope. Not yet.'

Vic kissed her. 'I hope one day we have a daughter as strong as you and your mother.'

She tried not to show on her face the jolt her brain had just received at the mention of kids, his simple assumption that they would have them together one day. He didn't seem to realise he had said anything momentous at all.

'What is it?' Vic asked.

'Nothing. Your turn,' Kate said. 'Thirty-one.'

It was his turn to take a moment before replying. 'That was the year everything went wrong.'

'God yeah, sorry. Shall I pick another one?'

'No, it's okay. I don't have anything to hide from you. I don't really know. I felt like a deflated balloon, and like however much I tried to breathe I couldn't blow myself up again. To start with I continued turning up to work, but I just sat there at my desk in front of a screen of numbers and

Room 706

I couldn't do anything. I couldn't type. I couldn't even tell anyone I couldn't do anything. I'd say to myself that this was just adulthood, that I was a grown-up. You know, I owned a flat, an iron, more than two towels. I wasn't some kind of loser who didn't know how to be an adult. But I felt lonely. So, so lonely. Even when surrounded by people.'

'That sounds terrifying.'

'It was. I managed to call Tom eventually, when I couldn't even get out of bed one day. He dropped everything and came to get me.'

Vic took a deep breath. 'In the beginning he even washed me, and helped me to put food into my mouth like a baby. And very slowly he coaxed me back to life.'

They walked together quietly, their ice creams finished, until Vic spoke again. 'It was also the age I was when I met you, so you know, not all bad. Your turn. You are fifty-six.'

'Oh, I am going to be a fabulous fifty-six-year-old. All velvet scarves and dangly gold jewellery and a sexy voice that sounds like I smoke but if you did an X-ray of my lungs, you'd be able to see that I definitely don't. And my children will have grown up and left home, but not had their own families yet, so my husband and I . . .'

'Will that be me?'

'Don't interrupt. My husband and I will be having amazing weekend breaks all over Europe and beyond, and he'll have to fight off beautiful older men with sparkly eyes and silver hair like silk thread, wearing handmade shoes, who are all vying for my attention and offering me flowers everywhere we go. It'll be my decade.'

'Mmmmm.'

'Your turn,' said Kate. 'A hundred and two.'

'I'll be looking back on a life well lived and drinking a daily double from my collection of fine malts, before shuffling from my city-centre flat to the concert hall downstairs for some entertainment.'

'That sounds nice.'

'Yes. Want to join me?'

There had been a kid in her class at school who used to talk about dying young, and how romantic that would be. Like Jesus. Like James Dean. Like numerous actors and singers. Kate had never felt that way. She wanted to be old one day. Old looked like it might be safe, like it might be full of kindness and wisdom.

But 102. Did she want to be 102 with Vic? Or rather ninety-two, the age difference would still be there. That seemed like a very long time to spend with one person. She stole a sideways glance at him waiting for her to reply, looking both vulnerable and handsome.

'Sure, why not?' The idea of getting old with Vic, it wasn't a bad one. He seemed relieved by her answer, pulling her close, leaving his arm draped around her.

'One more. Twelve and a half.'

'Twelve and a half. I started my period at school, but I didn't say anything. I just stuffed toilet paper in my knickers. And when I got home and saw my mum, she just knew and gave me the biggest hug. And we had takeaway that night, which was a big deal. And I got to choose what we watched on television.'

Chapter 21

Six years earlier

Contact from James came quicker than Kate expected, the day after the book launch. She'd given him her personal number before leaving his hotel but by the time she got home she regretted doing so. It was a one-off, a moment of madness, certainly not something to be repeated. And, while not ideal, they hadn't actually had sex, so it was okay; she hadn't even really cheated on Vic.

She'd picked her phone up that morning to turn off her alarm, and saw a message from him sent just after 6am. It was just two words: *Thank you.*

Kate felt like she might suffocate with embarrassment. It had been so out of character letting him watch her like that. She pulled the duvet up over her head and closed her eyes like a child hiding. If she couldn't see Vic then he couldn't see her.

'Hungover?' Vic asked.

She made a kind of grunt in reply from under the covers. She'd go along with that if it meant she could stay where she was. What if he knew just by looking? She was sure what she'd done must show on her face. What if he could smell the remnants of arousal?

He sniffed the air. 'You smell of cigarettes.'

'Yeah. All the young folk were doing it on the balcony. I ducked out for some fresh air and got it full in the face,' she said from under the duvet. Lying was easier when she didn't have to look at anyone. Her voice was croaky.

'Yuck. Poor you. And you've probably lost all your tolerance to alcohol over the past few years of pregnancies and breastfeeding. You sleep, I'll do this morning,' Vic said.

He got the kids dressed and breakfasted while she stayed in bed. When she heard the front door close behind them, the three of them headed for nursery before Vic went to his office, she finally felt able to sit up and drink from the glass of water Vic had left on the bedside table for her. Her head did hurt, but she also couldn't stop smiling. What had happened? It was wild and crazy and out of character, she thought. Or maybe this was her real character and she'd just never tried to find it before. Maybe she was still drunk.

When Kate woke the second time, the excited feeling had disappeared. She tried to find a word that would describe the heavy heart and sense of impending doom. Ashamed, she thought. But also, alive.

Oh God, she thought in the shower. What had she done? What was she doing? She willed herself to cry. Maybe she

Room 706

could weep away the guilt. But there were no tears. Just a thumping headache and the urge to laugh hysterically.

Lying on the bed again, exhausted by the heat of her shower, she picked up her phone. James had sent another message: *Would you meet me one lunchtime, not for lunch?*

Three weeks later she was on her way to a hotel. Most days she had planned to message James and cancel. Leaving a book launch together buoyed by alcohol and surprise was one thing. Deliberately, soberly, arranging to meet somewhere private felt like quite another. It was late November. She could just tell him there were too many Christmas commitments coming up. Work drinks. Nursery nativities. Dates to meet Santa. Life was busy and she was very sorry but meeting was impossible. Yet somehow each day ended without her cancelling. Okay, she'd just see him once and get him out of her system. Then she could write it off as an experience, tick that box and move on.

Both kids were at nursery and Vic was at work, which meant there had been some time alone at home to get ready and to get worked up. She didn't know whether her own flexible work schedule was a blessing or a curse. If she had to account for her every minute then maybe she wouldn't be doing this.

They would have sex, that much she knew, that was clearly why they were meeting, but she wasn't really sure how it might happen. What did you do when you were meeting someone for sex? Did you say hello? Would there be small talk? Would there be snogging like teenagers meeting someone at a club or a party? What did you do about having the light on or off? Oh God, would he want to watch her again? No, not in the daytime, not sober. She pushed that thought from her mind. Would she even be able to do anything, to clear her mind of Vic and the children and the logistics of their lives that spun around her brain all day every day like a never-ending washing machine?

He'd messaged her the day before with the address of a hotel and a note: *Can you bring the condoms, unless you already have it covered.* Well, at least she didn't need to bring up contraception then. She did not already have it covered. She didn't like the pill, didn't want to try anything hormonal, or implanted under her skin.

When she arrived at the hotel she'd hovered nearby, waiting for James to send her a message telling her where to go. *I'll meet you in the lobby – key card needed for the lift*, it said when it came. She felt sick with excited tension.

He met her as arranged and they locked eyes, stepping into the empty lift together. As soon as the doors were closed he had pulled her to him and kissed her long and hard, stopping only when the lift came to a halt on their floor. She didn't feel nervous any more, just excited.

They were kissing again as soon as they were in the room, clothes off, lights on, fucking very fast and very hard, hands everywhere.

'You're so soft,' he said, 'so beautiful, so sexy.' He'd held her face and looked into her eyes as they moved, and she'd thought of nothing other than how good it felt.

When they finished he held her, but they didn't speak. As

Room 706

Kate's body calmed down she had the overwhelming urge to cry; the release of emotion had been so intense. She held the tears in until James had left, then let them come once she was in the shower, tears of relief rather than sadness. Afterwards, drying on the bed, she felt incredibly relaxed, as if this morning was truly the first time she had ever done anything purely for herself. It was good to get him out of her system.

Chapter 22

5.20pm
Room 706

Kate couldn't stop thinking about the boy's voice as he'd called the lift. About how she and James might have been able to stop them if they had acted as soon as they'd heard anything.

Vic had been checking in on her frequently, but there were only so many ways of asking are you okay, when the answer was clearly no. Still, she needed his reassurance.

Do you really think I am going to get out of here? she typed.

He replied quickly. *I know it.*

I'm scared.

I'm right here, every step of the way, he replied.

She was wondering what to write next when her phone flashed. It was Vic again.

Room 706

Do you remember in Italy when we left our mark in the new road?

Kate did remember. It was mid-August. They were on a back street in Rome walking home from the grocery store to Nonna's apartment. She remembered they had a bag of first crop fresh plums and Nonna had promised to teach them how to make jam. Kate was due back in England in a fortnight, for her final year studying. She didn't want to go. Her year in Italy, with Vic and with Nonna, had suspended reality for her. England was where her mum was dead. Where she had few friends at her university, and even fewer once those on shorter courses had finished. The heat of the day had died down from oppressive to merely stifling when they realised the road they were walking down was blocked by cones and tape to stop people walking or driving over newly filled potholes.

Kate messaged back: *I remember.*

Do you remember what we wrote?

Kate thought about it. It was she who had suggested they make some kind of mark in the asphalt, Vic who had worried about getting caught. Kate had looked around. No one was coming. No one was hanging out of a window. There were no cameras.

'I just want to show that I was here. In Rome. That I existed,' she'd said to Vic. And he'd taken a pen out of his pocket and, using the non-writing end, he'd scratched a message into the edge of a filled pothole.

Was it 'Kate and Vic woz 'ere'? Kate tapped back to him.

No, it was 'V&K always'.

She remembered properly now. He'd marked 'V&K always'

and she had taken his pen and drawn a heart around it, pushing it deep into the road surface.

I drew a heart around it, she replied.

Yes, and then you asked me to come back to England with you, to live with you.

Kate smiled at the memory. She knew he was trying to distract her, and it was working to some extent. She closed her eyes and imagined being back in Rome with Vic. 'Maybe I could just stay here forever,' she had said to Vic. And he'd given her a sensible answer: 'You could. But I need to go back too. My savings won't last for ever and I have a flat I need to sort out. I need to work out what to do with the rest of my life.'

'Do you feel ready?' Kate had asked him as they walked back the way they had come, looking for another street that would lead them where they wanted to go.

'I do, actually,' Vic said.

'Will you come and live with me?'

And Vic's face had broken into a grin. 'I thought you'd never ask.'

'It's full of students.'

'I know.'

'And it's my final year. I'll have to study all the time.'

'I know that too.'

'It's not Rome.'

'Yep.'

'It's not even London. It's over two hours away by train.'

Kate had looked at Vic. Would he really come and live with her? What would he do for money? How would he fill his time?'

Room 706

'I love you Kate, and I'm ready to go back.'

He'd pulled her close to him. His arms were strong around her. 'We've got this,' he'd said, 'the two of us. V and K always.'

What are the kids doing? Kate messaged Vic.

She'd spent most of the last hour or so looking at pictures of them on her phone.

They're watching tv and eating biscuits.

Kate's chest hurt as she thought of Lenny and Annie. There was a very real possibility that she might never see them again. What had James read to her about previous attacks? That the one on the hotel in South America included bombs, but they hadn't gone off. What if they went off this time?

What have you told them? she asked.

I said you had to work late and you would see them in the morning. By the way, we picked up Fluffy. Annie reminded me on the walk back from school.

Can you give them extra kisses for me? she wrote.

Of course. But you'll be able to do that yourself too whenever you get home.

Kate appreciated Vic's optimism. She wondered whether he believed it himself.

Another message came through. *Do you want to tell me how come you are there?*

She'd been expecting him to ask, though it still made her feel dizzy when he did. Kate stared at the message. The phrasing was odd. He must know something was amiss, besides the situation she was in. *Do you want to tell me?* No, she thought, not really.

She typed her reply quickly. She didn't want it to look as if it was taking her time to think of an answer.

I met the sleep woman in the hotel bar. When she left I went to the loo but got lost on the way. Heard a commotion, realised something seriously wrong, ran to hide, found master key card on a cleaning trolley left in the corridor and locked self in room.

She pressed send before she could change the story. It had so many holes. If there was a master key card why didn't the gunmen have one? Why was she on the seventh floor? Though thinking about it, maybe Vic didn't know that detail. What was the commotion? Why did she go looking for a toilet near the guest rooms? And she didn't mean to say she'd met the psychologist. It was almost the story she had worked out earlier, but that one had been better. She should have taken her time to reply, typed more slowly, thought it through again.

What was that phrase her mum had always quoted? 'What a tangled web we weave.' Where did that even come from? Shakespeare probably.

He replied. *I love you.*

Did he believe her? Kate wasn't sure.

I love you too.

She opened the search page on her phone and typed. *What a tangled web we weave.*

It came up straight away. *O' what a tangled web we weave when first we practise to deceive!* It was Walter Scott.

Who even was Walter Scott? She was sure she'd never read him herself. What did it come from? She searched some more.

Room 706

It took a while, a few more clicks. She got there in the end. It was from *Marmion, A Tale of Flodden Field*.

Maybe I should read it now, she thought.

From Scott's epic poem, said the website. Epic meant long. She clicked on a link to a cheat's guide. *An epic poem of over 1,000 lines about Lord Marmion, a courtier in the time of Henry VIII, and his pursuit, with the help of a delinquent nun, of a rich woman in spite of her engagement to another.*

Kate closed the tab. Not today, she thought. Not today.

It seemed highly likely they could be in the room for many more hours. She picked up the pad of hotel notepaper and the pen from where she had left it on the bed. She really should write a proper note for Vic, and for Lenny and Annie. The top page still had the supermarket password on it. Without context it would help no one. But sending it now to Vic struck her as desperately sad. She picked up her phone and emailed it to herself with the subject *Supermarket password*.

What do you write to your loved ones to say goodbye? It was impossible. She recalled watching a television programme about the notes people left behind after the 2001 attacks on America, written by people who knew they were facing certain imminent death on a hijacked plane, and messages left on voicemails from people in burning towers. With not much time to go they had stripped it down to the basics. *I love you. Thank you.*

She flipped the pad to a new page and wrote it down. *I love you.* What if it looked like it was for James? She scrawled *Vic, Lenny and Annie* above the *I love you.*

Kate wished she had her special notebook with her. It

was duck-egg blue with a soft leather cover, slightly spongy to touch. Vic had bought it for her when she got the role at *Hidden Depths*. Embossed in the lower right-hand corner of the cover was the word *Mummy*. Kate loved it, but it was too personal for work, embarrassing even. She couldn't get it out at meetings and still look professional. She kept it instead on her bedside table, for going-to-bed lists and middle-of-the-night thoughts. She felt guilty that Vic had spent so much money on something, with extra for each embossed letter, for it to never see the light of day anywhere else.

This would surely be easier on her laptop. No, she should write it. She still had a box containing scraps of paper with her mum's handwriting, and she loved having something her mum had actually touched.

She took the notepad again and wrote three separate notes, each on a different page.

Vic, I love you so much. Sorry. Kate
Lenny, best boy, I love you, Mummy
Annie, my wonderful girl, I love you, Mummy

Would the kids want an example of every letter in her handwriting? Would they even notice such things? What was that sentence that used every letter? She tried to remember. The quick brown dog jumped over the lazy fox. Or was it the quick brown fox jumped over the lazy dog? Or was the lazy brown fox doing the jumping? None of them could be right – there was no S. Must be jumps, she realised.

She wrote it down on the pad in lower case letters, and again in upper case.

She really was going crazy. Surely no one else would think

Room 706

that about having an example of every letter. Would they spend ages trying to work out what it was code for? No, she knew Vic would get it, that he'd guess what it was she was trying to do.

This is ridiculous, she thought. They've got their writing examples now, I'll do the rest on my laptop. She opened it, connected to the hotel wifi and started a new document, saving it on her main drive. It synced with their computer at home so Vic would definitely find it if he looked. She saved the document as *Letter to Vic*, with the day's date.

She was still sitting by the sockets, in the space between the bed and the wall furthest from the window. She'd created a little nest for herself with some of the hotel cushions, taking the bedside lamp from the built-in shelf and placing it on the floor where enough of its glow was blocked by furniture for her to judge that it would not give away their presence either under the door or through the window. James was back on the bed, his laptop in front of him. She wondered what he was doing now. He was tapping very quietly on his keyboard. It was odd how they could be together in the same room, experiencing the same situation, yet seem to be occupying such different spheres.

Dear Vic, I'm in a bit of a situation as you know. I love you and the children so very much. You have made my life complete. Never forget that.

Never forget that. It sounded ridiculous.

Whatever you find out about me after reading this, please know you were the love of my life.

She read it. No, no way, what if he never found out? Why plant seeds of doubt?

She deleted the whole thing and started again.

Dear Vic, I love you very much. Please know that. You made my life and I hope I have contributed to your happiness.

Fucksake. Like a receipt. She deleted the last line and tried again.

You made my life and I hope I have brought you happiness too.

I want you to be happy and don't want you to feel bad if you have other partners.

No. Delete again.

I want you to be happy and to find love once more.

This was much harder than she thought it would be. Maybe, if death was certain, it was better not to have much time at all. This in between, not certain one way or the other, was impossible to navigate.

She deleted everything.

Vic, Lenny and Annie. I love you.

She looked at it. It just seemed so short, so unfinished. She thought about travel guidebooks with their handy round ups, before the internet and smart phones usurped them. *If you have twenty-four hours here then do this . . . If you have three days then do this . . . If you have a week then do this . . .*

What would it say for twenty-four hours in a terrorist hostage situation with your lover? *If you have two minutes write 'I love you'. If you have ten minutes write it twice and make a note of any passwords your partner needs. If you have an hour do the supermarket shop and finish the novel you are reading.*

She'd been in the hotel for just over six hours. What would

Room 706

it say for that? *Spend two hours fucking your lover, one hour wondering what the fuck to tell your husband and the rest of the time reminding your family that they are the ones you love really.*

A husband and two children each needing a letter, but what if she didn't manage to do them all before being killed, and one child was left out? That wouldn't do. It had better be a letter to all three of them at once. She'd leave Vic to determine at what age they would be old enough to read it.

She deleted the line she had written and started again.

Dear Vic, my true love, and Lenny and Annie, the most important wonderful people ever to come into my life.

I love you I love you I love you. Know that.

Kate stared at the screen. Her eyes filled with tears and she rapidly blinked until she had chased them away.

If it came to it, that was all that really mattered. She saved the note. Emailed a copy of it to herself and then opened the document again.

Kate thought about the inverse pyramid of news writing that she had been taught in her journalism training. Put the most important information at the top and the less vital information further down. Then, if your story needed to be cut, the editor could just take sentences from the bottom knowing that they were losing the least important ones in terms of the story making sense. She'd employed the technique plenty of times herself. Well, she thought, she'd done the I love yous, they were the most important. Yet she felt compelled to keep writing.

Lenny and Annie, when you were younger I'd go through

the many ways in which I loved you when I was putting you to bed. I would tell you that I loved you more than all the drops of water in the ocean and all the grains of sand on all the beaches in the world, and all the stars in the sky. Then we'd move out of this universe and talk about loving you more than all the stars in all the universes known and unknown. And in a funny way I now find myself in a universe unknown where I must write you a letter in case I am to shortly die, in the hope you never have to read this letter. And while I may have hours, or even days, to write it, I may get interrupted at any point. So the most important thing to know is I love you. I love you, I love you, I love you.

Kate reread what she had written. Everything she wanted to say seemed so ridiculous. Sod it, she was just going to let it come out, and she could delete the letter later anyway, once she was home safe and sound.

(For when you are older)

Be kind. To each other and to yourselves.

Have babies. There will never be a right time so just have them whenever you can.

Kate paused. Is that it? Is that all the maternal advice I have?

Vic, there are a million pieces of information I want to give you, practical things about insurance renewal dates and buying school uniform, but in the spirit of the inverse pyramid I am trying to follow in writing this note (I love you I love you I love you, you have completed my life and thank you, I am so sorry) I will leave that for now.

What else could she tell them?

Room 706

Annie – you are strong and fearless and wonderful. Remember you can be anything you want to be. (And, as extra advice, I want to tell you that when in doubt, take painkillers. For your period. For headaches. And definitely for childbirth.)

Lenny – when you were born I remember looking at you and thinking about the huge task of bringing you up not just to be a man, but a kind man. But I look at you now and see we have succeeded. You are so thoughtful, so kind. Hold on to that.

She read it over. The whole thing seemed so ridiculous. But if nothing else it was giving her something to do, so she continued.

I read once that when a mother knows she is going to die she should tell her children the things that only she knows, which really just boils down to what it felt like to give birth to them. I presume, Annie, that you will be more interested in this than Lenny, because one day you may go through it. But the truth is your birth was far less interesting that Lenny's. You didn't even cost me a night's sleep – labour started at 9am and you came bang on 5pm – just like a day in the office, we said at the time. Lenny, yours was terrible. I truly thought I was being ripped apart from the inside'. We learned at school once about a tribe somewhere in the jungle where one of the most gruesome punishments given out consisted of bending two tall trees towards each other and then tying one leg to each trunk before letting go, thus literally ripping the person in half as the trunks bounced back. That is how I felt. But the moment I saw you, clichéd as it may be, none of it mattered in the slightest. I just thought how incredibly clever I was to make such a beautiful baby.

No, Kate thought, reading it back, I can't tell them about feeling like I was being ripped in two. She deleted that and replaced it with *Lenny, yours was harder, as first babies often are.*

That was better. They didn't need to know everything. And Vic had been there too; he could tell them. Not that she thought it had even registered with him at the time, how she thought she was going to die, the bargains she had made with the God in which she didn't believe, the emptiness she had felt for months afterwards as she went through the motions of keeping a small baby alive, desperate to see her own mum.

And she had been ripped in two, not just physically, but emotionally. As soon as Lenny was born a part of her lived outside of her body.

Now that she thought about it, God had actually kept to their side of the bargain. Kate had asked for her children to be delivered safely, for herself not to die in childbirth so that she could bring them up, for the pain to stop. And all of these things happened. If she did believe in God perhaps this would be proof of their existence.

She thought of something else she should share with the kids.

Those days or months or years where everything seems dreadful, they usually turn out okay. When you feel everything is awful ask yourself, do you think it will always feel like this? Or can you see any glimmer of hope at all that it might change one day? Grab on to that hope and gradually it will get bigger and bigger and nearer and nearer and things will start to feel better.

What was it her mum used to say about having a child? Long days, short years. This was turning into a very long day.

Kate looked up at James. She had written everything she needed to write. There was nothing to do now but wait for something to happen. Had James written anything to his wife? Had he even told her that he was here?

'I used to worry that your wife would die.'

He looked up, his face frowning. 'Why would she die?'

'I don't know. Cancer, a road accident, whatever.'

He studied her face. 'Shouldn't it be me worrying about that, not you?'

'No, not the dying per se. I don't even know her. But if your wife died, or my husband for that matter, then we'd be finished too, wouldn't we? And I didn't want that.'

'I'm not sure I'm following you,' James said.

She gazed at him. It felt too hard to explain what seemed very simple to her.

'Every time I come to see you, I think it is the last time,' Kate said instead. 'I come ready to tell you that I don't think we should do this again.'

'But you haven't ever said that,' he said, looking puzzled.

'No. I haven't.' She ran her fingers through her hair, pulling hard as she went, as if she could release the words from her brain by yanking on her scalp.

Whatever her intentions each time they met, she'd never been able to bring herself to end things. The idea of that having been the last time she got to touch his body, that the deliciously secret trysts in hotels would end, would overwhelm her. Her whole body bristling with a kind of post-sex static electricity, she'd bat away any sense that she should fulfil her promise to herself to do this.

Kate stared at a picture on the wall. It was a typical hotel art print, coloured blocks in geometric shapes blending into each other. She could see no greater meaning in it beyond bringing some colour to the room. She tried to follow the line of the frame as she breathed, in on the short sides and out as she followed the line of the longer sides with her eyes. There was some lightness, she thought, despite the dire situation in which they found themselves, in knowing that if they got out of there this period of her life had run its course, that she would never see James again. She'd never meant to carry on seeing him after the first time. She'd never even meant the first time to happen. And now, even if she wanted to see him again, well, it wasn't like she'd ever be able to relax in a hotel again.

'What are you doing on your computer?' James asked.

'Writing a letter to my children, just in case. You?'

'Got to get this report to the Board by Monday.'

'Oh.'

No one gets to their deathbed and wishes they'd spent more time in the office, Kate thought, resisting the urge to say it out loud.

Several minutes passed. They both looked at their screens but neither typed.

'What are you telling them?' James asked eventually.

'I'm telling them that I love them.'

Room 706

'Don't they know that already?'

Did they? She didn't know. She told the children she loved them all the time, so much that sometimes when she said it they just rolled their eyes. Did she tell them too often? She didn't think that was possible. So yes, they knew.

'Do you think I could boil the kettle?' James asked.

Kate shrugged. Surely a kettle boiling in one room wouldn't be the kind of thing that would show up on any systems the terrorists may have access to.

James walked into the bathroom and filled the kettle at the sink, then brought it back to the desk and switched it on. It hummed quietly.

She watched him neatly rip open the square paper packets holding the teabags and put one in each mug. Everything was small, not just the kettle. The mugs looked like they held enough liquid for just a few mouthfuls. Kate remembered when she was a child and her mum had won a travel iron and kettle set in the school raffle. They found them hilarious, not because they rarely travelled and when they did they usually camped, but because they were so small.

'Perhaps,' her mum had said, 'you want less tea on holiday, or your clothes shrink.'

'Bikinis are small,' Kate had said, and they had laughed at the idea of tiny people ironing their tiny bikinis with tiny irons.

Kate and James stood silently watching the kettle. At exactly the moment it clicked off, the hotel phone on the desk rang.

They looked at each other and didn't move. Correlation

is not causation, Kate thought. It had been something that was hammered into them on her journalism course. Just because there are more storks and more babies doesn't mean the storks brought the babies. Just because the phone rang as the kettle boiled doesn't mean the kettle made the phone ring. She watched the phone on the desk. Correlation is not causation. Correlation is not causation.

James watched the phone too. It rang off eventually and then, faintly, they could hear the ring of a phone in the next room, and then in the room beyond that, though Kate was not sure whether that was in her head or not. They must be ringing every room.

Fuck fuck fuck, she thought. When will the door knocking and the phone ringing become kicking down the doors?

Chapter 23

Thirteen years earlier

When they returned from Italy they'd found a flat to rent together near Kate's university campus, in the basement of a house belonging to academics. Vic had started his life again, volunteering with a school reading programme for several months until he got his job at a literacy charity in London. 'Words,' he said, 'just make me so much happier than numbers ever did.' The job came at the right time. He needed to be in the capital in order to arrange the sale of his flat and look for a house to buy for when Kate finished her studies. He stayed at Tom's in the week, returning to Kate on weekends.

One Saturday at their flat, Vic showed her the listing for the house he had viewed that week. 'I went twice, the first time by myself and the next evening I made Tom come with me. It only took half an hour to walk from their place. It just felt right, you know. Solid and cosy and homely all at once. Plus it's currently empty, so the sale would be quick.' She liked this description. Kate had never lived in a house before.

'Has it got a garden?' she asked.

'Yes.'

She was sitting at the computer and he leaned over her shoulder and used the mouse to click through the photos of the property. 'A small one, but it's a decent size for London.'

'And its own front door?'

He kissed the top of her head. 'You can see that it has.'

She tilted her head back so that he was looming over her, upside down. His head the wrong way up made it look as if he had a full head of hair. 'Then I'm sure it'll be amazing.'

'Don't you want to see it first, in person?'

'No. I trust your judgement.'

He kissed her then, still upside down, until she pushed him away. 'I'm going to fall off my chair.'

'I'll catch you,' he said.

The house was on a quiet street between a part of London full of retail parks and train lines and a chic area of trendy coffee shops a couple of miles away, where they preferred to hang out. The large deposit came from the proceeds of Vic's trendy flat near the old docks that he'd bought when he was working in finance. Kate struggled to get her head around how much money he must have been earning at that time. That when she was a teenager buying most of her clothes

Room 706

from market stalls or in the sales, he was what her mother had disparagingly referred to as a yuppie.

They moved in as soon as they could, just as summer ended and leaves started falling from the trees. Vic had been right; it was a cosy house, full of nooks for bookshelves and armchairs.

Just a week after they'd moved in, Tom brought his wife, Polly, and their daughter, Clara, over to meet Kate and to show them the house. More than anything else, Tom's approval felt like confirmation that this was her life now. They ate pizza sitting on the floor, as the table and chairs they'd bought hadn't arrived yet.

Polly was kind, chatty and easy to be with. She was almost the age Kate's mum would have now been, and Kate wasn't sure they had much in common. But as future family, she was great, clearly devoted to Tom and extremely fond of Vic. She followed Kate into the kitchen to help with drinks and took her hands.

'I am so pleased Vic met you,' she said. 'We've never seen him so happy.'

Their daughter was the same. Now aged eight, Clara said thank you, she laughed, she dashed around the house being entirely age appropriate, neither precocious nor naughty, saying and doing nothing offensive or memorable.

Tom was different when he was with Polly and Clara, jollier and less intense. When it was just him and Vic, or him and Vic and Kate, he became more big brotherly, more concerned about their welfare. But with his family there too he just seemed to be himself. Maybe now that Kate and Vic had a house together he'd accepted that he wasn't the only stable presence in Vic's life.

Kate, in the main, felt happy too, no longer thinking of her mum every moment of every day. Her grief sat in her stomach like a pebble, but one that only made itself known every so often.

Kate had been toying with the idea of journalism for a while. She liked studying subjects from all angles and distilling them into something simpler. It was Vic's suggestion that she apply for a three-month journalism course in London.

'You've mentioned it as an option a few times. Why not give it a go? I can support us while you do it.'

'You don't have to do that,' she'd said. 'I'll find a way. I'll get an evening job.'

'Kate,' he said, 'stop it. We're a unit now.'

It was a bright morning about six months into living in their new place when Vic woke Kate up with his suggestion for a day trip.

'Let's go to the coast.'

She had sensed that Vic was planning something for that morning, but she had been expecting croissants in bed, a wander around the flower market, a walk along the canal and maybe a late lunch in a cosy pub. He was expert at creating what she called 'romcom days', ones that usually only exist in films.

She rolled over sleepily, but Vic was insistent. 'Come on, let's have a day out. We need to celebrate your job news.' Kate had been offered a reporter job straight after her course, and

Room 706

had just passed the three-month probation period. 'Besides, I want to feel the spring winds on my face and smell the sea air, skim stones on the water and eat your body weight in fish and chips.'

'Where are we going?'

'Southend.'

'The seaside in March. Really?'

'Yes really. I want to smell the sweet smell of fresh sewage pumping into the estuary. Besides, it's only an hour or so by train. We can pretend we're in Italy again.'

His enthusiasm was infectious.

'Okay,' Kate laughed, 'you win. A day at the seaside it is, though I am not sure the mudflats of Essex compare to the beaches of Ostia.'

They'd eaten warm sausage rolls on the train, bought at the station along with cups of strong tea, and walked straight to the seafront when they arrived. Vic had a crumb of pastry in his beard and Kate eyed the seagulls as they walked. Would one dare to take it from his actual face? Not wanting to take the risk, she pulled him towards her for a kiss and, while doing so, surreptitiously swept the crumb to the ground.

'Shall we take the train or walk?' Vic said, gesturing at the pier railway.

'We've just been on a train so ordinarily I'd say walk. On the other hand, it's the longest pier in the world and it appears to be raining,' said Kate, sticking out her hand to catch a drop.

'Good points. Stay there, I'll get tickets.'

She stood looking at the miniature beach huts and statues

of seagulls in the window of the small shop inside the pier entrance, and the reflection of Vic as he walked purposefully towards the ticket window.

He returned, brandishing two tickets. 'You're in luck, the next train leaves in five minutes.'

Although it was spitting when they got on the train, by the time they got off a short while later it was a glorious bright day a mile out to sea, the rain clouds having been blown into the distance. They walked hand in hand from the train platform to the lifeboat station at the very end of the pier, climbing the stairs to the top level for a better look and then peering through the windows downstairs, behind the shop, to see the lifeboat, before reading the small exhibition on lives saved at sea. A blackboard gave the stats for the month. *Out on a shout* was written at the top, underlined three times. Underneath someone had written, in chalk, *Total call-outs this month – five. Lives saved – nine. Fatalities – none.*

'Good stats,' Vic said. Kate nodded.

Vic took a note from his wallet and put it in the collection box, and they walked back towards the café.

'I'm going to nip in here for the loo,' Kate said.

Vic nodded. 'I'll be right here.'

When she came back, wiping her damp hands on the back of her jeans, she stopped suddenly. Vic was wearing a 'Kiss me quick' straw hat. Before she could ask where he'd got it, he had pulled her to the side of the café, out of sight from the other people on the pier.

'I want to do this properly,' he said, 'but I know you won't want a public fuss.' And he suddenly dropped to one knee

Room 706

and said it: 'Please marry me, Kate. You're the one, I know it, and I love you.' Kate, gobsmacked, happy, and almost certain, nodded and pulled him up, kissing him hard, his beard rubbing her chin and her upper lip as his mouth met hers. She looked at his hat again and laughed. He was crying now and, to Kate's surprise, so was she. 'We'll choose a ring together?' he said tentatively. She nodded.

Vic took from his bag two mini bottles of cava and two straws, and they sat on a bench to drink them. Then he produced matching temporary tattoos of anchors and branded their forearms, wetting the backs of the tattoo paper with the remaining drops from the cava bottles. They held them out to dry in the sunshine as a lone man stopped a few metres away from them and started feeding chips to the seagulls.

Kate tried to count the birds as they whirled and swooped and caught chips mid-air, but every time she was thwarted by the beaks and wings that swirled into one when a new chip was thrown. She tried to remember the collective noun for seagulls.

It's not a murder, she thought, that's crows.

Vic must have read her mind. He put his arm around her and kissed the top of her head. 'Colony,' he said.

Chapter 24

Five years earlier

The work trip was to represent *Hidden Depths* at a publishing conference in Minnesota. It wasn't a sexy destination, but Kate didn't care. It was her first time away from the children, and her first time in the United States, as well as potentially, hopefully, the first nights of unbroken sleep since Lenny was born. He'd only started going through the night even a little bit reliably after Annie was born, so the sleepless nights had been relentless.

Other than the conference, Kate had plans for her three nights and four days, which included sleep, room service, and a whole day at the Mall of America, the largest mall in the whole country. Kate had only brought a carry-on because, she and Vic had agreed, she was going to buy a suitcase in the mall and fill it with new clothes. She needed a revamped

Room 706

wardrobe for her grown-up job, and the kids were now old enough that she no longer needed to think about access for breastfeeding when buying new things.

She'd also promised herself time and space to get what was happening with James straight in her head. That summer she and Vic had taken the kids to Italy for the first time and, with time to relax and take stock of her life, she'd vowed to herself that she would end things with James. Except that when she got home and made arrangements to see him again, she couldn't bring herself to do it and had to admit the truth, that she didn't want to finish things, not permanently. She liked sex with James. And she liked having a secret. It made life exciting.

At five that morning, before heading to the airport, she'd given sleepy kisses to Vic, and to Annie who was between them in bed.

'We'll be fine. Have the best time,' Vic had whispered, 'and don't take any American lovers in that fancy hotel of yours.'

Kate stopped in her tracks. 'What did you just say?'

'Nothing, I was joking. I just said don't use your hotel room for lovers.'

Kate forced out a small laugh. 'Sleep,' she said. 'I will use it for sleep.'

Then she tiptoed into Lenny's room to kiss her son's sleeping head.

Of course Vic will be fine, Kate thought, as she carried her bag down the stairs. The cupboards are stocked and the kids will be at nursery and school. Their clothes are laid out and the timings of their clubs and playdates are written on a piece of paper on the kitchen counter. You literally have to do nothing other than carry out the things I have prepared for you, she thought. She banished this from her head and tried instead to be grateful for the prospect of three nights' uninterrupted sleep.

Quite unexpectedly, wholly wonderfully, just as she was settling down in her seat on the plane, shoes removed, two magazines stuffed into the seat pocket in front, there was a tap on her shoulder. 'Excuse me, could I have a word?' said a member of cabin crew. 'We have some capacity at the front of the plane and a family who are very keen to sit together back here. Would you be interested in an upgrade?'

Oh my God yes please yes please, thought Kate. Words didn't actually come out, but she grinned, took her magazines from the seat pocket and picked up her shoes as the cabin crew opened the overhead locker for her to find her bag and take it to the front of the plane.

The seats at the front had their own compartments, wide and comfortable with plenty of room to stretch out. There was a fleecy blanket in a neatly folded bundle, with *please take me home* printed on its cardboard wrapper. Even up front the airline did not use upper-case letters in its branding, she noticed. There were free fluffy socks and a small washbag containing a toothbrush and toothpaste. They also asked to be taken home. And already another member of cabin crew was walking towards her with a smile. 'Would you like some champagne before take-off?'

'I really would,' Kate said happily.

Room 706

She took out her phone and sent a selfie to Vic.
Upgrade baby.
And then another message. *All okay on school run?*

He replied immediately, a thumbs up and a champagne emoji. And then a minute later, a message: *That looks comfy, wish I was with you. All fine. Lenny's got his club and Henry's mum will drop him home after that. Me and Annie planning a takeaway feast. Love you.*

She reread Vic's message and felt a little cross that Vic's evening did not involve looking after two children the whole time, or cooking. It wasn't fair that time with Papa was treat time. She didn't want Vic to be getting takeaway. She wanted him to be nursing sick children and combing for headlice and hiding vegetables in pasta sauces and making medical appointments. He should be helping Lenny make a paper-mâché pyramid for his school project and filling out the questionnaire Annie's nursery had sent about childcare provision in the local area. No, that wasn't fair, she didn't want them to have a horrible time together. But she didn't want him to think parenting was easy either. It was only easy if someone else did the never-ending tedious tasks.

Don't shoot your load too early, Kate thought. Don't give them all the treats the first night I am away. She took a deep breath and replied: *Enjoy. Love you too x*

Four hours in and Kate was still having a pretty nice time basking in the luxury. This will ruin me, she kept thinking. I'll only ever want to travel this way. She'd read both of her magazines, looked over the speech she was due to give the next day, and watched half a film. She'd eaten lunch chosen from an actual printed menu with embossed writing – salad niçoise, chocolate brownie, wine, coffee, mints – and was settling back with the glass of whisky that she'd just been handed when the seatbelt sign came on. The pilot's voice was calm and authoritative as she spoke. 'Ladies and gentlemen, we are about to hit some turbulence. Nothing to worry about. Seatbelts on and hopefully we'll be through the worst of it soon.'

Kate's stomach dropped. Oh God. She suddenly missed her family. Had the kids wondered where she was that morning, even though she had told them many times that she was going away with work for a few days?

She reached for the whisky in front of her and downed it just before cabin crew came by to pick up all the loose trays and glasses. She was feeling a bit drunk now.

This is how it ends then, she thought. Over the Atlantic wearing fluffy socks. The plane wobbled. Okay, she could handle that. She gripped the armrests, muttering. The plane shook harder the second time. Things jangled. What was it – cutlery, luggage, her nerves? Another bump and Kate rose out of her seat a little, the seatbelt keeping her mostly in place. A shoe rolled past her down the aisle and the plane lurched like a rollercoaster, leaving her tummy behind.

There was a loud cough from the compartment next to hers, then a man's face came into view. 'Are you okay?' He looked concerned. 'Sorry to bother you, but some of your language was a bit . . .'

'Fruity?' Kate offered.

'Yes, colourful,' he said. 'Are you a nervous flyer?'

She didn't think she was, but she was a nervous everything

since having children. Even going to the playground meant being aware of where the gates were, which adults seemed to be there without kids, which dogs looked like they might be able to run across the park and eat her child in one gulp. Hadn't she once been brave and fearless, the kind of person who could move to a new country knowing no one?

That's what a few years of cutting every grape and cherry tomato in half and holding hands at every road does to you, she thought. In fact, that's what having babies at all does to you, in one moment changing you forever into someone with the potential to know the depths of human sadness.

Kate didn't know what to say. She shrugged and tried to smile.

He was older than her, this man. She guessed late sixties. He had a beautiful face. Craggy and smiley and kind. The plane wobbled again.

'Oh fuck shit bollocks.' Kate did not mean to say it out loud. She caught the eye of the man. 'Sorry.'

'Feel free to ignore me,' he said, 'but if you want I can talk you through it.'

Kate nodded. She couldn't really talk at all any more. This was her punishment for leaving her kids, for sleeping with James, for enjoying herself, for being upgraded. What had this kind man done to be included in such punishment though? She turned to look at him again. He was telling her about his garden. She tried to listen as he explained the borders and how he had designed the rock garden. As she focused on his explanations of the types of moss, she felt able to breathe a little more.

'You are doing really well,' he said. 'What's your name?'

'Kate.'

'How old are you, Kate?'

'Thirty-two.'

'Okay Kate, it is nice to meet you. You are doing just great. We're having a bit of a wobble but the plane is designed to deal with much worse than this.' Kate took a deep breath. He carried on talking calmly. 'Keep breathing Kate, and maybe relax your hands a little bit.' She looked at her hands. They were clutching the arm rests so hard they had gone white. 'My name is Michael.' She nodded. 'Shall I continue telling you about my garden?' She nodded again. He started to describe how to maintain a garden pond, and the ways he had devised to keep squirrels off the bird feeder. Kate tuned in and out. She was thinking of Lenny and Annie and how they wouldn't even remember her if she was to die now. She wished she really believed in something or someone to receive her prayers.

'Are you married, Kate?'

'Sorry?'

'You are married?' Michael was looking at her hands, and the rings she wore.

She nodded. 'Yes. To James. I mean Vic. I am married to Vic.' The plane shuddered and her whole head went fuzzy. She could think of nothing but holding on to the armrests. She held her breath.

'Kate. Kate?' She forced her eyes open. 'You need to breathe, Kate.'

The plane was moving around a bit less now. She released her grip a little and took some breaths.

Room 706

'Kids?'

'Sorry?'

'Do you have kids?'

'Oh, yes, I do. My son is four. He just started school this year. My daughter is two. This is the first time I have been away from them. In a different country I mean.'

The plane lurched again, just a small one, and she gasped.

'It's okay,' he said. 'That was quite scary. But I think it's tailing off.'

It didn't feel that way, though after another minute of deep breaths, she had to concede the wobbles were getting weaker now.

He smiled at her. 'We are definitely through the worst of it.'

'Are you a pilot?' she managed to ask.

'No, but I was a firefighter. And the one thing we are trained to do, better than any other profession, is to keep people calm.'

The plane seemed stable now. Cabin crew were coming along the aisles, checking the overhead lockers and picking up shoes and magazines.

Kate smiled weakly at him. Her breathing was nearly back to normal.

'Thank you.'

'Any time, Kate.'

The embarrassment she had felt at causing a scene, needing help, losing control, felt overwhelming. In another act of kindness, Michael had put his headphones on and was watching his screen, meaning she did not have to speak or thank him any more. She closed her eyes and dozed the rest of the way, waking only as the pilot announced their descent.

Kate had forgotten that passengers at the front were allowed off the plane before anyone else. She could definitely get used to this kind of treatment. She found herself just ahead of Michael in the immigration queue once they had entered the airport building. He smiled warmly at her but didn't speak until Kate was next in line for the immigration official.

'Do you know what I've learned about marriage?' he said quietly. Was he talking to her? He must be. Kate shook her head. 'Most marriage problems, they're not problems. They're just marriage. The good bits, the bad bits, the boring years. It's just marriage.' Why was he telling her this? What had she said while convinced she was about to die? She hadn't thought she had said anything. She must have said something to him about Vic or about James. People don't give marriage advice out of nowhere. What about Vic's comments this morning about having a lover in her hotel? Was that from nowhere too?

No, be sensible Kate, she told herself. Vic was making a joke. This man giving her marriage advice was just being kind.

Michael continued. 'It's not a magic thing. It's an arrangement. An economic arrangement if you like. It's how you afford somewhere to live. In evolutionary terms, there's more chance of two of you being able to put food on the table for your kids than one of you. And if you're lucky, if you choose well and you work at it and you stick with it through

Room 706

the boring bits as well as the exciting bits, well then it's an insurance policy against loneliness.'

A spot was becoming free at one of the booths. Kate still hadn't said anything. She really couldn't remember anything she had said to him on the flight now.

'It was nice to meet you, Kate,' he said. 'Remember it's a long game and you have to hold your nerve.'

And then she was called forward. When she got through the other side he was nowhere to be seen.

Chapter 25

5.30pm
Room 706

Kate checked her phone. One of her former colleagues, a French woman who had moved back to Paris a few years ago, had replaced her profile picture with one of Tower Bridge. *#ViveLondres*, it said over the top. *Hope and prayers to my London friends*, posted an American she had been at university with. *#NotScaredMate*, that was the hashtag Londoners were adopting. What would happen if she put a message out there on social media? *Stuck in the siege hotel. Think positive thoughts for me.* What would people do?

She knew what would happen. Hundreds of sad faces and likes to mean 'dislike' very rapidly. Shares. Pithy slogans. And then a reporter would no doubt find her number and send her a message – *Hi, I read online that you're actually*

Room 706

in the hotel. Can you send me a quote about what it is really like?

What would she say? *Thanks for contacting me. It is boring. I still feel a bit sticky. My lover is annoying me.*

Have you seen all the hashtags? Kate messaged Vic.

#IHave, he replied.

#HaHa, Kate sent in return.

#ILoveYou, he fired back.

He was funny, this man of hers. Audacious too, really, to make a joke at a time like this. She loved him for it.

She didn't want to stop messaging. She wondered what it would have been like for him to get the call from the police. She remembered them coming to tell her about her mum's accident, their kind yet detached manner. She should have called him herself, not left it to the police. It was so pathetic. She wondered how his day had been before he got the call. Of course, the dentist.

How was the dentist? she sent him.

Fine, he replied.

She thought again of the family who'd called the lift, and put her hands over her face, almost literally wiping her smile away as she dragged her fingers from her forehead to her chin. That poor boy, so excited for his day in London. How long would it have taken him to realise what was going on, that this wasn't a joke or just even a single bad person with a gun? She tried to imagine what it would have been like to call the lift and for the doors to open and, and what? For them to open to reveal terrorists with guns? Would they have been smiling? Wearing masks? Aiming their weapons as the door opened like the middle-finger roulette she and Eve had played as teenagers in the shopping centre, daring each other to hold up their swearing finger as the lift doors opened?

It was over two hours since that had happened. At home alone, with nothing else to do, this amount of time would have been a godsend, leading to a whirl of productivity. Enough time to put on a new load of washing and hang out the wet stuff. Stack the dishwasher. Chop the veg for dinner. Work through her inbox. Locate and write a card for whatever get well soon, in sympathy or birthday message was called for that week. She'd probably tidy away some toys, order the online shop and do some work too.

She looked up. James was watching her.

'What have you told your wife?' Kate finally asked aloud.

'I haven't told her anything.'

'Really?'

He shrugged. 'There's no need.'

Kate was lost for words.

'She's away for work in America, on the West Coast, consulting on a photography campaign.' He looked at his watch. 'She'll be getting ready for the day now I suppose, or starting work, and I'm sure she'll see the headlines, but I doubt she'd have any reason to think I'm involved in this.'

'Do you think . . .' Kate swallowed. 'Do you think that if we get home okay, if we are the hotel in South America not the circus in the Caucasus, you will tell her?'

He took a moment to answer.

'I think,' he said, 'that there would be no benefit to be had in that.'

Room 706

Was this James just being a man, or something peculiar to him? The idea that Vic might go through an event like this and not tell her was unfathomable. He told her everything, too much sometimes. It could feel as if he shared every conversation he had, every meal he ate, every new street he ever walked down. But mostly she loved it, loved him, loved the way he wanted to know her wholly and for her to know him. That was how he ensured he would never feel lonely again. She had not really thought about the fact that there may be men who did not share everything with their wives.

And, other than what she had with James, she did reciprocate. Sharing things with Vic was what their relationship was about. He genuinely wanted to know her thoughts, her experiences each day, the funny things she had noticed.

That's what had made this whole affair so difficult, the not telling Vic. It wasn't the sex that made her feel like a cheat, though she knew technically that was exactly what made her one, but the seeing a funny sign in a hotel, or irons with no ironing boards, and not being able to tell him about it. After all, he'd probably understand the actual cheating bit, if she explained how it had happened, how she couldn't stop it, how it reminded her that she existed in her own right. He wouldn't like it, but he'd get it.

What was James's wife like? She typed Beatrice into the search box, then paused for a moment before adding James's surname. Did Bea even use his surname? She pressed enter.

Kate couldn't really believe she hadn't done this before. Not knowing too much made her less real she supposed, and if she was less real then so was any guilt. The search didn't bring up much. There was a fundraising page for a charity walk, but when Kate clicked through there were no pictures and just generic good-luck messages from people who had donated. 'I'm doing this walk with my team to raise money for a cause close to all of our hearts,' the message said, giving nothing away. There was a page for a different person with the same name, who seemed to be a grandmother in Florida. And a Companies House entry for a business registration, Bea's business, registered to an address in the village where they lived, she presumed.

Kate did the search again using Bea rather than Beatrice, and the name of her business. This brought up a recent article in an American photography magazine. Kate remembered James once saying she was a food stylist, so that made sense. She clicked through. There was a short profile focusing on her work, but no photo. Kate scanned it. Most of the article was technical, about how to ensure food looked fresh on long shoots in hot weather. But something about the piece niggled. She read it again, more slowly this time. *Bea tried moving to California full time a few years ago as so much of her work was in the Golden State, but only lasted eighteen months. She missed the changing seasons, she tells us, and her garden in England.*

You don't just try moving to another country if your marriage is fine, Kate thought. Surely James and Bea hadn't split up? He'd have told her, wouldn't he?

She had to ask him.

'James?'

'Yes.'

Room 706

She looked at his hands. His wedding band was on as normal. She was relieved, though she was sure she'd have noticed if it had suddenly disappeared.

'Are you married?'

'You know I am,' he said.

'Are you still together though? Properly together, not separated?'

'We're together,' he said, though he seemed to very slightly hesitate first. 'Why do you ask?'

She couldn't think of any reason she could give other than the truth. 'I have just looked her up, your wife I mean. It says here that she moved to California at one point.'

He opened his mouth to speak, then stopped himself.

'It's just, well, I don't think you move alone to a new country if your marriage is going well,' Kate said. She regretted it immediately. What did she know about other people's marriages? She barely understood her own.

He did speak this time. 'We had a break. A few years ago. Lots of her work was there. Mine is here, as you know. And, well, things were a little strained.'

'Were we, you know, did we see each other then, when you were single?'

His voice seemed a little forced when he answered. 'I was never single. Not really.'

Kate leaned her head back against the wall.

'And she's there now?'

'She is,' he confirmed. 'But these days she only goes for a week or so at a time.'

'Why didn't you tell me?' she said finally.

'Why would I have told you?' James answered.

Kate looked at him in amazement. 'You just don't get it do you?'

'Get what?'

'This,' she practically spat. 'This. Us. It's what I was trying to say when I said I used to worry about your wife dying. This only works because we're doing the same. Because we're both married. Because we have the same amount to lose, to gain. I didn't sign up to seeing you, to fucking you, if you're no longer married.'

He spoke quietly when he replied. 'Kate. I am married. I like things the way they are with us and I didn't, I don't, want anything to change.'

'Well, they're changing now.'

He ignored that when he spoke again. 'And it was temporary. We tried some time apart and decided that we preferred being together.'

Kate let that hang in the air. She couldn't help but feel that he'd lied to her.

'Does she know about us? Did you tell her, when you had your break, your temporary separation, whatever it is you called it?'

'No, but she is a very don't-ask-don't-tell kind of woman,' he said.

Her heart sank at that. She'd always assumed they were equally complicit, that their married lives were equally at risk. Had James taken her for a fool? Kate suddenly felt very angry. What would she have done if she had found this out when there was the option of being properly cross? She wanted to

Room 706

shout, to slam a door, to walk out. And at the back of her mind there was a niggling voice. There was a time when he wasn't with his wife, it said. And yet during that time he didn't ask you to leave Vic, he didn't want any more of you than he already had.

At least she knew now, even if they got out unscathed, even if they made it home this evening, that they were finally over.

'What are you thinking?' James said. He was peering at her.

'That this is how we end,' she said slowly, keeping her voice quiet and controlled.

He didn't reply. He rubbed his thumb over his lips as if to stop himself saying anything.

'It had to end some time,' she said.

'Yes, I suppose it did,' he finally replied.

She couldn't meet his eye. Instead she looked at her phone again for something to do. Social media was mostly the churn of the same messages going round in cycles. The news sites were finding new ways of saying nothing. A television awards ceremony due to be held in London that evening had been cancelled. No trains were running in or out of Waterloo, or on the underground lines whose tunnels ran nearby, and commuters were posting about alternative ways home. The cordon around the hotel had been expanded so no one could even get near to the station. River-bus services had been suspended in both directions. The major teaching hospital nearby had implemented its emergency plan, including evacuating patients.

Transport is fucked, she sent Vic.

Completely fucked, his text agreed.

But you got home ok? She didn't know why she asked him that. He was home after all so it must have been okay. She just wanted contact with him, to know that he was still there for her, whether or not he believed her story about why she was in the hotel.

I guess it took a while for decisions to close things down to be made, he replied.

The significance of the expanded security cordon suddenly hit her.

They must think there is going to be a big explosion.

How would it feel to be blown up? Would she even know it was happening? She suddenly became aware of a throbbing pain on her left thumb. She'd bitten the skin by the side of her nail until it was red raw. She hadn't even realised she was doing it.

Her phone lit up. She thought it would be Vic again. It was a message from Nicole. *You'll never guess who I saw on a dating app last night.* Kate momentarily wondered whether it was a celebrity or someone from work, before remembering the ridiculousness of caring about that right now.

She thought about confiding in Nicole. She was kind of perfect for the role. Non-judgemental, sharp. She'd get it. But if this wasn't the end she didn't want Nicole to be the person who knew. She didn't want to have to discuss it with her in weeks and months and years to come, to answer the 'why didn't you tell me' questions she'd be bound to ask, to deal with knowing looks. She didn't want Nicole messaging

Room 706

her other friends to say *You'll never guess who's stuck in the hostage hotel.*

Ignore it, Kate thought, looking at the message again. She deleted it, enjoying being able to control something, even if it was something as small as deciding not to care about who was on a dating app.

Chapter 26

Thirteen years earlier

'Shouldn't we invite your parents to our wedding?'

Vic shrugged. 'I don't think so. It's easier not to. I mean, for the past fifteen years or so I have seen them every six months for about two hours, and everyone seems perfectly content with that.'

Kate thought of the time a few months ago when Vic had taken her to meet them, shortly after they had got engaged. They were friendly, polite, and entirely disinterested. They asked no questions, and encouraged none about themselves either. The four of them had sat in silence, drinking tea, until Vic had said they should be heading off, and his parents had done nothing to stop them.

'Don't you miss having parents?'

'I do have parents,' he replied.

Room 706

Kate thought of her own mum and blinked back the tears threatening to slide down her face.

Vic pulled her across their bed towards him. 'I wish I had met your mum. She sounds like she was wonderful.'

'She was.'

Vic stroked her hair. 'I know it sounds weird because your mum isn't here any more and you wish you still had her. But my parents, they did what they were meant to do. They fed me and clothed me and gave me stability. They made sure I went to school and they asked me what I wanted for my birthday and either got it for me or got me whatever version of it they could afford. But they never did emotion. Not with me and not with Tom. Don't worry though. I got my quotient of kisses and cuddles and unconditional love. Every summer Tom and I went to Italy and stayed with Nonna and Nonno. They never forgave my dad for moving away to marry my mum, but they loved us kids from the absolute bottom of their hearts.'

'When did your *nonno* die?' Kate asked.

'When I was ten. He used to sing old Italian songs and sneak us treats, even before dinner when Nonna wasn't looking.'

'I bet she knew.'

'Yeah, probably. She knew everything. It was sad when he died, but I think whenever we went to visit Nonna she was just so pleased to see us that it was always joy, not sadness, that came through.'

'I wish she could come to the wedding,' said Kate.

'Who, Nonna?'

'Yeah.'

'Me too. But at least she lived to hear about our engagement. You should have seen her, Kate, at the end. She couldn't really say much but I held her hand and told her I had asked you to be my wife, and you had said yes, and she squeezed my hand and smiled.'

Kate had heard this before, several times. 'And then what?'

'Tom and I went to leave the hospital for the night, and when I went to kiss her goodbye she handed me her own wedding ring. She'd taken it off while we were gathering our things, and she pressed it into my hand and said 'Kate'. She'd be so thrilled that you are happy to wear it as yours,' said Vic.

They lay there in silence for a few moments. When Kate felt that she could speak without crying, she tried one more time.

'So you definitely don't want to invite your parents to our wedding?'

'No. I'll tell them beforehand. I'll say we're keeping it very small. They won't mind.'

'And it's not because you are ashamed of me or think they don't approve?'

'No! You are the best thing that has ever happened.'

'Ever?'

'Yes. Not just the best thing that has ever happened to me. The best thing that has ever happened, full stop. In the universe. In all universes.'

'Wow.'

He kissed her. 'Look, you met them once yourself, you saw what they are like. Even at my lowest point they didn't check in with me. I thought maybe it was embarrassment, you know, at mental-health issues and all that, but actually I think they have just completely checked out. To them parenting is just something you do to small kids.'

'It's still weird, not inviting them.'

'Everyone's life is weird to some extent,' Vic replied. 'I got over this particular weirdness years ago.'

'And I'm sad for you. When we have kids I want them to know that we're always going to be there for them.'

'Of course we are.'

He met her eyes and reached for her hand. 'I am not my parents. I promise I will always be there for you and always be there for our children, whatever happens.'

She leaned into his body. She'd needed to hear it. 'Thank you.'

It was a relief she'd fallen in love with a man who was happy to have a small wedding. Kate didn't like big events. She'd agreed to Eve's pressure for the two of them to have a pre-wedding dinner a week before the ceremony, on the proviso that no fuss was made.

Eve had mostly stuck to her side of the bargain. Kate touched the plastic tiara on her head.

'This is silly.'

'I know,' said Eve. 'But if you absolutely insist on not having a proper hen night then you can at least indulge me in wearing the plastic tat I have bought you, and be grateful not to be roaming the street in a group wearing matching t-shirts and carrying blow-up boyfriends.'

Kate smiled. 'I am very grateful not to be doing that.'

'I know.'

'I am genuinely so happy to be here, with you. Look at the view,' Kate said. They looked at the sparkle of their city spread out beneath them. Eve had managed to secure a table at the sought-after restaurant on the top floor of one of London's tallest buildings, and had even persuaded the maître d' to give them a window seat.

'It is rather fabulous,' Eve said. 'In fact it's so nice I am too embarrassed to get out the penis-shaped straws I brought with me as part of the hen-night festivities.'

'You didn't!'

Eve winked and patted her handbag. 'Maybe later when we meet up with Tom and Vic.'

'This I love, however,' Kate said, touching the plastic necklace Eve had given her, which spelled out 'Bride' in fancy writing. 'Do you think it will turn my neck green?'

'I hope so.'

'Actually, I got you something too, to say thank you for being my Best Woman.'

'You didn't have to do that.'

'I know. But I wanted to. You really are the best friend anyone could have. And I know I am boring and crap at nights out, and now I am marrying my first proper boyfriend, and really you'd prefer to be on an actual hen night, singing karaoke while naked waiters serve us lurid blue cocktails, rather than be here.'

'Here is very nice.'

'Seriously, I wanted to say thank you.'

Room 706

She slid a small box over to Eve.

'Can I open it?'

'Of course.'

Inside the box was a delicate gold bangle.

'It's engraved,' Kate said. 'On the inside.'

Eve held it up to the light. 'The deepening of the spirit,' she read, a questioning tone in her voice.

'Vic found the quote for me,' said Kate. 'It's Kahlil Gibran. "And let there be no purpose in friendship save the deepening of the spirit."'

Eve had tears in her eyes. 'That's really beautiful.' She reached across to put her hand on Kate's. 'Thank you. I love it.'

They'd arranged to meet Vic and Tom later that evening, in a bar nearby. Eve and Kate arrived first and found a sofa in a quiet corner.

'So you're really not inviting his parents?' Eve asked.

'He's insistent.' Kate shrugged. 'We agreed we wanted it to be small, very small. But I didn't mean he shouldn't invite his family.'

'And did you tell him this?'

'Yes, of course I did. He said they wouldn't be interested in coming. I've only met them once after all.'

'I know. You described them as pleasant.'

'I did. I don't have any other word for it.'

'I'd rather die than be called pleasant,' Eve said.

'That's okay,' Kate replied, 'because you are most definitely not a pheasant plucker.'

'What's that about pheasant pluckers?' said Vic, approaching their sofa with Tom, having entered the bar unseen.

'Eve is not one,' said Kate. Vic looked confused.

'I'm not a pheasant plucker, I'm a pheasant plucker's son, I'm only plucking pheasants 'til the pheasant plucker comes.' Kate finished the rhyme and she and Eve dissolved into laughter.

'I thought you were a literary man,' Eve said, lightly punching him on the arm. 'Anyway, now you are here I am going to the bar to get us all some champagne.'

'How was the hen-lite?' Vic said to Kate as he hugged her.

'So nice.'

'And did she like her present?'

'She loved it.' Kate beamed and Vic rubbed her arm.

'Good.'

'And you guys. How was the stag-don't?'

'Wild,' said Tom.

'Well, a little bit wild. There were no strippers,' said Vic.

'I'm pleased to hear it.'

'But I beat Tom at bowling and had a very large burger.'

'I let him win,' Tom said. 'I always let him win.'

'He always says that,' Vic said.

The next weekend, Eve was pinning buttonhole flowers on Kate and Vic outside the town hall.

'This,' she said, 'is the best day of your lives, apparently.'

Kate looked at Vic. 'I bloody hope not.'

Vic laughed. He had a great laugh that started as a rumble in his stomach and ended up like a sonic boom spreading across the surrounding area.

'You're right,' he said. 'The best is yet to come.' And he

clutched her to him as Eve ducked out of the way to give them some space. 'I love you so much Kate.'

'I love you too.'

'So much?'

She looked at him, catching for just a moment a glimpse of the vulnerable Vic in the crinkles at the edges of his eyes. 'Yes,' she said gently. 'So much.'

'And are you sure that you want to marry me?'

'Yes, I am sure,' Kate said. She felt Vic relax by her side.

Keeping it small had also kept it simple. A civil ceremony and an Italian meal at their favourite restaurant, tucked away behind rows of Georgian houses, fake vines covering the ceiling.

'Kate, I will love you forever,' Vic said in his speech, heard only by Kate, Eve, Tom, Polly, Clara and their waiter. 'Or until the world ends. Whichever comes first.'

Chapter 27

Two years earlier

They were lying on the hotel bed, James flat on his back, Kate on her side facing away from him, his hand resting on her flank. His touch was tender and she was finding it ever so slightly annoying. She wanted him to have his shower and leave, giving her a chance to be alone before she had to re-enter the real world.

'Still good?' James asked. He meant the sex, she assumed.

'Yeah, still good.'

A few moments passed. 'Why, was it not good for you?' Kate asked.

'I don't think there's any reason to doubt that is there?' James said. 'You surely felt how much you turn me on.'

The reference to his hardness embarrassed Kate now that they were not involved in the actual act. Her cheeks reddened.

Room 706

'You're only as good as your last fuck aren't you, when you have an affair. Otherwise, what's the point?'

Kate had not thought of what they were doing as an affair before he said this. Affairs involved emotions, falling in love, wanting to be with the other person. They'd been seeing each other like this for four years now and Kate had trained herself not to think about James between their meetings, not usually. She liked having sex with him, more than liked it, but she didn't want to be with him in any other way. Sex with James was like a special treat to herself, something to make her feel good. It had nothing to do with Vic or the rest of her life. It was, she told herself on the occasional moments she let herself think about him, no different to women who secretly bought expensive shoes and hid them from their partner, or had cosmetic procedures and pretended they didn't.

James wasn't usually so keen to chat. She turned to face him.

'Do you like me, Kate?'

'Do I like you?'

'Yes.' He met her eyes with his.

'As a hot lover?' she teased.

'As a person.'

'Oh.' Did she like him? She found him attractive, appealing, of course, but that was very different from liking someone. She didn't really know him well enough to be able to answer the question. That was deliberate. The fact that she hardly knew him was part of the appeal. Nothing to know, nothing to find annoying.

His expression reminded her of when Lenny or Annie

looked to see whether she had noticed their well-executed cartwheel or the goal they had just scored, the need for their achievement to be externally validated, to be noticed.

'Yes. I like you.'

His face relaxed a little.

Earlier that year James had sent her a message shortly before they had arranged to meet. *Apologies. I won't be able to make our meeting next week. I need to have a little procedure at the hospital.*

It didn't matter, she hadn't had time to get excited about seeing him yet. That only really came the day before.

She'd replied without emotion: *Let me know when you want to rearrange.*

He had rearranged, a few weeks later. They met at a hotel near Tower Bridge that time, a cramped room in a building that seemed too narrow to be a hotel, where the rooms were as claustrophobic as the reception area. There had been no coffee shops in the immediate area so Kate had waited around the corner to receive his message with the room number. She didn't like that hotel. You couldn't walk in without being noticed. You had to acknowledge the receptionists' greeting even as you tried not to look them in the eye, and, she imagined, the receptionists had to pretend that they weren't playing at guessing whether it was a lover or whore when women who had not checked in walked through the doors and headed straight to a room.

Only in the lift had she realised she hadn't even asked him what procedure he was having, or how it went. Was she meant to? She didn't know the rules. She didn't even know him well enough to know whether 'little procedure' was code for a huge operation. Was he a play-it-down or play-it-up kind of man? There was usually no contact between meeting, beyond making arrangements, so it hadn't really occurred to her at the time to ask him for details any more than she would have asked him where he was going on holiday or what his weekend plans were.

She'd ask him later, she thought, just in case it was something serious. Not straight away, but before they went their separate ways. But when they had finished, when they'd made small talk and he'd washed her off him and was saying goodbye, she had forgotten she'd meant to ask.

'What do you like about me?' His question brought her back to the present.

It was a hard one to answer. She hadn't realised he was so needy. It was quite unsexy, this need to be liked. Kate was pleased he had asked her after they'd fucked, not before.

'You are easy company,' she said. 'I like the way you make me feel confident in my body, in being a woman. When I am with you I feel sexy, and strong.'

She was aware that all of these things were more about her than about James, but it seemed to do the trick. He smiled and seemed satisfied with her answer.

Kate picked her words carefully. 'I don't think we'd carry on meeting like this if we didn't like each other would we? I don't know, maybe you can have sex as a one-off with someone you don't like, but to do it again and again, I'm not so sure that would be possible. We have something extra don't we? We have a bond; we're friends of sorts.' Yes. She hadn't had to articulate it before, but this felt like an honest description of their relationship.

'You're right,' James said, sitting up, looking more like his usual self. 'And for the record, I like you too. Though I sometimes wonder why it is we do this. Is it that we like taking risks?'

'Sex. I thought we agreed on that,' said Kate.

'Ah yes, we do have good sex. But it's not just that is it?'

'Validation?' Kate offered. 'Of each other as independent beings. Not just as a spouse, a parent, an employee.' James nodded. 'Also,' Kate continued, 'the sex I have with Vic, it's different to the sex I have with you.'

She faltered. She usually had one rule when it came to fucking James. Well, two if you included don't get caught. And that was don't cuckold Vic. She didn't make fun of Vic to James, or spill his secrets, or think of Vic when fucking James or James when fucking Vic. She did her utter best to keep them separate, even in her mind, entirely discrete compartments of her brain.

'In what way?' James prompted.

'Sex with you, it's . . . I don't know. It's freer.'

How could she say it, that the sex was great but not just because it was good sex, even though it was, but because there were none of the resentments that came with having sex with your husband. She didn't have to put aside irritation about who put the bins out or who was making dinner, or wait a decent time after finishing to confirm who was taking the car in for its service the next day.

'Why are you asking all this?' Kate asked. She realised the

Room 706

answer as she asked the question. He wanted to check she was sticking to the deal, that she wasn't falling in love with him.

Kate rolled her eyes. 'No, I have not fallen in love with you. That's what you want to know, isn't it?'

It took Kate the whole of James's shower to think to ask the question back. As he buttoned up his shirt, she asked him.

'Have you fallen in love with me?'

He smiled. 'I love the taste of you.'

'I know.'

'And the smell of you.'

'Oh shut up.'

He looked her in the eyes. 'No, I have not fallen in love with you.'

'In fact,' he added, 'it's just right. No demands. No expectations.'

'Other than good sex,' said Kate.

'Yes.'

Kate wasn't quite sure whether to be relieved or disappointed. It was one thing not to want someone to fall in love with you, another to realise that they hadn't, even though she knew they'd make a terrible couple. She couldn't imagine ever having a conversation with him about what to cook for dinner, or showing him an interesting article she'd spotted in a magazine. It occurred to her that maybe he would like the drama of her falling in love with him, even while protesting that she mustn't.

'I'm not going to fall in love with you,' Kate said. 'But when we are old I will come and meet you for lunch in your London club and we'll reminisce about the times we used to fuck, and we'll have a lovely afternoon and then go back to our spouses and grandchildren and photo albums and television detectives and Sunday supplements and kitchen gardens maintained by well-meaning younger neighbours.'

'No we won't,' James said. 'We'll book a room and you'll get down on your arthritic knees and take my still-hard and still-smooth cock in your mouth as far back as your false teeth allow.'

'Not sexy, James.'

'It is for me. Besides, I am already quite old.'

There was quite a long pause before James spoke again. 'Do you know the joke, the one where the man walks in on his wife and her lover? One of those old-school comedians, the type who have gone out of fashion, used to tell it, in between the mother-in-law jokes.' Kate shook her head. 'He says to his wife, "Look here sweetheart, you've got to be more careful. Next time it might not be your husband who walks in on you."'

'Very good,' Kate said. 'But I don't necessarily think my husband would see it that way.'

'Perhaps not, but would he leave you, or would he sulk for a bit and then get over it?'

'I don't know. Would your wife leave you?'

'I doubt it,' James replied.

'Let's not put it to the test.' Kate tried to keep her tone light.

'Yes, let's not.'

Chapter 28

5.48pm
Room 706

It came to her suddenly. They would need the recipe for chocolate cake. The kids would want that, if she didn't get out of here. It had been handed down by her gran, and she'd never seen a similar one online or in a recipe book. It was made with oil rather than butter, and less flour than you'd expect. Her gran had told it to her in ounces and Kate had converted everything to grams and memorised it when she was about eleven. She had eaten it every family birthday that she could remember while her gran was alive, and took over the cake-baking duty herself once her gran had died.

The next time they'd have it would be for Annie's birthday in March. Actually it would be for Vic's in January. 'Make your cake Mummy, the one you always make,' one of the kids would say a week or so before the big day. It was, Annie always declared, exactly what birthday cake should taste like: 'Gooey, chocolatey . . .'

'And filled with love.' Kate always finished the sentence for her.

'I am going to make this for my children,' Annie would say.

'Me too,' Lenny would say, joining in. 'I'm going to have four boys.'

'You don't get to choose what you have, do you Mummy?' said Annie.

'That's right, sweetheart. You get what you are given.'

Kate had always meant to write the recipe down for them rather than rely on it being in her head. She started on the hotel notepad. Plain flour, baking powder, eggs, cocoa, milk, vegetable oil, boiling water, vanilla extract, caster sugar. How much sugar? Shit, she didn't know. She'd been making this for years and now her brain chose this moment not to remember. There must be a version online. Her gran surely didn't make it up. She searched for a similar recipe. *Gooey chocolate cake.* It brought up loads but none that looked quite right. She wrote it down with a question mark by *sugar* and a note next to it: *Can't remember but more than you think.* It contained a lot of sugar. Maybe the kids would have fun one day working it out.

She took a picture of the notebook on her phone and emailed it to herself. I'm going mad, she thought. Why didn't I just type out the recipe to begin with?

Kate listened for the helicopters. She wasn't even sure when they were there and when they weren't, what was in her head

Room 706

and what was outside the window. It was funny, she thought, how they'd not noticed anything when they didn't know there was a situation and now they couldn't escape the noise. One of the pieces she had read online had mentioned drones. She hadn't really taken it in then. Who had the drones, the police or the terrorists? Or maybe it was the army. Surely they'd have been called in by now. Would drones be outside their windows, taking pictures? Could they get images through net curtains or, what had she read somewhere once, paint a picture of the room based on heat-seeking technology? Whether this was a comfort depended on which side had the drones, she supposed. Her head felt as if it was going to explode. And now she'd had the thought, she was convinced she could hear them, drones buzzing by the window.

Thinking about it, this might be the noisiest place she'd ever been. The low buzz of the mini fridge was booming. Kate's skin felt prickly, in a noisy way. She picked at the carpet, which seemed to make a continuous low rustle.

Perhaps she should be finding joy in the smallest of things. There was that book she had read some time ago by someone who woke up completely paralysed, unable to move or communicate. Once they'd recovered, years later, they wrote about how during that time they had meditated on the beauty of a single petal they saw when their carer took them into the garden, and the complexity of a fly as it buzzed around the room. She didn't know that she had that kind of brain, to appreciate things as small as that. She thought instead about playing a game on her phone, that always helped pass the time. It would be okay if she lived, she supposed, a totally normal way to pass an hour, two hours, ten hours, sixteen hours, however many hours this was going to be. But what if this was it, her last moments on earth, wasted bringing similarly coloured blocks together only for them to self-destruct, to no end other than a place on the game's own entirely inconsequential scoreboard. What would Vic say? He'd make a joke. He'd tell her to appreciate the beauty of each pixel.

She thought about asking Vic to distract her again. He'd probably try to play their age game. That was their usual way to calm things down, to get back on track after a row or to remind each other of their love. Name an age, past or future, and describe where you were or where you might be. What if he chose the age she is now, thirty-seven? She tried to think what she had said in the past. They played it often enough that most ages had been covered at least once.

Would it have been this? That I'm thirty-seven and I have a nine-year-old boy and a seven-year-old girl and I'm married to a wonderful man who I love, but sometimes I want more, so I have sex with a man who may or may not be wonderful to his own wife and who I definitely do not love, but I have sex with him anyway, and it makes me feel alive and wanted so that I can come home to my wonderful draining exhausting beautiful happy family and mostly be the mummy and wife they want me to be.

She looked at James who was, as he had been doing for most of the day, reading something on his laptop. She kind of knew him, but kind of didn't. She knew the precise spot on his neck to lick to elicit a low whistle, but not how he voted. The

Room 706

exact shape of his thigh, and the face he made as he climaxed, but not whether he went to concerts and who cooked the meals in his house. Yet she knew the depth of his breath when he paused before saying something outrageously filthy to her in hotel lifts. Intimate things only a few other people in the world could know, if any. But what did she know of him really? Who were his friends? Did he have any pets? Were his parents alive? Did he have siblings? Their relationship, based wholly around meeting, having sex and then going home, was probably the single most simple relationship she had ever had. She didn't even know his favourite colour.

They'd been fucking for nearly six years now, every three months or so. That was over twenty meetings purely for sex. Over twenty times bringing each other to orgasm, sometimes more than once, of becoming familiar with each other's bodies and secretions and smells and tastes, and over twenty times perfecting the post-sex nonchalance, the pretending to watch television while he showered, not saying anything too keen, too sarcastic, too anything. Their affair depended on at least pretending to be distanced.

It wasn't a pretence, Kate reflected now. She really didn't care for this man, not in the way she cared for Vic, and for the family they had created together. She cared for James, she thought, the way she cared for her hairdresser, who she saw with similar frequency and who also touched her intimately and made her feel good about herself.

How many of her friends had she had twenty meetings with over the past six years? The women she'd met at baby classes and playgroups when the kids were small all seemed to have left London. She had no friends from university, most were gone when she returned from her year abroad, by which time she had Vic anyway. She had worked with Nicole so saw her daily at one point, but they probably met in person for a drink two or three times a year now, relying on emails and social media in between. She had lunch with Tom's wife Polly, just the two of them, once a year or so. It was always nice, but neither of them ever suggested doing it more often. And Eve, of course. Eve was ever present in her head, but she hadn't seen her for over nine years.

Kate had no siblings, but she did have cousins. They weren't even first cousins though. Her mum, like her, was an only child. They were the children of her mum's cousins, the descendants of her grandad's brother, so they were actually her second cousins. She saw them at weddings and funerals, and, as a child, at family events. Probably not even twenty times in her life. The barista who made her coffee each day that she went to the office, which was not that often. She had met him more than twenty times, but their conversation never got beyond small talk about the weather and raised eyebrows when the person before her in the queue had some kind of demand about which brand of syrup to use or what temperature the milk in their coffee should be.

It came to her out of nowhere. 340g. That was how much sugar was in the chocolate cake. She was relieved she had remembered. Kate picked up the notepad and added it to the recipe. Then she took another photo of that page and emailed it to herself again. It was an insane amount of sugar,

Room 706

she always thought that when making it, but it did make the most amazing cake.

Kate knew Vic's favourite colour, of course she did. It was blue. She knew the exact shade, the exact tone, that would always make him buy a tie, a pair of socks, a scarf. The colour, he said, of the sea in the picture Nonna had in her kitchen. Not, he'd always point out, the real colour of the sea, just the colour the mass-produced postcard had been tinted to show.

'James?'

'Yes?'

'What's your favourite colour?'

'Kate?'

'Yeah?'

'I'm fifty-nine years old.'

'You don't see in colour when you're fifty-nine?'

He turned back toward his laptop.

Chapter 29

Thirteen years earlier

Eve was having a party at the flat she shared with two friends from her work. It was mostly packed with their colleagues, though Kate could also spot at least two of Eve's ex-boyfriends, and some people she knew to be their neighbours.

'I hate parties,' Kate whispered to Vic.

'I know,' he said, pulling her in for a kiss.

'Do you hate parties too?' she asked.

'I detest them.'

'Liar,' Kate whispered into his ear. 'I think you are enjoying yourself.'

'You're right,' Vic said. 'I like nosing around other people's houses, and seeing who their friends are and how they interact. I like judging their bookshelves and rifling through their bathroom cabinets.'

'What do you think of the fairy lights?' she asked him.

'Did you hang them?'

'I did.'

'Then they are the best fairy lights I have ever seen.'

'Ha, they should be. It took all bloody afternoon. They kept falling down, like one of those practical joke television shows. I would get to the last one on the string and just as I put that one on its hook the first one would collapse.'

'So how did you get them to stay up in the end?' Vic asked.

'It's a secret.'

'Oh.' He reached across to a plate on the sideboard and grabbed a handful of cheese and pineapple cubes on sticks.

'Are we in the 1980s?' he asked, holding them up.

Kate giggled. 'I guess so.'

'I'll share these with you if you tell me the secret.'

Kate looked at Vic, his eyes twinkling. He was still the person she most wanted to speak to in the room and she felt it even more keenly since their wedding earlier that year. He was the only person she wanted to speak to at all really, other than Eve, who was in hostess mode, topping up glasses, introducing people to each other, flirting with everyone. Kate didn't mind parties, she decided, if she could spend the whole evening talking to Vic.

She leaned in to his ear and told him. 'I doubled up. Sticky hooks for each light, but there's also masking tape every ten centimetres or so.'

'That's a lot of masking tape,' Vic said, holding his handful of snacks out to her. 'Did you know it was invented for the car industry, as normal tape was taking off newly applied paint?'

'That's completely irrelevant information,' Kate said.

'It's wholly relevant,' Vic replied. 'It's exactly what we were just talking about.'

How could he make talking about masking tape seem fun? Yet he did.

Eve stopped by them, pouring more wine into their glasses and grinning.

'People came!'

'Of course they came,' said Kate. 'They're your friends.'

'Do you like the retro snacks?' Eve asked, turning to Vic.

He smiled. 'Love them. It's a great party.'

'Kate hates parties,' Eve said. 'Did you know that?'

Kate blushed.

'Actually,' Vic said, 'she was just telling me that this is the best party she has been to this year.'

'That's because it's a new year's party.'

'Ah, but it's not midnight yet. She's had 365 days to go to a better party than this and yet she hasn't.'

'Kate,' Eve demanded. 'Have you been to any other parties this year?'

Kate shook her head, laughing. 'Not unless you count our wedding.'

'That was a celebration,' Eve said. 'But it wasn't a party.'

'True,' Kate said. 'Do you know why it was a celebration but not a party?'

Eve and Vic looked at each other before answering in unison: 'Because you hate parties.'

The three of them laughed then and Kate felt happy, next to her husband and her best friend, drink in hand.

'Well, I am pleased you came. And thank you for helping prepare all afternoon.' Eve gave Kate a hug, slopping wine from her glass on to Kate's shoulder as she did so. 'And,' she said, tipping her head towards a tall man with glasses standing by the arch that separated the kitchen from the living room, 'do you see that man over there standing behind my sister? That's the man from work that I think something is happening with.'

'Shall I go and ask his intentions?' Vic said.

'Don't you dare,' Eve told him, winking at Kate. 'Though I hope they are the same as mine.'

At midnight, Kate and Vic slipped away from the singing of 'Auld Lang Syne' and sat together on the stairs that led up to Eve's bedroom in the converted loft. They could see fireworks through the skylight above their heads.

'Do you think they're having a new year's kiss?' Kate asked him.

'Who, Eve and the guy from work?'

'Yeah,' she said.

'Probably.'

'Can I have one?'

'Oh yes. Yes please,' he said, leaning in to kiss her. 'Happy new year, wife.'

'Happy new year, husband,' she said as they finally pulled away from their kiss. She sat leaning against him, her eyes closed.

'Any resolutions?' Vic asked after a few minutes.

She opened her eyes. 'For the new year?'

'Yeah.'

'I can't think of any. You?'

Vic shook his head. 'No. I'm happy with our lives. Just more of the same please.'

Chapter 30

6.04pm
Room 706

If it had been Eve in the room with her, she was sure they'd have devised fun ways to pass the time. She thought back to their Spain trip, their list of people to talk about, one each day.

'I don't know that many people,' Kate had said, when Eve suggested it.

But she had sat down the day before heading to the airport and made her list. Her mum, her grandparents, teachers, everyone she remembered from her class at primary school, the people who mattered from secondary school, the boy who lived in the flat below, the people she had met in Freshers' Week and the lecturers who had inspired her that year, the nameless man who slept on a bench in her local park, the next-door neighbour who took in their parcels. It wasn't hard at all. She could have kept going, reached a hundred at least.

She had shielded it from her mum when she came into the room. That she might talk about such personal things, even to her best friend, felt a bit like cheating on their own relationship.

Plus she felt guilty. She knew she should really stay in the UK and work that summer to save up for her second year at university. 'No,' her mum had insisted. 'Go and have fun, live a little, see the world then come back and tell me all about it. I might have a gap year myself in the not-too-distant future, now you're all grown up, and I want tips. You can work in term time. Enjoy the summer.'

Now, eighteen years later, Kate thought of this list. If she had to do it again and make a list of people to talk about, who would be on it? She tried to remember who had been on the original. She hadn't even met Vic then, or James. There had been no concept of Lenny or Annie.

Kate thought about the hotel she was in. How many other people were here too? Even if only half the rooms were booked, and even if most bookings were only for one person, that was over one hundred and fifty people. And at least one room had been booked by a family, they knew that, so surely others would have been too. She felt sick at the thought of the boy, the family. How many other kids were in this hotel? And how many rooms had lovers like her and James, there but officially not there, booked in for the day only? And then there were the staff. How many cleaners

Room 706

and waiters and doormen and receptionists and cooks and maintenance staff? She didn't know how many people were still in their rooms when the hotel was taken over, but there could potentially be hundreds hiding in the building or being held hostage downstairs. More people than she had ever known by name.

What if in one of the infinite multiverses it was not her in the hotel, but someone else she knew? What if it was Nicole? Or Vic? Would they be fucking James in that version of the multiverse? Of everyone she had ever known, she wondered, who would be most likely to also be in this hotel? Was it men fucking women, men fucking men, women fucking women? Suddenly her affair with a straight married man seemed awfully vanilla.

Kate tried to think logically, to keep her brain in order and away from thoughts of numbers and multiverses. Outside was the dark of 6pm on a November evening, although the lights from the building opposite were bright and some filtered through the net curtains of room 706, giving them enough light to be able to see. Had all the buildings around them been evacuated? They must have been if they were within the cordon. That would be a lot of buildings. A lot of flats and a lot of offices. Any thought she had of going to the window to look was tempered by the realisation that by now they probably did have guns as well as cameras trained on them. She did not want to be shot through the window by a police sniper. She decided not to share any of these thoughts with James.

He was on the bed staring at his mobile phone. 'Do you

have any signal?' he asked. Kate looked at her own phone. She didn't. 'No, just wifi, that's how I've been messaging my husband.'

At least she thought that was how she'd been reaching him. She doubted herself now, and her understanding of how her phone worked.

James didn't say anything, but looked concerned.

'What is it?'

'Do you really want to know?' he asked.

'Of course I do.'

'I've been reading more about attacks like these. How security services approach them. There are articles everywhere if you search for them.'

'Right.' She wished he hadn't been reading more, then she wouldn't have to know any more herself.

'They turn off the mobile signal if they think there might be IEDs.'

'IEDs?' Her brain went blank at the acronym.

'Improvised Explosive Devices.'

'Bombs?'

'Yes.'

The word hung in the air between them. She felt sick.

She needed to know she could still contact Vic.

Still here, she messaged.

Me too, he replied.

Her thoughts were drifting all over the place. Maybe this is what shock and fear do to the brain. And hunger. She was so hungry. Right Kate, concentrate. Is there any evidence of James at home? Did she need to clean anything up? She was

Room 706

sure there were no clues at home. She had been so careful about that.

It was feasible that she could die but her phone survive. Kate picked it up and deleted James's messages from that morning. She usually did this straight away and wasn't sure why she hadn't today. Then she opened her contacts and deleted James's number. She was never going to need it again anyway. Of course if they died they would be found together. A used condom in the bin. A tube of lubricant too. Even if their bodies did not give up the secrets of what they had been up to, that surely would. Maybe any bomb would obliterate all the evidence. Or perhaps Vic would not be told the details of where his wife had been found. What would be better for him, she asked herself, to know for sure or to always wonder?

What was it the Swedes called it? She'd read a pitch about it for *Hidden Depths* earlier this week. It was a good pitch; she was going to recommend they commission it. Oh yes, that was it, *dostadning*, death cleaning, the Swedish concept of decluttering your home when you know you will die soon. She loved Scandinavian culture, and always thought of herself more as a cinnamon bun kind of person than a *pain au chocolat* one. She had a habit of buying overpriced candles with the word *hygge* on the front. Vic took the mickey out of this, even though he would buy them as her Christmas present from the kids.

'You know it's just a marketing con,' he would say. 'Well it works,' Kate would reply, and he would roll his eyes and they would laugh, before he pressed on. 'What about Finland?

That's the same part of the world. And Estonia. Why don't you like those? What's Estonian for *hygge*?'

'No idea. But their police dramas are less exciting,' Kate replied.

'How do you know? Have you ever watched Estonian drama?'

'*Nej.* Never.'

How much death cleaning could she do from the hotel room? She opened her laptop again. She'd *dostadning* her inbox. At worst it would save Vic having to plough through it. At best she'd no longer have a cluttered inbox to deal with once this whole mess was in the past.

There were 13,432 messages in it, 3,148 of them unread. Most were marketing emails and newsletters. She moved the ones she had sent herself earlier into a folder and named it *Important – for Vic*. She did a quick search for ones from Vic and went to save them in a folder too. They might have important info in them, the reference number for the car's service, that kind of thing. No, actually there was no need, he'd have his own copy in his sent folder if nowhere else. She selected the entire inbox and pressed delete. *Delete all messages?* the computer queried.

I'm the fucking boss here, she thought. She clicked *Yes*. Then she went into her sent messages. There were even more there, every message she had sent since getting her email account. Delete sent messages. *Delete 38,409 messages?* the computer asked. She clicked *Yes* again. The computer blinked. And froze. Fuck, she'd not cleaned up the machine, she'd killed it. Then it bounced into life again. *Clearing inbox*, a grey

Room 706

box on the screen announced, followed by half a minute of the colour prism wheel and a completely blank sent messages file. Wow. Kate felt sick. That was her life in all its electronic glory. It didn't feel cleansing at all. She looked at the clock. In less than eight minutes she had cleaned up her inbox. She went into the deleted messages and clicked on the icon of the bin to send all of the deleted to permanent oblivion.

What next? She closed her eyes and rubbed her forehead. Photos. Of course.

There were probably even more of those than emails. Kate checked her phone. No, a few thousand fewer. She'd meant for years to sort them out and get the good ones made into albums. Her phone was the keeper of family memories. What if the end came now? If the door was kicked in or the building exploded, or the terrorists finally got hold of a master key and used it. She listened. Was the end coming? How the fuck would she even know? She wished she'd thought of sorting out the photos earlier in the day.

9711 photos. Forty-six videos. Bugger. Shit fuck bollocks bugger. She searched for free online storage for videos. Kate chose the one at the top of the first newspaper 'best buy' list she found, downloaded it to her phone and created an account, emailing the log-in details to herself. Her inbox and sent messages folder were no longer empty. Uploading each video was calming in its rhythm. Choose the file. Wait for the symbol to indicate it had all been uploaded. Press save. Repeat.

She looked at the time. Just after 7pm. It had taken her almost an hour and she hadn't yet started on the photos.

Time flies, baby, when you're having fun, she thought. She felt drunk.

Transfer all 9,711 photos? The app asked her. *Yes*, touched Kate. And it immediately started uploading her photos, each one flashing onto the screen momentarily, so quick as to be like a comic book, photos of the kids as babies then toddlers then fully formed human being children, too quick for her to register the detail of their faces but enough for her to see them grow, their lives literally flashing before her eyes. She felt a physical pain in her tummy and could look no longer, letting her phone's screen turn to black while it continued uploading behind the scenes.

She looked at James. She hadn't even thought about what he was doing to fill the time since she had decided to start her *dostadning*. He was on the bed with his eyes closed.

Her phone flashed. It was an alert from the photo storage app. She hoped the wifi continued to work. The connection looked to be strong. The electricity had not been turned off, then. Would they be able to tell where in the hotel the free guest wifi was being used? She hadn't had to give a room number when she connected, she'd just ticked the box agreeing to the terms and conditions. No, if that was possible they'd have found them by now, she'd been connected to the wifi for hours. *74 minutes left of upload*, the phone flashed.

Okay, she thought, praying for the first time in she didn't know how long. Since that time she thought she was going to die on a plane probably. Please God don't end things until the seventy-four minutes are up.

James stirred. 'What are you doing?' he whispered.

Room 706

'Praying,' Kate said. 'For another seventy-four minutes.'
'Do you think it will work?'
She shrugged. 'Time will tell.'
'Kate?'
'Yeah.'
'If prayer works, do you think you could ask for longer?'

Chapter 31

Ten years earlier

They were carrying takeaway hot drinks – coffee for Vic and mint tea for Kate – and walking through the cemetery in Highgate where all the famous people were buried. It was Vic's idea for a day out. The ideas were always his.

'I grew up next to a graveyard,' he said. 'And I knew that it was a place for dead people. But I hadn't realised that they used to be live people. I thought they were just a separate type of person. I remember the day I found out. I was four. Apparently I didn't speak for six months after that, not properly. Tom tells this story sometimes. He says I was a child when I stopped talking and when I came out of it I was heavier, a four-year-old man.'

'That's sad,' said Kate, reaching over to place her hand on his arm for a moment as they walked.

Room 706

'It is. I'm sad for four-year-old me. Sometimes I wonder if what happened to me, when, you know, when things fell apart, if all of that was a delayed reaction to that whole period. I must have been so overwhelmed.'

'I'm sorry,' Kate said. Was that enough? She never quite knew how to respond to Vic's vulnerabilities. He often shared them matter-of-factly, and only some time afterwards would she reflect and realise that he wasn't really like most other people. He was like an ancient monument, strong and stable yet also always at risk of total collapse.

'I love you,' he said. 'And it was a long time ago.'

'I love you too.' She should have said it first, that would have been the right response.

'Do you know, I've never actually asked you where your mum is buried,' Vic said a few minutes later, as they walked slowly past ornate headstones.

'Really?'

'Uh-huh. I'd remember if you'd told me.'

'It's a massive graveyard on the edge of London. Actually she had planned and paid for her funeral in advance, so I had nothing to do, no decisions to make.'

Vic stayed quiet, giving her the space to expand. Kate knew he'd heard this bit before, that they'd spoken about it years ago when they'd met, but she appreciated the chance to retell and remould the story. Her mum used to say that to her when Kate had bad dreams. 'Tell me what happened again and again and each time you can lose some of the bad bits and eventually it will just be a story you tell.'

'I think it must have been as a kindness to me,' Kate said.

'I mean, she wasn't expecting to die when she did, I am sure, but I guess she was expecting to die before me. She even left a list of people to invite. Her cousins, her colleagues, some old school friends. It was small but the people who came, they mattered to her. I imagine she'd have made the sandwiches herself if she'd had a day's notice.'

They walked for a bit more. 'I'm like her really. I doubt there would be many people at my funeral if I died now.'

Vic stopped walking. 'Don't say that.'

She looked at him. 'It's true though. You know I'm not one of those people with loads of friends. You're not either. It's not a bad thing. At least I don't think it's a bad thing. And I have never really understood those people who collect friends like they're coins or stamps or whatever people collect these days. There's only so much of us to go round isn't there? Only so many people we can share ourselves with.'

When it was clear she had finished speaking, Vic spoke again: 'Have you ever visited her grave?'

'No. Not since the burial.'

He seemed to be picking his words carefully. 'I thought you might like to tell her, about the baby I mean.'

Kate took a moment to reply. He was so sweet and so earnest that she didn't want to ridicule the idea she needed to visit the grave in order to tell her mum that she was pregnant.

'No, it's okay. It's not her any more is it? Dead bodies, they're just shells of the person they used to contain. Besides, I told her already, in my head I mean.'

But Vic looked like he wanted more from her than this. Finding out he was going to be a father had made him ask her more questions about her childhood, and Kate felt she owed him a story. 'There's a square near the flat I grew up in. It's a public square, but it was mostly used by the people in the flats around it. Weirdly it has an empty plinth in the middle, surrounded by a flower bed and railings. It's just that little bit too high to be able to get on it easily so it was never somewhere the teens sat and smoked. Sometimes I think of my mum being there, a statue of her, overseeing the goings on in the park.'

Was that even true? She had always noticed the plinth and had always wondered who it was intended for. But had she ever imagined it was for her mum? No, she didn't think so, though now she wondered if she had thought that all along.

'I suppose, if I am lucky, if I avoid car crashes and other misadventures, there will be a time when I become older than she ever was,' Kate said.

'Remind me, how old was she, when she died?' Vic asked.

'Thirty-eight. She was eighteen when she had me.'

They walked in silence for a while until Kate broke it.

'What about when you die?' she asked him. 'Where do you want to be buried?'

He took his time answering. 'I don't care where I am buried,' he said finally. 'But maybe plant a tree or something. Somewhere you can go to remember me.'

'Okay,' Kate said. 'And what if I die first?'

'Then I will plant a tree for you.'

'Thanks.'

They stopped at a bench to have their drinks. Kate took a sip. 'I wish this was coffee.'

'Have some of mine.' He offered his cup to her.

'I can't. I want it, then the mere smell makes me want to throw up.'

He cuddled her. 'It'll be worth it.'

Kate wished she could have told her mum in person about Vic, and about the baby. She thought they would have liked each other, not that she had ever introduced her mum to any boyfriends. There hadn't been any, none that would constitute an actual relationship. There had been teenage flirtations and trips to the cinema and the local pub with a boy the year above her at sixth form. Her first sexual encounter had been on holiday the year between lower sixth and upper sixth, when she'd had sex with a boy on a campsite in France, just like her mum before her. Though who said that each generation repeats the mistakes of the previous one? Kate had used a condom, had insisted on it. He'd gone to buy it at the vending machine by the bar while she waited in the tent, resisting the temptation to rifle through his bag for clues into his psyche.

Then there had been a couple of incidents of drunken sex at university, people with whom she had nothing at all in common. But there had been no one you would want to spend a whole dinner talking to, let alone take to meet your mum.

And Vic wasn't even a boyfriend now. He was her husband, her mum's son-in-law, the father of her future grandchildren. Can you even be a son-in-law to someone who is dead, or a grandmother to someone not yet born? Maybe. She was still a daughter and her mum was still her mum.

Would she even have fallen for Vic if she hadn't just lost

Room 706

her mum? She didn't usually let herself ask this question. She looked at him as he bent down to pick up an acorn from the path.

Of course I would have, she thought. She might not have been so happy to speak to him in the cinema. She might not have cried on him afterwards. But if she had met him, surely she would have fallen for him anyway? He was the most interesting person she had ever known, delighted by the minutiae of life. Look at the way he was studying the acorn now, really studying it. He'd tell her five facts about acorns in a minute, and maybe quote a poem about oak trees. His face in profile looked kind and thoughtful. His neat beard gave a sense of quiet intellectualism.

'I like your face,' she said, giving voice to her thoughts.

He grinned. 'Thank you. Any reason for saying so?'

'I just thought you'd like to know. I hope the baby has your face.'

'I like your face too,' Vic said.

'That's good. It's the only one I've got.'

'What else do you like about me?' Vic asked.

'Oh, that is very needy.'

'I know. But you started it. Come on, you like my face, what else do you like?'

Kate thought for a moment.

'I like the way you throw salt over both of your shoulders when cooking.'

'I can never remember which one it's meant to be.'

'And I like the way you have a head full of facts and words and things that will interest me.'

'I do.'

'And all the ideas you have for days out and things to do and places to go.'

'Anything else?'

Kate thought for a bit. 'I love the way you love me, as if you really mean it, as if it is the most natural thing anyone can do.'

'It is. I do. I always will.'

Would her mum have been okay with Vic, she wondered, or would she have been suspicious of all that love, of the ten-year age difference, of his breakdown and the fact he barely saw his own parents?

She often imagined telling her mum about him. 'He thinks about the world differently, he's kind of complex,' she would tell her.

'Does he love you?' her mum in her head asked her.

'Yes.'

'Do you love him?'

'Yes.'

'Well then, there's nothing complex about that, is there?'

Chapter 32

7.31pm
Room 706

'You think you're better than me, don't you?' James spoke even more quietly than they had been doing all day.

'What? No. Why?' His accusation seemed to come out of nowhere.

'You think that just because you can quote poetry and because you are sending control-freaky messages in case you die, that you love your family more than I love mine. You think I've not told my wife where I am because I don't love her, but I've not told her because I do love her.'

Their last exchange had been about praying for more time. She hadn't been sure whether or not he was serious then, but nothing in his tone had suggested he was about to lose it. Now he seemed barely in control, his voice jerky, his face twisted.

He said it again. 'You think you're better than me.'

Kate had never seen him like this. Never seen him anything other than polite and controlled. He seemed so resentful, as if it was her fault they were in this situation at all.

He put his head in his hands and spoke quietly but forcefully. 'We're both here because we are liars and cheats. Because much as we love the comfort of having a partner and homecooked meals and in-jokes and friends in common and dinner parties and Christmas card lists and family occasions and people to go on holiday with, it's not enough for us. We both want more. And we get it by fucking each other's brains out every few months and pretending to everyone else around us that we haven't. And that's great – I love fucking you. I love that you love fucking me. What we have is something special. But please do me a favour and don't think that somehow, though we are both as culpable as each other in this deceit, you do it because you love your family and I do it because I don't.'

Kate couldn't think of a word to say. She'd said nothing of the type to him, though he was right, this was almost exactly what she did think. Perhaps they were more similar than she had thought. She stood up and got onto the bed, then reached across and stroked his hand.

'It's okay,' she said. 'It's okay.'

He seemed calmer now.

'Really though, why do you do it?' she asked quietly.

'What?'

'Us, why do you see me?' Kate asked.

She thought she knew. They'd danced around the topic before. But she needed to know again. She'd always thought

Room 706

it was because of the chemistry they had felt on that very first lunch, and their subsequent encounters. That the universe was moving them together in mysterious ways. But now she wanted to hear it from him.

James was quiet for so long she thought he wasn't going to answer.

'Because I want to.'

Kate nodded. She could hear in her head a Greek chorus of thoughts answering the question for her.

Because he showed an interest.

Because you're not in love with Vic.

Because you don't love yourself.

Because you do love yourself.

Daddy issues.

Mummy issues.

You're depressed.

You want to have it all.

You have a self-destruct button.

'And you?' James was asking her the same question.

She thought for a while. It was none of the reasons her mind was throwing at her.

'Also because I want to.'

This was the real answer, she knew that as she said it. Why did there always have to be a deeper reason? I wanted to fuck him. There you go, nothing deeper. Just sex. With someone I found attractive. No strings. No emotion. No reason. No playing a part. Just sex because he was there and I wanted to. End of story. She could imagine Vic's face, taking this explanation in.

'No emotional attachment?' he'd ask.

'No emotional attachment,' she'd confirm.

'No plans to leave me?'

'Never,' she'd reassure him.

No, who was she kidding? He wouldn't just accept it like that. He'd be beyond hurt. Maybe it would even cause another breakdown. Is that why she was doing it, a counterbalance to all the protecting she did? Maybe every act of love needs an act of betrayal for balance, Kate thought.

No, she told herself. Make all the excuses you want, but you chose to do this, knowing the potential it has to cause hurt to the person who loves you most in the world. James was right, they were both liars and cheats. She swallowed hard and breathed as deeply as possible, letting the air out slowly through her nose. It felt good and she did it again, taking air in as deeply as possible, until her lungs felt full as deep as her navel, then slowly exhaling.

'Sorry, I should not have had a go at you. Everything is just a bit . . . unreal, I suppose.' James was talking. She forced herself to listen to his words.

'As you get older the fact that you are going to die one day isn't just something you vaguely think about every so often. It starts to be there the whole time. I'm fifty-nine, sixty is looming in a few months and I've had enough friends and colleagues pass away before their time to know it's just luck that keeps you here. You can distract yourself of course, and make it feel like your actions have an impact. You wear a helmet when you cycle. Do whatever screening tests the doctor sends you. But really, it's just luck. And to have your

Room 706

mind focused, as it is now, it's intense. I know I probably look like I don't care. I was brought up not to show emotions.' He blew a long slow breath out. 'But I'm terrified, Kate. I've been reading about these people. They don't mess around. They usually have some kind of demand, but it's sometimes bogus. Their *raison d'etre* is to create fear and panic in the societies they see as their enemy. Instability is their goal, or their interim goal anyhow, something like that. I don't think they will hesitate to kill anyone, everyone.'

She reached across to his hand again and this time held it. She'd focus on the personal. The bigger picture stuff was too much to even think about.

'I get it,' she said. 'My mum died when I was twenty. In a car accident. It wasn't her fault. And ever since then I have known that life can be taken away just like that. I didn't have a dad or siblings or anyone else. I could have gone off the rails I suppose. If I'd gone wild no one would have been there to stop me. But you know what I did? I carried on with my plans as if nothing had changed and I married the first person who made me feel looked after.'

'Vic?'

Kate winced. She hated it when James said Vic's name.

'I love him. I really do. I mean I genuinely fell for him. He's brilliant. But if I look on it now I have spent my whole adult life trying to ensure nothing happens, trying to be steady and stable and safe and boring. As if by being average the fates might leave me alone. Even the number of kids I have is average.'

He squeezed her hand. 'I'm sorry about your mum.'

'Yeah. Then when I was pregnant with my son, my best friend, Eve, she died.' It sounded so stark to say it like that. 'It was cancer. It happened very quickly. And, you know what, it wasn't even a shock because after my mum died I expect everyone to die. I don't tell anyone, I don't want people to think I'm mad, but every time I pick my kids up from school or childcare I expect there to be a disaster. It used to be that I expected the nursery to have caught fire. When they started school, if I saw an ambulance on my walk from the station, I always assumed it was on its way to our school where my child would have choked on something. When they go to a friend's house I worry about gas explosions or carbon monoxide poisoning. So this, today, I mean I didn't actually expect this exact scenario, but I'm almost not surprised you know.'

She extracted her hand from his but neither of them moved their body away. They sat on the bed, leaning against each other. She couldn't let her brain continue down the path of thinking about disasters, not right now.

Think of something else Kate, she told herself. She looked at her phone. The photos were still uploading to the storage she had chosen.

Kate's stomach rumbled so hard that she almost shushed it. 'I'm so hungry,' she said. Only then did she remember the wrap she'd bought this morning, still in her bag. She got up and fetched it. The wrap was split in two halves, and she passed one to James.

She wondered what Vic was having for dinner, whether he even felt able to eat. Shit, the slow cooker. She had left

Room 706

it on that morning to cook the chicken stew, and it needed turning off, even if they weren't going to eat it, otherwise it would just cook all night. She should have bought a fancy one that turned itself off.

She messaged Vic. *You need to turn off the slow cooker.*
Roger that.

Laughable really. No one ever thought that being given a chance to sort out your affairs might boil down – she noticed her own pun – to turning off the casserole for that night's dinner. Or sorting out her affair, singular.

Chapter 33

Nine years earlier

'I asked what happens when you die,' Eve said.

Kate was visiting her in the hospice, as she had every day for the past week. She swallowed hard. She knew she had to let Eve speak about dying, that it was her job to be there and to listen, but it was so very difficult. Knowing that her best friend was receiving palliative care, had gone from well to unwell in just a few short months, had an aggressive tumour that had been dismissed by the doctor several times until it was too late, it was almost unbelievable. Kate had already been pregnant when Eve was diagnosed, and she was going to die even before the baby arrived.

'What was the answer?' she managed.

'No one tells you anything. They throw it back to you.

Room 706

"What do you think will happen?" they say. I said, "Will it be quick?" and they said, "Do you want it to be quick?"'

'What did you say to that?'

'I said I don't want it to hurt. No one ever answers a bloody question.'

'Oh love.' Kate reached for Eve's hand. 'You're wearing your bangle.'

'The deepening of the spirit. They keep trying to get me to take it off as it gets in the way of the IV. But I said no. I want to be buried wearing it.'

There was ringing in Kate's ears and she swallowed hard. She couldn't talk.

'They say life flashes before your eyes when you're about to die,' Eve said. 'But I have days, maybe weeks, and I am too tired to do anything but sit and remember. Even being pushed around the garden here is exhausting. And it turns out it's not really flashing before my eyes. It's whole vignettes.'

Kate held Eve's hand. She could feel the baby that would become Lenny kicking the inside of her womb. His due date was in eight weeks.

'I had one the other day, of our Spain trip,' Eve said. 'Do you remember how exciting everything was then, like we'd live forever, like life was just about to begin? What were we, nineteen? We were on a beautiful beach with the sea stretched out in front of us and mountains in the distance behind us, and we were running into the ocean and laughing. I can't remember why. But it was so nice to be back there. The sun was so hot and the water so perfect. We were young and beautiful.'

'You are still beautiful,' Kate said. She didn't know if it was the right thing to say but Eve let her say it.

'It was before you met Vic.'

Kate nodded. Vic had come with Kate to visit the day before, but she'd said she wanted some time just her and Eve today.

'I told you he was a keeper. Do you remember that, the first time I met him?'

'Yeah, you did.'

Yesterday Eve had been quieter, preferring for the three of them to just be together without talking. But today she was in a chatty mood. 'Is he excited?' She gestured at Kate's bump.

Kate nodded. 'So excited. He wants the baby to call him Papa. You know, once it can talk . . .' She trailed off.

'You're holding back. I can tell.' Eve rubbed Kate's arm gently. 'Come on, I'm not dead yet. Tell me.'

Kate had tried not to talk about the pregnancy too much. Since Eve's shock diagnosis it just seemed to emphasise how cruel life was. But Eve was looking at her expectantly, and the silence needed to be filled. 'I'm not worried about what kind of mum I'll be,' Kate said. 'I had a great mum, I can just do what she did. Love and cuddles and acceptance and time together. That's all of it really. But I don't know what dads do and, having met Vic's dad, I don't know that he knows either.'

Eve nodded. She seemed glad of the distraction. Kate carried on. 'I can't help but worry how he'll cope. Everyone I meet says we'll get no sleep, that however well we prepare we'll be shocked by being responsible for someone so utterly

Room 706

dependent on us, all of that. I worry I'll be too busy with the baby, too tired to protect Vic the way I usually do.'

Was she wrong to burden Eve with this? She felt incredibly disloyal to Vic.

'You still worry about that?'

Kate shrugged. Though she hadn't told Eve that much about Vic's mental health when they first met, Vic was always very open about it, and as he and Eve got to know each other properly, once they were all living in London, he'd told her himself.

'How do you still protect him?' Eve pushed.

'Will it sound awful if I say it's by being a willing repository of his love?'

Eve looked at her. 'How so?'

'It's so hard to articulate. I don't know. Just by having someone to love, having someone who lets him love them, who appreciates the facts in his head, he thrives on it you know. I'm not being big-headed, but me being there is his protective shield.'

'But aren't you going to be doing just that by giving him a son or a daughter, giving him someone extra to love?'

'Yeah. I guess. It's just we've never put it to the test. There haven't been any high-pressure situations since we've been together. He loves his job. We could afford a house and we're okay for money. We make nice food, go on nice walks, read books, have holidays. Saying that we sound so middle-aged already. And maybe we are. But it's nice. I know how lucky I am. And now maybe we're going to ruin it all by bringing in the unknown.'

'It is nice,' said Eve. 'And it's all anyone really wants isn't it? You just got it a bit earlier than lots of people.'

'Yeah.'

'Do you ever wish you'd met him later, had a chance to have some fun first?'

Did she? The kind of fun Eve meant, dating and partying and sharing houses with strangers and taking some years to find what she wanted to do for a job, none of it actually sounded that much like fun to Kate.

'No. I think I met him exactly when I needed to. We both did. I needed him. He needed me. But now, I don't know. Maybe when I have this baby to love I won't need him so much, and I think he needs me to need him.'

'That sounds overly complicated,' Eve said.

'Yeah, I don't even know what I am saying, what I mean. It's probably hormones or lack of sleep or something. I get up to wee every couple of hours.'

They sat there holding hands, looking out of the window of Eve's room. Kate tried not to think about what she was going to lose when Eve was no longer here.

'I wish I'd had a chance to have babies,' Eve said.

Kate didn't know what to say again. 'I wish you had too.'

'But mostly I just want to know, will I realise it is happening or will it be bam, dead,' Eve said.

'Will it come with a whimper or with a bang?' Kate said.

'Yes, that's it. What's that from?'

'T. S. Eliot, *The Hollow Men*.'

Eve nodded. Then, with impeccable comic timing she

Room 706

arched an eyebrow, took a sip of her water, and said, 'I prefer *Cats*.'

Kate got the call when she was at the hospital, just as she left an antenatal appointment where she'd been having her blood pressure checked and her bump measured. Dying had been quick in the end. Eve's mum, Sandra, had been there, but there had been no time to summon anyone else. It was Eve's sister who had rung her with the news.

Outside the hospital, Kate called Vic at work.

He answered with a concerned tone and all Kate could do was sob.

'The baby,' Vic said, 'is the baby okay?'

'Eve's dead.'

'Stay put. I'm on my way.'

Forty minutes later Vic was there, scooping her up from her position crouched against the external wall of the hospital.

'I've got you, I've got you,' he said as he held her up and walked her to the waiting cab. 'I've got you.'

Chapter 34

Earlier this year

'One side always likes the other more,' Nicole said.

'What?'

'In a relationship, one side always likes the other more. There's always the one who needs to be loved and the one who gives that love and feels good for it. What would you even call that?'

'The supplicant and, whatever the opposite is, the supplier I suppose,' Kate replied.

Nicole had called Kate that morning in a distressed state, asking if she'd meet for lunch. She had just been dumped by her boyfriend of three years, a financier called Chris, who Kate had only met once in passing and who she'd struggled to recall much about when she'd described him to Vic just a few hours later.

Room 706

Kate had plans to meet James that day but they were, unusually, going to meet in the afternoon rather than the morning. She'd told Vic she had an editorial planning meeting until 5pm, so he was scheduled to pick up the kids.

'I have a meeting near London Bridge at 2pm,' she told Nicole. 'I can meet you there first, in the café opposite the entrance, on the hospital side.'

'So who liked who more?' Kate asked. A bunch of daffodils was in a vase on their table, making Kate feel joyful in spite of Nicole's sadness.

'He liked me more, of course.'

'Of course.'

'I mean I liked him too,' Nicole said. 'He was fun and generous. He never looked at the amount on a bill before paying it.'

'Is that generous or is that showing off?'

'Both. I found it sexy,' Nicole said.

'So why did he end things?'

'He said he liked me too much.'

Kate looked at her, confused. 'He liked you too much, so he had to end it?'

'Yes. Though now you put it like that I am doubting things.' Nicole's eyes were glistening.

'Come here,' Kate said, pulling her in for a hug.

'He said we either had to get married or split up, and since I'd always said I had no interest in marriage it had to end. His picture of the future included a wife and kids, a double garage and membership of the tennis club, and he didn't think I wanted any of that.'

'Oh Nic, that's shit. Do you want that though?'

'Fuck no. I don't want to be tied to anyone. I have no interest in tennis. I don't need a garage – I can't even drive. And I'm definitely not going to have more kids, this time is mine.'

'So he was right?'

'I don't understand why we couldn't just carry on as we were. We enjoyed each other's company. Sex was good. We were having fun.'

It's not the fun bits you need to think about, Kate thought. It's the un-fun bits. When someone is sick, or depressed, or in a boring phase. The day-to-day tedium. The farting in bed. The doing the same things over and over again with the same person. Making the same cup of tea and going on the same walks. She remembered the firefighter from the plane, what was his name? Michael, she remembered. He'd given her this marriage advice, unbidden, five years ago.

'Did you ever just hang out at home doing nothing?' she ventured.

Nicole sniffed. 'Not really, no.'

'Oh love, I am sorry.' Kate hugged her again and held her for a moment. 'How's everything else?'

'Oh, it's fine. Finn hates me, but only in the way sixteen-year-old boys are meant to hate their mum.'

'Doesn't that go full circle and they end the teenage years loving you as much as they did when they entered them?' Kate asked, trying to cheer Nicole up.

'Here's hoping. The thing is, when they're the age your kids are, you think it's really hard because they just want to

Room 706

be with you all the time, whether you're on the sofa or going to the toilet or whatever. You're their witness to existing. But you know what, it turns out they need you more when they are older, except they want you to be out of sight rather than next to them. And if you're not within their range, well they're furious, even though they don't want to talk to you or even acknowledge you.'

'Can't wait,' Kate said.

'Uh-huh. Then you look in the mirror and realise you're old.'

'Hang on, young mama,' Kate said. 'You're almost the same age as me. When my kids are Finn's age I will be way older than you are now. Whereas in a couple of years he will have left home and you'll have the chance to reinvent yourself any way you want.'

'I just don't want to get old,' Nicole said.

'Why not?'

'Old age is shit. You're invisible. Your body hurts. Either your friends die and you are lonely or you die and you're actually dead.'

Kate shrugged. She thought of her mum, and of Eve. She was sure they would have both liked the chance to grow old. Her mum used to talk about it, even though she was still in her thirties. 'I'm going to watch a film a day and eat buttery toast then pretend to be young and flirt with hot men online using your picture,' her mum had said.

'Don't use my picture, I'll be old too,' Kate had laughed. 'When you are eighty I will be sixty-two.'

'Age cannot wither her, Kate. You know that.'

'Besides,' Kate had said, 'the internet will be old news. There will be some kind of new technology for meeting people.'

'I'll use that then.'

Eve had wanted to be old too, Kate was sure of it. The thought made her angry at Nicole and she had to remind herself that Eve dying was not Nicole's fault.

She snapped herself back to the present conversation. 'I don't know. Vic's *nonna* used to say getting old hurts but it's better than the alternative.'

'How did she know?'

'No one knows, do they?' Kate said.

'Is she alive now?'

'No, by the end she did want to go. She was tired.'

'What's that saying?' asked Nicole. 'Age cannot wither her.'

'Age cannot wither her, nor custom stale her infinite variety.'

'Yes, that's the one.'

'It's *Antony and Cleopatra.*'

'Shakespeare?'

'Yep. My mum used to say it all the time. I've forgotten his name, but the one who's the friend of Mark Antony says it, that he's never going to fall out of love with Cleopatra because however old she gets she's never going to be boring.'

'That's an ambition for us all, eh?' Nicole laughed hollowly. 'Never be boring. Maybe Chris thought I was boring.'

'More like he was too boring to appreciate you.'

Room 706

Did one half of the couple always like the other more? Was Nicole right? Kate was still thinking about this after she had waved off a tear-stained Nicole, checked she really had gone into the train station, and doubled back towards the hotel. She'd barely had time to think about James and about what they would be up to that afternoon. Now, as she approached the hotel and checked her phone, the familiar nervousness settled in her stomach. She checked that the condoms she'd bought before meeting Nicole were still in her bag, and thought about James and what they were about to do.

Last time they had met he'd asked her about her fantasies. She didn't know that she really had any she wanted to live out. What did he want her to say? Two men? Two women? Restraints and gags and blindfolds? When pushed, she told him that the only fantasy she really had was the idea of meeting and fucking and doing what they did, but with no talking at all.

'None at all?' he'd asked.

'None at all,' she'd confirmed.

She didn't want to tell him why. That sometimes she just wanted no one to make any demands. That when James whispered in her ear as they fucked that he needed her, sometimes it was a huge turn on, but other times it repeated itself in her brain while she thought, what about my needs, what about my need not to be needed.

She wanted to say, 'Look, what I want is to come to the hotel and for you to be there on time, and I want to come up to the room and I don't even want to say hello or pretend to be shy or make small talk or even ask how you are. I want to come in and I want to be touched and fucked and consumed and to consume and then to be completely and totally alone without having uttered a word to each other.'

His text arrived at 2.05pm. He was in room 112 on the first floor. It was followed immediately by another text. *No talking.*

The sex was hot without talking. They were even more attuned to each other's bodies, to picking up the cues on what felt good, what was wanted next. But the lack of a goodbye, the dearth of spoken compliments, the absence of any chit-chat at all, left her feeling slightly used and uneasy.

As she lay in the hotel bath using all the free toiletries, she pondered again what Nicole had said. Did James like her more or did she like James more? He was the one helping fulfil her fantasy. But she hadn't asked him to do that. He'd insisted on knowing what her fantasies were.

Another demand on me, she thought.

When she got out of the bath and checked her phone, he'd sent her a message. *You are magnificent. Thank you. Next time let's allow ourselves to talk. I like you too much not to.* The uneasy feeling disappeared as soon as she read it.

She was still thinking of Nicole's theory on the way home. Who liked who more out of her and Vic? At first she thought it was Vic. He had so much love for her, a puppy-like enthusiasm. He wanted her and he wasn't afraid to show it. But, Kate concluded, if it wasn't her it would

Room 706

have been someone else, he would have found another lost soul to receive all that love and adoration. She didn't know whether the same applied to her, whether she would have found someone else to love.

Chapter 35

8.26pm
Room 706

The photos were all uploaded. While she was being practical she may as well look at what else was on her to-do list. Kate had an app on her phone for this. It had three sections – *Do Now*, *Do Soon*, and *For The Future*.

Kate clicked on *Do Now*. There were two things on that list. The first was *Sign permission form for school trip*. She had done that yesterday and Lenny had taken it in his bag this morning. Hopefully he'd remembered to give it in. She clicked on the tick beside it in the app. *You've got this*, it flashed at her.

Do next door's bins was the second thing. Their neighbours were on holiday and she had promised to put the bins back in their front garden that evening so that their house didn't look empty. Should she message Vic to tell him? Surely a message about bins was just too tedious to be her last message to him. Even if not the last, it just didn't sit right. No, it was fine. If she died then there would be enough people popping in for next door not to get burgled. If she was alive, she could do it when she got home. She ticked it even though it had not been done, to enjoy the frisson of nothing to do on the *Do Now* list. *Take some time for yourself. Have some bubbles,* the app told her, with a picture of both a bubble bath and a glass of fizz.

She moved on to the *Do Soon* list.

Pay balance of holiday. The deadline for payment was in two weeks' time. The holiday was for immediately after Christmas, a lodge in the Scottish Highlands. Kate had no family. There was no tradition of visiting Vic's parents. Tom would be with Polly's family. So they were going to spend time, the four of them, in a holiday cottage that looked ever so cosy online, all tartan rugs and real fires. They'd watch films and drink hot chocolate and maybe they would even see snow. The kids would love that, building a snowman, having a snowball fight. They needed waterproof gloves. She should add that to her list, except she didn't want to put anything new on it today.

She wrote an email to Vic, scheduling it to send to him in exactly one week. *Balance on holiday due next week.* She added the reference number and the website and the amount left to pay. Would he even want to go without her if it came to it? She hoped so. Maybe they could scatter her ashes there. Was suggesting that by email too controlling? Yes, a step too far, she thought. Besides, she had never been there before, she might not even like it. And it was a long way to make the kids go for the rest of their lives if they wanted a special place. But a holiday, yes, they should definitely go even if the worst happened. She checked the button on her app next to that item. Done.

Good job, the app flashed at her. Kate liked it, these little pre-programmed affirmations.

Yes, good fucking job indeed, she thought. She may not have paid the balance, but she had sent an email about it. That was good enough.

She extended her legs as far as she could in front of her. Everything was tight. She did a few stretches then lay back against a pillow. The app flashed at her again. *You have an item on For The Future with a deadline of three weeks. Do you want to view it?*

No, Kate thought. She pressed *Yes*.

Lenny, Invader Day. Costume needed.

Oh God, she'd promised to help him make a homemade costume for Invader Day. It was such an odd day, a celebration of all the armies who had come to the UK and won, and scheduled just a week before all the Christmas concerts and parties started. They'd planned to fashion a Viking hat out of tin foil and make a huge blond moustache from yellow cardboard. Would Vic do that if she wasn't here? She searched the web. There was a Viking costume in Lenny's size available to be delivered within five days.

Surely this is cultural appropriation, she thought to herself. No, it can't be, they invaded us. It was eighteen quid and then an extra six quid for postage. She barely hesitated. Little Lenny Victorsson shall go to the ball. She ticked the box on the app and it disappeared.

Amazing. You are on fire! flashed the app.

If only you fucking knew, Kate thought.

Ticking things off was making her feel a little calmer. She looked at what was left. *Christmas teacher gifts* was next, a reminder to buy something for each of the kids to give their teacher at the end of term. Not that it mattered, she was sure. How many boxes of chocolates or bottles of cheap wine or *Best Teacher* mugs did they need anyway? She deleted it from the to-do list. She could add it again later, if she remembered, if she made it. She shook her head to try to rid it of that thought.

At least the kids' own Christmas presents were mostly sorted. She bought little things throughout the year, the novelty toys and cute stationery and Christmas-themed joke books that did not really change regardless of the kids' ages. She kept a list of them on a different app on her phone. Would Vic know about the app or where the gifts were hidden? She wrote an email, also scheduled to send next week, telling him where they were, in separate bin bags in the cupboard on top of the built-in wardrobe in the spare bedroom, the one neither of them could reach without standing on a stool, where the children couldn't reach even standing on a stool. Whatever happens today, she thought, the kids will get Christmas presents. There was just the main present, the big one that ostensibly came from Santa, left to buy.

Kate knew that Annie wanted a specific gift for her big

present. A very expensive doll from an American brand, with a matching outfit that Annie could wear herself. She'd wanted it for years now and had convinced herself that this Christmas would be the one.

Fuck it, Kate thought. She typed in the address of the website that sold them. The price made her baulk and was even more once the extortionate postage charges were added. *All our prices include tax. Nothing to pay on arrival*, the website trumpeted with a flashing gold star. Deep breaths, Kate thought, as she ticked the box to allow the website to use the card details saved on her computer, and entered her security code. She reopened the to-do list app and added *Buy doll for Annie* to the *For The Future* list. *When would you like a reminder?* it asked her. She ticked *Never* then immediately marked the item as done. A shower of stylised confetti fell from the top of her phone screen in congratulations.

Check in with Sandra was the last unticked thing on her list. Kate tried to make contact with Eve's mum every so often, to maintain the link. She'd send her an email to say hi, update her on the kids, be a connection to her dead daughter who had died way too young. Eve had only been twenty-seven. Sandra had other children, and grandchildren, and was immersed in their lives. But she always replied to Kate, thanking her for maintaining contact, sharing a memory of Eve, asking after her handsome Italian. Kate didn't have the stomach to message her right now. She clicked the notification icon next to it on her list, asking to be reminded again in a week.

If Eve was alive Kate could have told her everything. Eve

Room 706

would have been there for her. She may not have approved of whatever it was Kate did with James, but if she had called her from the hotel room she would have listened and supported her unconditionally. She was her dead-prostitute friend after all. It was almost unbearably hard to think of Eve now, even though she had died nine years ago.

At least I've had my babies, Kate thought. If it all ends today, I've done that.

'We could have sex?'

'Sorry?' Kate whispered.

She'd thought James was asleep, but perhaps her stretching had woken him. Without opening his eyes, he started talking.

'I don't mean it,' James said. 'Not really. Just it seems appropriate. What do you do when you know the world is ending? You fuck.'

Kate shook her head. 'Could you even, erm, get excited, knowing it was only because it's the end of the world?'

He shrugged. 'I mean, probably. My cock is not always rational.'

'Let's not.' Kate smiled weakly.

'Okay.'

She didn't know whether James had actually meant it or not. Was it his idea of a joke? It must have been.

'What would you be doing this evening if the day had gone as planned?' Kate asked.

'I would be at my choir rehearsal,' James replied.

'You sing?'

Kate had not expected that. She was reminded once more how little they knew about each other.

'I do.'

They lay there side by side, not touching.

Kate wondered whether she should call the police again. She had the number they had sent to her after her initial call, to message if she had any new information. What if she rang it and said she had no information but would they mind just telling her what was going on? She wanted to ask them, have you remembered we are here? Are you coming to get us? The news updates on her phone showed her that no one had forgotten. The Prime Minister had returned early to London from making a speech in Paris. A special meeting was being convened.

Hey. She messaged Vic.

Hey.

There was nothing to say. She wasn't even sure why she had messaged him.

I just bought Annie a doll for Christmas. It'll arrive in a couple of weeks.

Kate could imagine Vic's face if she had told him this in real life, incredulity at the cost, not because he resented the money but because he couldn't believe anyone would spend it on a doll.

Ask me how much it cost, Kate messaged him.

How much did it cost? Vic replied.

You don't want to know.

You're right, Vic replied.

Will it make her happy? Another message from Vic.

Actually, Kate thought, it probably would. Annie would

Room 706

feel that she had been listened to, that the universe had granted her wish, that the doll had special powers to understand her innermost thoughts and desires. And who were they to say this wasn't true anyway?

I think so, she sent Vic. Then, in another message, *Lenny needs a big present too.*

What do you think he'll want? Vic asked.

She'd hoped that Vic would have ideas for that. After all, he was the only one of them who had been a nine-year-old boy before.

Dunno. If all else fails then probably the most recent strip, the official expensive one. Lenny loved any clothing from his favourite team.

The mundanity of the conversation was almost laughable. But Kate was pleased he had replied so quickly and was going along with it. When they were messaging she felt so much calmer than when time passed with no contact.

Would you call the police for me?

He responded even more quickly this time. *What's happened? Are you okay?*

Shit, she'd confused him. *Nothing new has happened*, she quickly typed. *I just want to know what to do, what's going on, when this will be over.*

Vic's reply took longer this time. It came through eventually. *I'll try now.* She sent him the number the police had sent her.

Kate looked at James. He appeared to be asleep again.

You possibly have just hours left on this earth, she thought, and you spend them sleeping.

Kate almost laughed out loud at that. Well he wouldn't be in charge of his family's memories would he? He'd not be the keeper of photos and guardian of videos. He would not have to send the online shopping password to his wife.

Chapter 36

Nine years earlier

'I don't want to. I can't.'

'Why not?' Vic asked gently. 'It'll do you good.'

'I'm eight months pregnant. I am huge and uncomfortable and tired. They are not pregnant and not uncomfortable and not tired. I couldn't feel less in a going-out mood.'

'Anything else?'

'Yes Vic, my best friend is dead.'

'I know.' Vic stroked her back underneath the duvet.

'You don't know though, do you?' Kate said. 'Losing Eve is not just losing Eve, as terrible as that alone is. Losing Eve is also like losing my mum all over again. She was the only person I knew who had known my mum. Now, without that, sometimes I find myself thinking I must have made my mum up.'

'I know. It's awful. I get it. But Kate, this might be your last chance to go out for a while. It'll be harder once the baby is here, and, well, I am worried about you. I've barely seen you smile since Eve died. She wouldn't want you to be so unhappy, not when we are about to meet your baby, our baby.'

'I don't want to go out. I don't even want to get out of this bed and get dressed and go to work. I want to stay at home and be miserable,' Kate said.

'I think it would be good for you to go,' Vic persisted.

Nicole had asked Kate to go for a drink after work. 'Come on, you're going to be away from work for a whole year. We should have at least one more night out first.'

'I won't be any fun sober.'

'I'll drink for you,' Nicole said.

Kate was at her desk still dithering over whether to turn up when she looked out of the window and saw Nicole walking back from her lunch hour carrying a big gift basket. Shit, that must be for her. She couldn't pull out if there were presents. She messaged Vic. *I'll go tonight.*

Good, he replied. *Get a cab home if you need to. I love you.*

The gift basket, Nicole explained that evening, was a combination of a staff whip-round and some gifts just from her. The communal money had bought the baby clothes and the posh blanket. The present from her was the stash of lotions and potions for all the bits people didn't speak about. Aloe vera wipes for piles, cream for cracked nipples, a special bubble bath recommended by midwives for soothing bruised vulvas.

Room 706

'You're not making this sound fun,' Kate said.

'That's because it's awful,' Nicole said cheerfully.

They were joined after half an hour by another of Nicole's office friends, Cheryl.

'Is she going on about haemorrhoids?' Cheryl said as she took off her coat.

'She is,' Kate said.

'She scared the shit out of Kelly on the sales team before she had her baby,' Cheryl said.

'Rubbish. Women need to know these things,' countered Nicole. 'This whole conspiracy-of-silence thing, the whole isn't-motherhood-all-peachy-and-aren't-our-bodies-amazing line. Our bodies are amazing but oh my God pregnancy fucks them up. Kate, you might never again feel attractive naked, but I just want you to know that's normal, every mother experiences it and, also, that any product with numbing cream in it is a good idea.'

'I need food,' Kate said. They ordered plates of loaded nachos and a lime and soda for Kate, while Nicole and Cheryl shared a bottle of wine.

After half an hour of office gossip, Cheryl could keep it in no longer.

'I met someone,' she said.

'You met someone,' Nicole echoed.

'Yes. It's wonderful. We have the most amazing sex. And, get this, because he is married I don't have to do any of that emotional stuff. We have sex. We chat. We give each other compliments. We go home.'

'An affair?' asked Nicole, raising her eyebrow.

Cheryl nodded. 'Yes, yes I suppose it is. For him. I am single, remember. Well I suppose I'm not now, if I am seeing him, but other than him.'

'I had a married lover once,' said Nicole.

'Tell us everything,' said Cheryl. Kate nursed her drink and rubbed her belly under the table. She thought of Eve, already just a memory, and swallowed hard.

'There's not a huge amount to tell. I met him at work years ago when I was a marketing assistant and he did something in accounts, and we would smoulder at each other across the office. We got together at a drinks thing and he'd come back to my flat for an evening every few weeks when Finn was at his dad's for the night.'

'Where did his wife think he was?'

'I have no idea. But then after about a year and a bit he brought her along to the office summer party. It was a black-tie thing in a marquee, and partners were invited. So I kept my distance and didn't even look over his way. Respect for the institution of marriage and all that. In fact I was working very hard at chatting up someone else from one of our advertisers.'

Cheryl laughed.

'Yeah, wild times. Anyway, the next day in the office he cornered me in the kitchen. "She knew," he said, and I was all like, "Knew what?" and he said, "She knew we were lovers. She said she could tell by the way you walked past me to get a drink." Well, I knew this was bollocks, that she had no way of knowing. She could only know if he had told

Room 706

her. I said to him, "Look, mate, what you are describing is not some kind of sixth sense knowledge your wife has – it's the feeling of your own guilt."'

'So what happened next?' Cheryl asked.

'Nothing. It turned me right off, him trying to make his guilt my problem. A problem shared is a problem doubled and all that. I got a new job shortly after, where we all work now in fact, and never saw him again.'

'He never just turned up at your flat?' asked Cheryl.

'No. It had run its course I think. He wanted someone who would beg him to leave her, so that he could feel good about not doing so.'

'And did you want him to leave her for you?' Kate asked.

'Oh my God, no way, that would have been the worst. He wasn't a long-term prospect, he was a bit of fun.'

'I wonder whether they're still together,' Cheryl said.

'Probably.'

Later, when Cheryl left to go and meet her lover, Nicole and Kate dissected her news.

'Wow, what do you think about that then?' Kate asked.

'I'm not surprised to be honest. Everyone seems to be at it.'

'I'm not,' Kate said.

'Yeah, but you've only been married, what, three years?'

'Four. But we were together for a few years before that.'

'And now you're pregnant. It's all still new and exciting. But I was talking to someone on my team the other day. She's been with her bloke for twenty years. We were trying to arrange drinks after work. I suggested Thursday and she said, I kid you not, "Oh, darling, I can't do Thursday. Adrien is over from Brussels and I am meeting him in Claridge's to fuck."'

Vic was still awake when she got home. 'How was it?'

'Eve is still dead.'

Vic stayed silent.

'Sorry. I just, well, it's just not something that a night out is going to fix. She's dead. Forever. She is never going to be alive again.'

'I know that, Kate,' Vic said.

Once in bed, wrapped up in the duvet, Kate spoke again. 'I'm sorry. I'm just so sad.'

'I know you are. I wish I could make it better,' Vic replied.

'We spoke about sex with married men, broken vaginas and sore arseholes.'

'Oh.'

'They got me this.' Kate pointed to the large gift basket she had put on the floor by her side of the bed, in the space they had cleared for a crib.

'That's nice,' Vic said. 'That's really nice.'

'Yeah, I know.' Kate felt totally flat.

'Who's sleeping with married men?' Vic asked.

'Everyone. Cheryl is now. Nicole used to. And someone in Nicole's team who has been with her partner for twenty years meets a Belgian man called Adrien in Claridge's to fuck every so often.'

'Don't assume that because he is foreign and stays in a swish hotel that he is sophisticated,' said Vic. 'I bet you

Room 706

Adrien is a middle-aged, mediocre, middle manager who cannot believe his luck.'

'Yeah, probably.'

Vic rubbed Kate's pregnant tummy and kissed her neck.

'And you?'

'What?'

'Are you sleeping with a married man?'

'Well, yes, if you count yourself, then I suppose I am.'

He gave her a kiss. 'I know you are sad. I know she is dead and it's shit and nothing I can do or say will make it better. But I'm still pleased you went out.'

Chapter 37

9.06pm
Room 706

Kate pressed her fingers hard against her eyelids, making patterns of grey and green and red. Her temples throbbed. She heard Eve's voice in her head.

Go on, Eve said, *choose someone to talk about. Pretend we're in Spain. What about him?*

She moved her fingers and the patterns started to fade. Hearing Eve's voice, even though she knew it was not really there, felt very odd.

You're dead, Kate said in her head.

I know, said Eve's voice. *It means you can tell me things. I can't tell anyone.*

And Eve's laugh echoed in Kate's ears.

Go on. Tell me about him.

Room 706

Who?
Him, that fella you've got in there with you.
Kate waited a few moments. It was silent.
Okay, she said in her head
I'm still here, no rush, Eve replied, laughing again.
I don't know what to say.
Say anything. Whatever comes into your head. It's like our travelling game.
Okay.
There was quiet. Kate wasn't even sure she knew what was real or not any more.
Eve?
Yeah?
I'm in a bit of a pickle.
Oh love. I wish I could give you a cuddle.
Yeah. What's it like being dead?
Oh, y'know, nothing much to say really.
Kate shook her head, her eyes still closed. This was crazy.
You can't get rid of me that easily.
Yeah.
So, who is he?
I don't know.
Yeah you do.
He's called James.
Eve said nothing.
I don't really know what happened. It just did. It's amazing sex. Great sex. Sex-you-wouldn't-have-with-your-spouse sex.
Sounds fun.
Yeah.

How did you meet?
Long story. Work lunch. A picnic. A book launch.
You love him?
God no.
He loves you?
Nah.
It's just sex?
Yeah.
You time?
Kate's voice in her head laughed a bit. Yeah. Me time.
Could be a massage?
Yep.
A facial?
Uh-huh.
A secret gin and tonic in the pub after work with a book?
I do that too, sometimes, and pretend I've gone to yoga.
Atta girl.
Sometimes I really do go to yoga.
What about Vic?
He pretends not to know, but I'm sure he sees the gym kit is unused.
Not about the yoga, silly.
No. He doesn't know.
Are you sure?

Was she sure? Could it be that he'd known all along, that after the very first lunch he could tell something in the universe had shifted, or that when he'd said he could smell cigarettes on her the night after the book launch what he meant was he knew something out of the ordinary had happened? No, she wasn't sure he didn't know. How could she have imagined she could do something like this and him not know?

Oh God, Eve, maybe he does know.

Well he hasn't stopped it if he does.

No.

Does he still adore you? Does he look at you the way he used to look at you in Rome?

Will you hate me if I say yes?

Absolutely.

Eve?

Yeah.

I might die today.

Cheer up sweetheart, the end hasn't been written yet.

It was such an Eve thing to say. It really felt as if she was in the room.

I love Vic you know, she told Eve silently.

'Kate, are you okay?' It was James's voice.

Kate opened her eyes.

'What?'

'Are you okay? You look, I don't know, you look very far away.'

'Not really, no. I'm not that okay. What with being a hostage and all.' She had no patience left to do anything other than snap.

What would she be doing at this time if she was home? Just gone 9pm. Kids would be in bed hopefully, dishes put in the kitchen at least, even if not loaded into the dishwasher. She'd be on the sofa with a book and a glass of wine or a mug of peppermint tea, waiting for Vic to stop pottering and join her for an episode of whatever series they were watching, before heading to bed themselves. Is that how they spent their evenings? They'd had thousands of them together and now she wasn't even sure what they did each night. She'd give anything to be there now, on the sofa, getting cross that she was still waiting for him before she could press play.

She realised she should ask James the same question.

'What about you, how are you doing?'

'I've had better days.'

'Yeah.'

If this was a film, Kate thought, it would focus on Vic, not her or James. It would be a story of transformation from wronged husband to avenging hero, with a dose of forgiveness. His wife goes missing on the day of a major terrorist attack and he tears through the city looking for her, shedding layers of clothing as he goes. Kate couldn't help but smile at the idea of Vic, topless, having acquired a bandana, angry. All clues would lead to the hotel. An address scribbled on a scrap of paper found in the bin maybe, or an email in her inbox advertising the special day rates. And when he arrives at the hotel he doesn't know who to kill first, her lover or the terrorists. No, he wouldn't kill the lover, the lover would die but not at his hand. Yes, that would be it. The terrorists would try to kill both Kate and James but Vic would leap in front of them saving Kate but, sadly, not James, while killing the terrorists at the same time. She would cry out and he would hold her. 'It'll all be okay,' he would say. 'It's over

Room 706

now. Let's go home.' She was sure she'd seen something like this at the actual cinema in her teens.

She shook her head to empty it. If only this was a film rather than real life.

As if Vic could tell she was thinking about him, her phone flashed.

I called them.

Who had he called? What was he talking about?

The number went straight through to a special incident room but they weren't able to tell me anything. They said the advice is the same – stay hidden and as quiet as possible. They only really want to know if you have seen or heard anything, or if you have moved room.

Oh, the police. Of course, she had asked him to call. When even was that? At least half an hour ago. What had taken him so long? Maybe the kids had needed him. Maybe he'd been making some food.

Had she seen or heard anything? How could she even begin to tell Vic about the boy and his parents calling the lift, and the gunshot. Or that she had done nothing to stop it. What could she tell him, or the police, that could be helpful? People knocked on the door. No, I didn't see them. No, I didn't recognise their accents. No, they didn't say anything identifying. No, I am not sure I didn't imagine it.

Did they say what the demands are? Whether the government will meet them? When this is likely to be over? She typed her message quickly.

They didn't say anything. I don't think they share that kind of information. I've been reading everything. I think if there are demands then there must be some kind of media blackout on printing them.

Oh yes, that's what she'd read earlier in the financial newspaper. She remembered now. The government does not negotiate with terrorists and therefore their demands are irrelevant, officially at least.

Thank you for trying, she messaged back.

It'll be okay. This can't last forever, Vic messaged.

No, but the world might end. Her world might end. *Love you*, she sent back. She wondered whether he had eaten anything, whether he might be annoyed if she were to ask. She decided not to.

Kate took a deep breath and refreshed the news app on her phone. She needed to face reality and to read it for herself, even if every time she did so it made things too real and made her feel like she wanted to throw up.

The live news feed was being updated pretty regularly, even when there was nothing new to report. She liked the word 'live' she thought, until her eye caught its opposite – dead. She knew that even looking at this was a bad idea, like searching for symptoms and a diagnosis online before seeing a doctor, but she couldn't stop. The latest entry on the live feed was an anodyne comment from the Home Secretary. Everyone was apparently doing their best. But, below that, that was the place from where the word 'dead' had jumped out. *Two bodies have been pushed out of the revolving door, both now confirmed dead.*

'Oh my God.' Kate put her hand to her mouth. James

looked over and she passed him her phone. He read it silently and passed it back.

'I hadn't read that yet. I'm on another site.'

She had nothing to say to that. On one website people were dead. On another those people were still alive. Her whole body felt cold. She concentrated on not giving in to the static feeling in her head that made her feel as if she would pass out. On social media people were already sharing images of the bodies. Who were they? Staff or guests, terrorist or hostage? So much had been pixelated that it was impossible to tell. Kate was sure she would be able to find clearer photographs if she searched for them, posted and reposted by ghoulish people. She did not search for them.

Despite the blurring of the images you could see what the dead people were wearing. One was in bright green, all the same colour, maybe a jumpsuit or a trouser suit. The other had black trousers and a white top. Would their spouses, their kids, their parents, be able to recognise them from this? Did people generally know what their loved ones were wearing that day? She wondered whether Vic knew what she was wearing right now. Had he seen her dressed this morning? Yes, he'd made her a cup of tea in his *World's Best Papa* mug and they'd had a conversation about her made-up plans for the day. It all seemed a long time ago. Whether he would remember though, that was another question. Her navy knee-length dress was pretty standard office wear, entirely unmemorable. She'd worn it partly for that reason, so as not to stand out as she entered the hotel and made her way to the room, and partly because she liked the jersey material. It was easy to take off, unlikely to crease.

She messaged Vic again. *There are dead people. I saw online.*

He took a while to reply. Maybe he was looking up the details. She'd have thought he'd have it on the television and the live feeds on his phone or computer, but maybe that was too much, maybe he'd turned it all off. When he replied he didn't mention the bodies.

Sit tight, you'll be home before you know it.

How would she be written about if it were her dead body pushed out of the door? Women were never allowed to exist in their own right in the news. It would be mother of two, or wife. Wife and mother. Wife and lover. Woman. Child. We're all someone's child, she thought, or we all were once. She missed her mum so much.

Chapter 38

Eight years earlier

She'd finally realised she was pregnant again because of the huge amount of crisps she was eating, roast-beef flavour mostly, craving salt and that meaty savoury taste. She bought a test at lunchtime and peed on it, knowing even before the two lines showed that it would be positive.

They hadn't been trying to conceive, but they also hadn't been using any contraception, which now seemed the same as actively trying. Kate felt embarrassed that she hadn't noticed her missed periods, though they had been sporadic since returning after Lenny's arrival anyway. She should have realised from the nausea alone, but she had thought it was from tiredness and being back at work and worrying about Lenny's nursery catching fire and the ridiculous lunches with James who she now intended never to see again. No wonder she had been sick when running away from his picnic a few weeks ago. That wasn't guilt. Or not just guilt. That was a baby.

She took the test home in her handbag to show Vic. He was thrilled: 'Lenny will have a sibling.' And suddenly she was filled with anger and sadness. This baby's life was not there in order to be a sibling, she railed at him.

'Don't do that,' she had said, 'don't define this one by what already exists, by who already exists.'

'I'm sorry,' Vic said. 'I'm sorry. It's just that my brother is so important to me I can't think of anything better than a sibling for Lenny. That's what we're defined by isn't it, our connections to other people? Me to Tom. Tom to me. Me to you. Us against the world.'

She nodded and wiped her tears. It was meant to be a happy moment and she had snapped at him, ruining it.

'Sorry,' she said. 'I'm so sorry.'

He held her. 'It's okay. I love you. I love Lenny. I love this baby.'

They sat there silently together in their cuddle for a while. She let him rub her tummy gently while she transmitted secret messages to the baby inside her – you're you, you exist, you are more than your relationship to other people.

'Kate?'

'Yeah.'

'I mean it you know. We're a unit. I know you find it hard to let people in sometimes. I know that other than me, and Lenny, everyone you've ever loved has been taken away from you prematurely. But that's not going to happen to us. You

Room 706

know that don't you? That it's you and me and Lenny, and now this baby too. And we're not going anywhere.'

'I know.'

A week later they were walking along the South Bank of the Thames. Lenny was asleep in his buggy, Vic pushing. For once Kate had her hands completely free – no buggy, no toddler, no bag. She had her phone in her pocket and that was it.

'I learned a new word this week,' Vic said. 'It was sent round at work. One of my colleagues saw it online.'

'What is it?'

'Sonder.'

'Sonder.' Kate tried it out, feeling it in her mouth. 'That's wonder and sound. What does it mean? Is it something about wondering where sound is coming from?'

'Not quite. Hold on.' He stopped pushing the buggy and got his wallet from his pocket, taking from it a folded-up piece of paper.

'It's the realisation that everyone around you is living a life as vivid and complex as your own,' he read from it.

'Oh, that's lovely.'

'It's a good word for us isn't it? Like those days on the beach wondering about people's lives. Maybe what we were doing was sondering.

Kate smiled. She loved Vic's enthusiasm for language, for knowledge.

The tide was low and a small beach was visible at the water line. A man was crouching on the stones, digging at something with a small shovel.

'What do you think he's doing?' Kate asked.

'Mudlarking,' Vic said.

'Mudlarking?'

'It's kind of metal detecting in the mud. Though not necessarily metal. They don't even use a detector. In fact, not necessarily mud – it's pretty stony down there. They're looking for treasure and things from the past.'

'Bodies?'

'No, they usually end up further east.'

'You seem to know a lot about this.'

Vic shrugged. The man had picked something up and was examining it.

'He's found something,' Kate said.

'Mudlarking. What larks.' He pulled her to him and kissed her. 'I love you.'

'Oh.'

'What?'

'It kicked. That was a definite kick.'

Vic put his hand on her belly.

'Where?'

'Here.' She placed his fingertips to the right of her navel.

'What did it feel like?'

It was her second pregnancy and in theory she should have remembered what a baby kicking felt like. But with Lenny the books had all said it would be like butterflies, so it duly felt like butterflies. This time was different. It felt like something else. She thought for a moment.

'A fairy,' she said, 'on a miniature trapeze.'

Room 706

They stood watching the riverbank as the mudlarker threw his find into the water.

'Oh, it can't have been anything worth keeping,' Kate said. But Vic was staring at something else now. The tide rose quickly on this stretch of the river and the beach was already smaller than it had been a few minutes earlier. The mudlarker was moving towards the stairs leading back to the river path and Kate was still watching him pick his way carefully across the stones. But Vic seemed to have spotted someone else further away.

'That doesn't look right,' said Vic, pointing to a figure sitting at the end of a wooden jetty sticking out some way over the river. 'Call the police and an ambulance. Say we might need the coastguard.'

Kate was still waiting for the call to be answered when Vic reached the man he had spotted, having jumped over the locked gate and walked carefully but quickly down the slanted wooden structure. She saw him greet the man, who did not appear to respond, then crouch down next to him.

The operator answered and Kate described what she could see. A man sat at the end of the jetty, his feet dangling, the river waters rising, one small jump from freezing oblivion, not doing anything, just sitting. But something about his demeanour had made her husband concerned, and he was there with him now. One small push away from freezing oblivion himself, Kate realised.

Please don't take him with you if you do anything to yourself, she tried to transmit to the man. She put her hand on Lenny's buggy and held it tightly. The operator assured her that emergency services were on their way. Kate could see Vic moving, as if he was nodding with his whole body at whatever the man was saying.

And even as the police arrived and she waved at them to show where Vic and the man were, she could see Vic move closer and put an arm around him. Vic seemed to have succeeded in persuading the man to shuffle back a little. Their bottoms appeared to be slightly further from the edge than they had been, though Kate wondered whether she was telling herself this just to make herself feel better. The police officer spoke to them from a few feet away and Vic turned to him and said something, his other hand on the man's knee. The police officer stayed back and some time later Vic gestured him forward. Together they helped the man to stand, Vic holding on to him the whole time. They walked back down the jetty together, to where an ambulance was now waiting. A small crowd was watching. Vic climbed in with him. After ten minutes or so Vic came out of the ambulance. As the paramedic opened the door, Kate could see Vic embracing the man and kissing his forehead. He was tender and strong. Vic had saved the man's life, she was sure of it.

'Home?' she said to him as he came and stood next to her.

He took the buggy and kissed his sleeping son gently.

'Home,' he said.

Chapter 39

9.51pm
Room 706

There was nothing to do in the room except sit and wait, refresh the news feeds, listen for noises and be prepared, though for what she wasn't sure. To hide? There was nowhere. To run? Also nowhere. To fight? She didn't think they'd manage to hold anyone off for long.

Bored is a funny word, she thought. Kids are bored all the time, but she wasn't sure when she had last been bored. There was always something to do, something to think about.

Kate wished she could bring her mum to life in her head today the way she was doing with Eve. She often could, but not always.

Mum, she made her brain call out. Mum?

Nothing.

If only she could make herself believe in all that religious stuff about seeing each other again one day. Maybe if she did she wouldn't feel so scared now. What would her mum say about this situation? It was hard to guess. Kate realised she didn't even know whether her mum had lovers. She couldn't remember ever being introduced to anyone. But maybe there had been nights out while she stayed with her grandparents, or perhaps it was like mother like daughter and she had made use of the daytimes while Kate was at school.

Kate remembered once asking her mum if she regretted being a single parent. 'God no,' she'd said. 'Bringing you up alone has been glorious. Not easy, necessarily, I have barely any time to myself and we don't have that much money. But I never have to convince anyone to do things my way. I am not resentful of anyone not pulling their weight or not loving you enough. Someone once asked me if I wanted someone to share the joy, but why would I want to share it? The joy in you is all mine.'

She remembered the night before she went to university, when the two of them went out for dinner. This was, she knew, a big deal. Dinners out were for special occasions only. Kate would have preferred a takeaway in the comfort of home, or to be able to help by paying for the meal from her summer-job earnings, but she also knew that it was important for her mum to be able to do this for her. They both instinctively declined the suggestion of a starter and chose from the cheaper items on the menu.

'Has it been a good childhood?' her mum asked.

Kate smiled at her. 'The best.'

Room 706

'Now I know two things,' her mum said.

'Which are?'

'First, that you are lying. And second, that I haven't done that bad a job if you are kind enough to lie.'

'I'm not lying.'

Kate's mum looked at her. 'I know it has been hard, just me and you, not really enough money for all the treats your friends had.'

'I had plenty of treats.'

'You've been amazing. You never asked for anything. But I know there were school holidays you couldn't go on. Clothes you wanted but couldn't afford. Fewer days out than other people.'

'Mum, I had you. It was great. And you're talking rubbish. We had holidays. I never went without, not anything I needed, not even much that I wanted.'

It was true, it had been great. Picnics in parks and film nights at home with supermarket popcorn. Hugs on demand and not too many recriminations for staying at Eve's house longer than agreed, getting home late. And always Kate knew that her mum had her back.

Kate kept her eyes tightly closed and tried again to summon her mum. Most of the images she could bring to mind were not of a living and breathing woman, but of photographs. They were memories of memories. She scrunched up her eyes and concentrated hard, willing her mum into focus.

What came was the two of them sitting on a green-and-white chequered blanket that they had put on the grass next to their tent one summer. It was hot, they were in France and they'd been to the supermarket on bikes. Kate was about eleven, she supposed.

'Right then Katie, we could buy mini quiches and French cheese and pots of chocolate dessert,' said her mum. 'Or we could take the same amount of money and buy bread and apples and as many different types of sweet as we can find.' Kate chose sweets, of course.

'I was hoping you would choose that,' her mum said.

They sat on the blanket by their tent and Kate drew up two copies of a chart on the pad of lined paper she had bought especially for the holiday. They were each to mark every type of sweet according to look, texture, flavour and overall experience. They spent a whole afternoon doing this. Kate could still taste the winner now, a kind of boiled orange sweet that would suddenly break apart when sucked for long enough, and deliver a hit of fizzy sherbet, though her mum had preferred the two-tone chewy snakes with one end that was supposed to be sweet and one that was supposed to be sour.

Her mum had loved sweets, and challenges. Once, Kate remembered now, they had been for a walk somewhere, near her gran's house probably, somewhere that felt rural but was in reality part of the Greater London sprawl. She must have been thirteen or fourteen, because her gran had died when Kate was sixteen, and had been in hospital for almost a year before that. They were walking down a path in a forest. There was still the occasional late conker to pick up, so it must have been mid-October, around the time of her birthday. And her mum had produced a packet of strong mints.

Room 706

'How many of these do you think you can keep in your mouth at once?' she asked.

'Easy,' said Kate, 'at least five.'

'Go on then.'

And Kate took five mints and popped them on her tongue until the burning feeling spread across her whole face and it felt as if her nostrils were going to freeze off. She spat them into a pile of leaves, her mum laughing and laughing before taking just one mint herself.

Kate knew her mum was dead, but remembering that fact now made her catch her breath, as if she was finding out afresh. She wished she had a recording of her mum's voice. Was there a recording of her own voice for the kids? Yes, there surely must be, on the videos she had uploaded earlier.

What would Lenny and Annie remember of her if she did die today? Would it also mostly be the sweets and treats? Why had she never rated all the sweets available in the supermarket with them? Why had she not yet taken them camping in France? Kate tried to think what else she remembered from her childhood. She could remember watching television gameshows cuddled up with her mum on the couch. The weight of a bag full of books on their weekend trips to the library. The exact number of steps it took to walk each street on the way to her primary school and the weight of her mum's hand as she held it. The smell of her mum after a bubble bath. Were these memories real or what she wanted memories to be? It didn't really matter she supposed, if she believed them to be true.

Was she a good mum herself? Kate wasn't sure. She loved

her children with all her heart. But was she a good mum? Good mums don't fuck their lovers in hotel rooms, she thought. Good mums don't have affairs. Good mums are fulfilled enough with their husbands and their kids and their normal lives. Oh God, would that override everything? If she died today, if Vic found out the truth and one day told the kids, would that be the main thing they knew about her? Our mother, who cheated on our father, who got what she deserved, who brought it on herself.

What if James had been there on time rather than turning up at 11am? Would they have finished fucking half an hour earlier too? Then he'd have surely left the room before the television news channels got hold of the story. Would he have got out in time or would he have been met at the lift or in the lobby by people with guns, and taken to be with all the other hostages? Then she'd be in the same situation as she was now, only without James in the room. His presence annoyed her, but being alone would be worse.

In the multiverse, Kate thought, there is a world where I didn't fuck James today. There is a world where I did fuck James but in a different hotel. There is a world where Vic did not have a breakdown and did not go to Italy to recover. And there is one where he didn't have a breakdown but he did meet me anyway. There is a world where everything is the same except I fucked James yesterday not today. There is a world where we fucked yesterday but the terrorists were also here yesterday. There are infinite worlds with every form of me in it and infinite worlds without me in it.

And yet, Kate thought, if she could live her life again, this

Room 706

life, she would probably make every single decision the same. She'd have married Vic. She'd have taken the jobs she had taken. She'd have fucked James. She couldn't see any way in which anything could have been different.

There are worlds, Kate thought, where in a few moments I could cease to exist.

And there is a world, she thought, in which this all works out just fine.

Kate got off the bed and stood at its foot, looking down the small hallway towards the door. What would happen if she just walked out of it?

She really wanted to talk to Vic. She walked back to her spot between the wall and the bed and sat down in the gap.

Wish I could hear your voice, she sent Vic.

He replied immediately. *Call me.*

Police told me not to use phone.

I feel so impotent. I wish I could make you safe.

She wasn't sure what to write in response. *I love you*, she sent.

I could just talk to you and you not reply.

No. I'm scared.

Okay, we can just message, Vic wrote.

Yes please.

Do you remember how Nonna knew everything? Vic messaged.

She did remember. It was nice to think of Nonna now. Vic had chosen a good subject.

Yes.

Remember how she knew it was your birthday?

Kate had only been living in Nonna's apartment for a few weeks. She hadn't told anyone it was her birthday. Without her mum there to mark it, such an event seemed meaningless anyway.

But somehow Nonna had known, and during dinner that evening she had just announced it. 'It's your birthday,' she said. Vic look confused, questioning his understanding of the Italian words.

'Really?' he said. 'Your birthday? You didn't tell me.'

Kate had shrugged, embarrassed. 'It's not a big deal.'

And then Nonna had handed her a beautifully wrapped package. It contained a square of patterned silk in a flat box. It had seemed so grown up, so sophisticated.

Nonna gestured at the dishes. 'I will do these,' she said in Italian. And to Vic, 'You will take her dancing,' handing him a piece of paper with a nearby address on it – a bar with a dancefloor that neither of them had even known existed.

I wonder how Nonna knew, she messaged Vic back.

I don't know. She knew everything. She knew that you and I were meant to be together from the moment I brought you into her apartment. That's why she invited you to stay.

Kate still had that scarf, the square of silk. She'd worn it around her neck at Nonna's funeral.

She thought of Nonna standing in her kitchen, teaching Kate to make ravioli from scratch, showing her how much filling to put in, how hard to press her wooden-handled cutting wheel.

'She only lets people she really loves touch that,' Vic had said.

Room 706

Her phone flashed into life again. Maybe, she thought, maybe Vic was having the same memory at the same time, thinking of the ravioli too.

Hey lovely lady. Don't forget to give yourself the once-over and check for lumps and bumps.

It was her monthly reminder to check for breast cancer. She had signed up for it when Eve died, even though that hadn't been the type of cancer Eve had. It gave Kate a sense of control, and a feeling that she was doing something.

She swiped the reminder and dismissed it, just as another came up reminding her to log her Kegels. Three times a day she had to either log that she had done them, or the phone would remind her. *Squeeze squeeze squeeze, it's time to take care of your pelvic floor.*

The copywriter could have done a better job on that one, she thought. Instinctively, she clamped her vagina, counting to ten in her head. It reminded her that earlier in the day she had been having sex. She could still feel it. She did ten long squeezes and ten short ones, then checked the box on the app.

Chapter 40

Five years earlier
Italy

The plan was to give the kids their first taste of Italy with some late-summer sun just before Lenny started school. They'd started the trip with a two-day city break, pushing a double buggy around a too-hot Venice even though at four years old Lenny was too big and too heavy for the buggy. None of them had ever been to Venice before.

'Look at it Lennio. Isn't it beautiful?'

'People. Pigeons. Boats.'

'That's right Lenny. People. Pigeons. Boats.'

Cobbles, steps, bridges, she thought to herself, cursing the buggy for the umpteenth time that morning. Stop being grumpy, Kate told herself, and admire the people, the pigeons and the boats. Add buildings into the mix and he'd summed

Room 706

the whole place up. Not that they could do much other than absorb it all from the outside. The kids had no patience for galleries or nice restaurants. Still, just being there was a thrill and the hotel was nice and the coffee was strong and the pigeons, well they were Italian pigeons not British ones, so might as well have been exotic birds.

And now five nights at the beach, in a resort hotel, Venice itself so near yet so far. The hotel was mid-range and the four of them were sharing a room in a block five minutes' walk from the pool and bar area. Holiday resorts made Kate think of open prisons, not that she'd ever been in one. They'd had images of swimming in the warm sea and eating pasta together, then the kids napping at the same time as each other while Kate and Vic drank wine in the shade at the side of a beautiful piazza. The reality was a bit different. Infected mosquito bites, heat stroke, tantrums over sunscreen, nap times all over the place.

'We'll always have Venice,' Vic said to her as they scrabbled around for the right coins to buy a ball filled with plastic tat for each child from a vending machine.

'In memory,' said Kate, 'this will become a wonderful holiday. The kids will look at the photos and won't remember anything other than the image of them on the beach, chocolate ice cream all over their faces. They won't see the peeling skin, the bites, the sand in every imaginable fold of their bodies, the bags under my eyes. Annie won't remember the real thing at all, but you know what I think Lenny will remember?'

'What?'

'Being allowed his first ever fizzy drink, straight out of a glass bottle, on the beach.'

It had blown his mind. 'Bubbles. Bottle. Drink,' he had said delightedly over and over again.

'Thank you for booking everything,' Vic said. She inclined her head in acknowledgement. Not that Vic knew the half of the planning that went into holidays. She wanted to tell him how every holiday they ever had, even in the UK, was the result of hundreds of hours of research, before even getting to the actual packing and paperwork stage. All that booking the popular attractions in advance, the buying summer clothes in the right sizes and sunscreen that rubs in properly without causing a rash, and sticker books to use while waiting around for trains or planes, and the ointments and plasters and the just-in-case antibiotics she had procured from the GP for Annie's recurring earaches. The diarrhoea tablets and headache pills and antifungals and antihistamines. The paracetamol and the ibuprofen, adult and kid strengths. And then the negotiating on the size of the teddy that can fit in the suitcase and the *yes, we do have to take cardigans as it might be cold in the evening* and the *no, you can't take the very heavy set of building blocks even though you do like playing with them every day.*

What would happen if she did none of that, she sometimes wondered. Vic would probably just pack some T-shirts and underwear and they would all go and have the loveliest time and he'd think all the stress and all the planning and all that thinking she always did on the family's behalf before every

Room 706

trip was unnecessary. 'They have shops abroad you know, if we need anything,' he'd say.

Kate had barely thought of James while in Venice itself, but at the beach, as Vic splashed in the water with the kids and she watched from afar, she'd had a chance to reflect on the past year.

They'd met up four times since the book launch and each of these Kate thought that it would be the last. If she left the hotel thinking that was the end of this, then there was nothing ongoing, nothing to hide, nothing to worry about. But then, after a couple of months, James would send a suggested date to meet, or a diary invitation, and she'd say yes again.

The longer it goes on the more chance there is of getting caught, she thought. She'd end things soon. Maybe just one more meet-up then that was it, she'd tell him that she didn't want to do it again.

Except she did want to do it again. Sex with James felt like part of her self-care routine now. For days afterwards she'd be in a good mood, less resentful of time spent rushing home from work to make quick dinners and lying in the dark by the kids' beds, willing them to sleep. It was benefitting everyone really, she told herself.

The flight home from Italy was the first time both kids napped at the same time the whole holiday. Lenny had the window seat and Annie was in the middle, the armrest up and her head and arms on Kate's lap, gripping tightly onto Kate's skirt.

Vic sat on the aisle seat across from them. 'They are so

beautiful,' he said, looking over at their sleeping children. 'I can't believe Lenny will start school next week.'

'There was a pitch at work a couple of weeks ago,' Kate said. 'Someone wanted to write a *Hidden Depths* article on why you shouldn't tell your children too often that they are beautiful, as then they will grow up thinking that beauty matters.'

'And was it commissioned?' Vic asked.

'No. I successfully argued that it's a sorry state of affairs if a mother . . .' She looked at Vic. 'If a parent, I mean, can't tell their children they are beautiful.'

'I totally agree,' he said. 'We need to tell them so much that they just know it to be a truth. That doesn't mean we can't teach them other things are also important, that they should be kind to others and interested in the world, loyal and hardworking. Besides,' he said, nodding at their sleeping faces, 'they really are beautiful. Look at them.'

Kate studied her sleeping children. 'Yes, so beautiful.'

'And you know what?' said Vic.

She knew what. But she asked anyway. 'What?'

'We made them.'

'We did.'

At home the children ran around touching their things, as if they'd been away for months, not a single week.

'Look Mummy, my teddy. He is still here,' Lenny shouted delightedly as he went around the house checking every room.

Kate put the washing on, made a cup of tea and checked what time the supermarket delivery was coming that evening. Only later, when everyone else was in bed, did she look at her emails. She had another week off booked straight after this one so that she could take Lenny to school and pick him up each day of his first week, but preferred to check for any pressing messages now rather than wait for them to become urgent in a week's time.

A notification of a diary invitation popped up on the home screen. It was from James, four days ago. And in her inbox there was an actual message, sent two days later. *Are you okay? Are we okay? Just checking in.* He'd have got her out-of-office reply so she'd wait and reply in a week, she decided. Yes she wanted to see him, but she was sticking to her side of the bargain. She wasn't going to need him, or fall in love with him.

Chapter 41

10.05pm
Room 706

Kate needed the toilet. She couldn't hold it much longer. The bath was still full of water, the bubbles a grey scum. She dipped her hand in. It was cold.

The bathroom smelled of unflushed urine. She sat down on the toilet and tried to breathe through her mouth. She wiped and stood up, then without even thinking about it she flushed, realising what she had done the moment her hand left the metal lever, staring at the swirling water with horror.

'Kate!' James opened the bathroom door. He'd said her name in a whisper, but in an angry tone, as if he was yelling at her. His eyes and neck bulged and Kate could see he was trying not to lose his temper.

'I'm sorry. I'm sorry. I forgot.'

'You forgot? What bit? The terrorist bit? The keeping quiet bit? The fact they shot someone in the fucking hall bit?' He hissed the words at her.

'Shush. I'm sorry. It was instinct. I reached for the flush without thinking.'

The pipes had calmed and only a faint sound of them refilling was coming from the cistern.

James looked tired. His shirt was crumpled and his hair somehow looked greyer than it had this morning. She would no longer describe him as elegant.

They returned to the bedroom. James lay on the bed, his eyes closed. Kate took up her position between the other side of the bed and the floor. She decided to write an extra note to Vic and the kids. She ripped a page from the hotel notepad and carefully folded the top of it about one centimetre down, using her fingernail to go over the fold before carefully tearing the strip off, then writing on it.

Vic, Lenny, Annie. I love you all so much. Kate/Mummy xxx

She folded it up into the smallest shape she could and tucked it into her bra. Vic had once told her that it was impossible to fold a piece of paper in half more than seven times. They'd spent half an hour trying, but he was right. Something about diminishing surface area.

She remembered a woman that she'd met at a local playgroup who had once, over a cup of tea while the toddlers ran around, said that she could write a book about life through the prism of objects found in her bras over the years. A tenner for the cab home. A condom. Socks to increase a teenage bosom.

Drugs when she was a clubber. And nowadays breast pads for leaky nipples. She'd probably never considered including notes to loved ones during a terrorist attack, Kate supposed.

James's cross words over the flushed toilet were whizzing round her head. That was it, toilet roll. Toilet roll! That was on her shopping list. Thursday evenings were when she did the online shop, to be delivered the next evening. It was so routine that she didn't even need to have it on her to-do list. Taking in and putting away a supermarket delivery on a Friday night might not be everyone's idea of a fun way to start the weekend, she and Vic sometimes joked. But she liked it, waking up on Saturday morning knowing they had everything they needed. There were a few minutes left until the 10.20pm cut-off for the order. She logged in. It never stops, Kate thought to herself. Even now, waiting for the whoosh or boom or whatever noise it would be just before a bomb went off, she was doing the grocery shopping.

Her virtual trolley contained two bottles of champagne, put there as a placeholder, the easiest way to meet the minimum-spend threshold and reserve the delivery spot, even though they never drank champagne at home. She removed them. *Do you want to copy last week's order?* the website asked. What was in last week's order? She had no idea. She clicked yes, then had a look at the list it gave her. Not those sausages, no one had liked them. She took the sausages out of the virtual basket. No need for purple and green pre-made icing either – the Votes for Women cakes had gone down very well for Annie's class 'bring in food that represents famous people you admire' day, but she

Room 706

had no plan to make those again. The irony of the mum and daughter slaving all evening over suffragette cakes had not been lost on her. If she was to die – aargh, it was hard to unscramble her brain. She took a breath and tried the thought again. Right, if she was to die, Vic and the kids would need food. Everything else on the list seemed okay. What was it she had made a note of that morning? Oh yes, pearl barley, and ketchup had been on the list too. She added both of those and two multipacks of toilet roll.

Then she remembered the other kind of rolls. The bread rolls. Toilet rolls, bread rolls. Had Vic bought any of either? She searched the supermarket site for rolls and added a pack. The kids would need lunches next week regardless of what happened to her.

She clicked *Complete purchase*. The computer flashed at her: *Your purchase is complete. Do you want to reorder the same shopping for next week?* She thought about it. At some point, if she didn't make it, Vic would have to start doing the shopping himself. She clicked *No*.

She leaned back against the wall and closed her eyes. She felt overwhelmed by how much she missed Lenny and Annie already. When she opened them something had changed. The room suddenly seemed very quiet. She listened. There was nothing.

'Things feel different,' she said to James. 'Can you feel it?'

He opened his eyes and sat up. 'Yes.'

Kate looked around. Of course, it was darker. The lamp on the floor was no longer on.

The red standby light on the television had gone. The

continuous low buzz of the fridge wasn't there any more. Even the noises from the helicopters seemed a bit quieter.

'They've turned it off,' she said. 'They must have just done it. They,' she continued. 'I don't know who I even mean by that. Terrorists? Government? Does this mean the end is coming?'

'No, it means the electricity is off,' James said.

'How do you think they'll do it?' Kate asked.

'Who?' His voice sounded weak.

'I dunno. Whoever rescues us. Police? The Security Services? Special Forces?'

'Special Forces, I think.'

'Do you think there will be a shoot-out? How will we know the goodies from the baddies?'

James didn't answer. He shut his laptop and leaned back against the headboard, his head facing upwards.

Kate checked her phone. The hotel wifi no longer worked, but a pop-up message asked if she wanted to connect to the public wifi of the office block next door. She tapped *Connect* and held her breath. It worked. There was no new news.

'I wonder, will it be quick at the end? Or will there be confusion, fire, smoke, a hail of bullets?' Kate couldn't stop herself from speaking. It was all spilling out.

'I have no idea Kate. I don't imagine it will be that orderly.' He didn't move position or look at her.

Kate felt overwhelmed by the feeling that she barely knew this man.

'Am I the only one?' she asked James. She knew that she sounded mad but this suddenly mattered to her, urgently so.

Room 706

Now he turned to face her. 'What do you mean?'

'Do you fuck anyone else other than me?'

It came out quickly, like a demand. She needed to know. If James noticed the change of tone in her whisper, he ignored it.

'My wife.'

'Other than me and your wife?'

'No, there's only you. Only the two of you.'

The idea of James fucking anyone else other than his wife made her feel incandescent with jealousy. If this was the way things were going to end then she wanted to be someone specific, someone special, not one of a revolving cast of women any of whom could have been in this room, in this situation, with James. If they survived, she didn't want to be just some random woman in the retelling. Or perhaps his wife was in on the whole thing. Kate pictured James at a dinner party in his large house in a small village, a beautiful, elegant woman at his side. Bea. She had a posh English voice and she started regaling the room with the promise of a story. 'Let James tell you about the time he was caught up in a terrorist situation. Do you remember? It was the one in the London hotel. He was there with one of his many mistresses while I was in the United States working.' Imaginary Bea laughed and all their guests joined in.

'Kate?'

She snapped back from her imagined scene. Maybe she had fallen asleep for a moment. She was still hungry. Half a wrap had not been enough. She was cold too, and so tired. She yawned a huge yawn, so big that she could feel the stretch in her jaw, and at the corners of her mouth.

'Sorry, what?'

'I said no, that there are no others. You are my only lover.'

'Good.' She meant it.

'It's a strange thing to ask me right now though.' He gestured around the room. She shrugged in response.

'Are you jealous?' James asked. He looked almost amused.

Tears prickled at her eyes but she blinked them away. She was so tired. What had he asked her? Oh yes, was she jealous. She should answer him, she had raised it after all.

'No, I am not jealous. Not of your wife. I have my own husband. I love him. I like my life.' She took a deep breath and wiped her eyes before trying to answer again. 'I am not jealous of your wife, no. Maybe if there are others, other lovers, then yeah, but not your wife. But this, us, it's not that I want it to mean too much, but, you know, it has to mean something. If this is how things end, it has to have been for a reason.'

'A reason?'

'Yeah. There has to have been a real connection. Something special. Not just that we were there and bored and convenient for each other, you know.

James spoke slowly and deliberately, picking his words. 'Kate. I am not here with you because I was bored. Or because you were convenient. I like you. You captivate me. Since the very first time we met I felt a connection with you. I didn't meet you that first time looking for anything other than lunch and maybe some favourable coverage in your publication.'

'And the second time?'

Room 706

He paused for a moment then answered. 'The second time I hoped for more. There had been a connection, I was sure of it. I wanted to see you again.'

How was it they were only discussing this now? It was ridiculous.

'Did you fall in love with me?' Kate asked.

'No. It's different to that. But I wanted to be in your orbit. I wanted to touch you. Every time I have seen you I have felt, as soon as I left, the desire to see you again.'

That sounded a lot like love to Kate. It was certainly how she felt about Vic, how she had always felt about Vic. Had she felt that about James? She thought so, but it was hard to remember now. There must have been something, she must have felt something, to have let things happen, to have done it repeatedly. She tried to think back to how she felt even just that morning, how exciting it was going to meet James, the anticipation of touching him and how it felt once she was in the room and able to actually do so.

They were quiet for a couple of minutes until James spoke again: 'Of course if I did have other lovers I wouldn't tell you.'

Kate lifted her head to look at him. 'Excuse me?'

'It's why you've chosen me isn't it, because of my discretion?'

Chapter 42

Two years earlier

'What happens when you die?' Annie asked. She'd been asking several times a day for weeks. Kate changed her answer depending on the day, fighting back her own tears. 'I don't know.' 'Nothing happens.' 'You fly away.' 'You return to dust.'

Images of her mum and of Eve came into her mind and she concentrated on pushing them away, staring at an area of chipped paintwork on the wall of Annie's bedroom.

'Sweet dreams, darling. Don't think about it. Don't make yourself sad.'

But Annie never was sad about death. She was curious.

When you get asked a question and you don't know the answer, then throw it back at whoever has asked it, said Eve's voice in her head. Kate remembered Eve saying this in real life

Room 706

too, in the hospice, that all her questions about death were just thrown back at her.

'What do you think, sweetheart?'

Annie was too clever for this though. 'I'm asking you, Mummy.'

Annie was obsessed with all death, not just her own. Flowers. People. Ants.

'Where do we even come from?' she'd ask.

'I don't know, my love, but it's bedtime now.'

Lenny had been obsessed with death too, for a time. Kate remembered as she lay in the dark next to Annie's bed, stroking her hand. She remembered him, aged three, noticing some decaying bluebells on a walk to the library, and obsessing about them in the middle of the night.

'Where do the dead ones go Mummy?'

'The dead what?'

'The dead flowers. The blue ones.'

'It's 3.30am. Not now Lenny, please not now.'

'But Mummy, I just want to know, what does it feel like to be dead?'

Kate thought urgently. What would make him go back to sleep? 'Do you remember what it felt like before you were born?'

'No.'

'It feels like that.'

'But what does that feel like?'

'It feels like lying in the park with the sun on your face knowing Papa will be back in a few minutes with a treat from the shop.'

'That sounds nice Mummy,' Lenny said.

And then he'd turned over and gone back to sleep. Just like that. One moment an existential crisis, one moment fast asleep. And what did it matter anyway, Kate thought, when exactly you die? You live five years, thirty years, fifty years, a hundred years. In the history of the universe it's nothing. Like that meme that circulated every so often showing how if the world was a day old then dinosaurs only became extinct in the last hour.

She remembered another fact she had seen online somewhere. A million seconds is eleven days, a billion seconds is over thirty-one years.

'I love you hundreds and thousands,' Lenny would say when they decorated their homemade fairy cakes, inspired by the jar of sugar strands.

'I love you millions and billions,' Kate would reply. That was the way it should be, her love for them way outnumbering their love for her. One two loads. Hundreds thousands millions billions.

Last term Annie's class project had been 'My family'. She'd been sent home with the outline of a family tree to fill out, as well as a worksheet called *Families come in all shapes and sizes*. The two seemed slightly contradictory, Kate thought. Your family must fit neatly into a tree. Yet your family can be anything.

Annie had sat at the kitchen table, concentrating hard, her pen hovering over the space on the tree for kids to fill out their parents' names.

'What's your full name Mummy?'

Room 706

'Catherine Rachel Bright.'
'But everyone calls you Kate?'
'Yes, different people call me different things.'
'Who calls you Catherine?'
'The government, and banks. Official people.'
'The police?'
'Yes, I suppose so.'
'What do I call you?'
'Mummy.'
'What did your Mummy call you?'
'Usually Kate, sometimes Katie.'
'Why doesn't Papa call you that?'
Because I reinvented myself as a grown-up, Kate thought.
'Papa calls me lots of things.'
'Like what?'
'Sometimes he calls me Kate. Sometimes darling. Sometimes KitKat.'
'That's funny.'
'I suppose it is.'
'What's my full name?'

Chats with Annie were rarely so linear. She was approaching the age now where she could hold a thought and really mull over its implications. So much better than the *why why why* stage, even when conversations seemed to go on forever.

'You know your full name, darling.'
'Annie Giulia Evelyn Mariani.'
'That's right.'
'Why am I called Annie?'
'Because I love the name.'

'Why am I called Giulia?'
'After Nonna, Papa's grandmother.'
'Did I ever meet her?'
'No, sweetheart. She died before me and Papa got married.'
'Why am I called Evelyn?'
'After my friend Eve, who you never met.'
'Did she die too?'
'Yes.'
'Did you have a cat called Annie?'
'No.'
'A dog?'
'No.'
'Was your Mummy called Annie?'
'No.'
'What about a dolly?'
'I don't remember the names of any of my dollies, so probably not.'
'Why do you love the name?'
'I just do. It sounds right. You came out of my tummy and I looked at you and thought yes, your face is just perfect for this name I have always loved my whole life.'
'Just like you have loved me my whole life.'
'Yes, exactly like that.'

She and Vic hadn't been sure about actually using the name. Was it weird to give a child a name meaning grace and elegance? That was surely setting her up for a fall.

'Are we overthinking this?' she'd asked Vic.

'There's no such thing as overthinking,' Vic had replied.

Room 706

Lenny had been easy to name. Vic had said it early in the pregnancy. 'If it's a boy, I would like to call him Leonardo.'

'Why?'

'Because I like it. I like it so much that when I was allowed a kitten as a child I called it Leonardo.'

That was why Annie was so obsessed with whether she too was named after a cat.

'Just to be clear, Lenny is not named after a cat,' Vic said, walking into the room and joining in with the conversation. 'Lenny and Leonardo the cat were both named after the same thing. That is different.'

'What thing?' asked Annie.

'Leonardo,' Vic said, enveloping her in a hug, 'means brave as a lion. And though I may look like a pussy cat, and though Leonardo the pussy cat was in fact a pussy cat, inside we all, me and Leonardo the pussy cat and Lenny Leonardo your brother, and even you though it is not your name, are lions.'

'Does Annie mean lion?'

'No. You are a secret lion. There are no clues in your name to your fierceness. In fact in some languages your name means grace. Your name,' Vic told her, 'means that even though you have the power to hurt someone, you will be kind to them and love them unconditionally. That,' he said, 'is even stronger than a lion.'

And he roared and pretended to eat her tummy as Annie laughed and pretended to fight him off.

Chapter 43

12.46am
Room 706

Eve was back.

Tell me about him.

Sorry?

You were going to tell me more about him before you got distracted. You know what to do. Say anything you want and just speak until you have nothing left to say.

I don't really know what to say. We met through work. I told you that already. He's posher than me. He's funny, sexy. I don't know. Something clicks with us, physically. Sometimes I don't even know if I like him, but there's a chemistry there. He's totally different to Vic.

Eve's voice said nothing.

Room 706

It's not really an affair. There's no emotion. We don't have any contact in between, you know.

More silence.

No honestly, we don't have deep and meaningfuls. We, well, we fuck. We make each other feel good. We go home.

Is he married?

Yes.

Does Vic know?

You asked me this already Eve, a few hours ago.

Well, you've had a lot of time to think since then. Do you think he'll leave you, if you make it home?

The idea of that happening hit Kate like a tsunami. Her head went fuzzy. For a moment she thought she might black out. When she regained the ability to form words in her head, Eve was still there.

These aren't the rules, Eve. The rules are we let the other one speak and no questions until the end.

Okay.

James stood up and stretched and Eve's voice disappeared from Kate's head. She watched him for a bit as he put his arms over his head and leaned his body in each direction. He put his arms out and rotated his torso from side to side then put each foot in turn on top of the bed and balanced. His movements distracted her. He was probably right to stretch like that. Her body felt incredibly stiff and tense.

She wanted to know more about this man she was trapped with. She wondered where he had grown up, shocked she didn't know this already. She barely knew him. He barely knew her. She didn't even know whether he even knew what her kids were called or how old they were. Annie was only one when they met again at the book launch. She couldn't not have ever mentioned their names, she was sure. Then again, she didn't know the name of his stepson either.

'My kids are called Lenny and Annie,' she said.

'Okay.' James looked a bit confused.

'What is your stepson called?'

'James.'

'James?'

'Yes. He was called that before I met Bea. It wasn't deliberate, just coincidence.'

'Oh. Is he ever Jim? Or Junior? Or another version of James?'

'No.'

'Or you? Maybe you are the Jim.'

She was babbling. And besides, he didn't look like a Jim. James eyed her warily.

'Where are you from?' Kate asked.

'From?'

'Yeah. Where did you grow up? She let out an inadvertent high-pitched laugh. James gave her a look but didn't shush her. She was feeling slightly hysterical, like the whole set up was just a scene in a situation comedy. She just needed the audience to laugh and then she could laugh herself.

There is no audience Kate, she told herself. And this is real. Very fucking real.

'I'm from Somerset,' he said.

'Tell me something interesting about Somerset.'

Room 706

James thought for a moment. 'It has more thankful villages than any other county in England.'

'What's a thankful village?'

'Villages where no one died in the First World War. Everyone who left to fight came home again.'

'Oh. Wow.'

'There are two doubly thankful villages there too. They lost no one in the Second World War either.'

'Are you from a thankful village?'

'No. You just wanted a fact.'

'It's a good one. I'll file it away for the future.'

She knew she sounded snippy. She couldn't help it.

'I'm not even from there really,' James said. 'It's just where my parents lived for the longest. They moved around for my father's work.'

'Oh.' Kate felt a bit disappointed by that.

She didn't like how brusque she was sounding, but his normality was annoying her. Why had she risked everything for this man, who didn't even come from anywhere, who was just as ordinary and boring as anyone else?

'Have you got any siblings?'

'No.'

How many more questions could she get away with asking? What had his parents done for work? Did he get on well with them? Were they still alive? When is his birthday?

He hadn't asked her where she was from. Not that the answer was interesting. Grew up in London. Returned to London. Likely to die in London. What was that statistic she'd read? They rolled it out every ten years at census time. The majority of people die within twenty miles of where they are born, something like that.

The background on Kate's phone caught her eye. It was a photo of her and Vic last year at a village fete, holding a foot-long hotdog on a cardboard tray, sausage poking out of either end. Their niece, Clara, was home for a visit from her studies and they'd all gone into the countryside together for a walk – Tom, Polly, Clara, Vic, Kate, Lenny and Annie, stumbling across the most English of scenes. There was a dog show, a cake competition, giant vegetables, bouncy castles and local bands. They'd immediately abandoned their plans for a pub lunch in favour of the festivities. Vic's hand was outstretched, making sure the middle of their hotdog didn't collapse, and their faces were side on, their mouths open like crocodiles about to take a bite. The picture did neither of them any favours, with their mouths wide open in profile, but she loved it anyway. It was so full of joy. At her end there was a neat line of ketchup and a few onions spread along the top. Vic's half was piled high with ketchup, mustard, a brown sauce of indeterminate nature and onions falling all over the tray. She remembered Vic laughing at her before asking 'Do you want a knife and fork with that?' as Tom insisted they pose like this for a photo, framed by a line of bunting. You could see the kids in the background, almost eclipsed by a giant stick of candyfloss. Vic had really gone for it, sauce all over his beard. The whole scene was a snapshot of a happy family. It was hard to believe that she'd ever worried Vic wouldn't cope with being a dad. They'd fed the leftovers

Room 706

to the gulls hovering nearby, even though there was no sea within thirty miles.

'Careful Squawky,' Vic had said to one as it swallowed a chunk of smoked sausage down in one go. 'It'll bring about an early end.'

Chapter 44

2.53am
Room 706

Kate sat up straight. She could have sworn she'd heard noises somewhere. Not near their room, but not from outside either. She strained to hear but all her brain could focus on under pressure was the noise of a helicopter, to which she had grown so accustomed during the past twelve hours that isolating it as a sound was now difficult, and she did not know whether it was even real or not. She heard the noise again, a kind of dull thud, more than one, somewhere below them.

'James,' she said softly. He was lying on the bed, his eyes closed, but sat up immediately she said his name, completely alert.

'Can you hear that?' she said quietly.

He listened.

Room 706

'No.'

She listened again too. There was nothing.

He lay back down.

Another message came from Vic. *How is everything?*

Poor Vic, he must be exhausted. She wanted to tell him it was okay, he could go to sleep, either she'd still be here in the morning, or she wouldn't. He didn't have to stay up messaging her.

No, she didn't really want to say that. She desperately wanted him to stay up messaging her.

The same, she replied.

What are you doing?

Nothing. Time passes, Kate replied.

At what speed?

He was misquoting Beckett. So was she. Which one? *Endgame?* No, *Waiting for Godot*.

She sent back a shrug emoji then immediately followed it with another message.

How are the kids?

Sleeping, Vic replied. *Annie's in our bed.*

I wish I could speak to them.

A moment later she messaged Vic again. *What about you? Are you okay?*

He replied. *Yes. No. Ish.* And a moment later, *Tom's here.*

Of course Tom was there. Tom was Vic's life support. She should have known Vic would call Tom and that he would dash to his side. She was pleased that he was there for him.

Don't hurt him. She heard Tom's voice from the day she first met him in Italy, years ago.

I'll try.

Had she tried? She didn't know. She hadn't actively tried to hurt him. But had she tried hard enough not to hurt him?

Kate's head pounded. It was almost 3am. Surely Special Forces wouldn't launch a rescue operation at this time. They'd wait until morning. Maybe she should try to get some sleep. Or maybe they'd count on the terrorists thinking that, so they would do it now to take them by surprise. Bluff bluff double bluff. What about the terrorists? They wouldn't bomb the place with the markets closed, would they? Wasn't terrorism about economics as much as anything else? She wondered if the terrorists had brought food with them or whether they'd got the hotel chefs to make them something. She'd love some room service herself. A burger maybe, or some breakfast pancakes.

She suddenly felt an overwhelming need to know what Vic had said to the man on the jetty many years ago, when she was pregnant with Annie. She remembered seeing him kiss the man on the forehead when the ambulance doors opened. Why had she never asked him before now? It had seemed sacred somehow, a moment between two men. She'd sensed that he had never wanted to speak about it and, until now, she had respected that.

She picked up her phone and typed a message. *Do you remember the man on the jetty, who you saved?*

Vic replied immediately. *Of course.*

Why was he there? What did you say to him?

It took slightly longer for Vic to reply this time. She supposed he was thinking about his answer.

Room 706

He wanted to die because he was frightened to die. I told him what we were going to have for dinner, that you were pregnant, that I was hoping for a girl, that I used to feel the same way. It wasn't that logical, it was whatever came into my head.

Do you ever think of him? Kate sent back.

Every day. Another quick answer.

Think, Kate told herself. Think. What is it you want to tell Vic? This is the end. What do you want him to know? She messaged Vic again. *I love you so much. I love the children so much. Say sorry to them from me.*

Her phone flashed. She expected it to be Vic. It was Tom.

Kate. Shit. Can I do anything?

It was to the point.

What could she say? She appreciated that he didn't ask her anything direct about the situation or why she was there.

She quickly replied to his message.

A bit scared. Not sure how this is going to end. Am emailing you some info in case Vic ever needs it.

She sent the message before she could change her mind.

Of course she could send info to Tom. She should have thought of that before.

She reached for her laptop and started an email. She wrote down everything she could think of, taking care to keep the noise of the keys as quiet as possible. James was lying on the bed again. He opened his eyes for a moment then closed them.

'It's okay,' Kate said. 'Nothing is happening.'

She wrote down everything she could think Vic might need. The supermarket password. The online banking login. That the life-insurance details were in a folder on the shared drive, in case Vic forgot. That her mother's jewellery – nothing valuable – was in the wooden inlaid box in her bedside drawer and was all earmarked for Annie, as was hers. That she'd bought the expensive doll for Annie's Christmas present and that they still needed to buy Lenny's big present and that Vic knew all this but might need reminding. She told him that she had emailed Vic about paying the balance of their holiday. That if she died he must make sure Vic knew he had her blessing to meet someone else. She wrote it all down, gave it a subject of *Just in case* and pressed send.

She didn't know why she was so worried. He could work all that out if he needed. Passwords could be reset. Documents could be ordered. Bills came with reminders. And when she wasn't there the kids were always fed and dressed, even if it wasn't exactly how she would do it. He knew that birthdays and Christmas need presents and cake. He'd even managed to pick up Fluffy this evening.

Life will go on, Kate thought, whether I am here to be part of it or not. The thought was as comforting as it was upsetting. It was over fifteen years since he'd had his burnout and he wasn't the same man he was when they met. She wasn't that young woman either.

We'll reset, she promised herself. If I make it home we'll reset, two equally capable adults.

Tom replied to her email within the minute. *Roger that.*

Like brother like brother, she thought.

Would Tom work out the real reason she was in the hotel?

Room 706

She wasn't sure. Would he tell Vic if he did? Of that she was more sure. He wouldn't do anything to hurt Vic.

Would Vic stop loving her if he found out? She didn't know. Would she stop loving him if it was the other way round? She didn't think so. Would she even be cross? She tried to imagine it, Vic with another woman in a hotel room. She tried to imagine what it would feel like, whether she would be hurt or relieved, whether it would absolve her own guilt.

There was no order to her thoughts now. She tried to quiet her racing brain for a bit but it wasn't working. Maybe she should confess all in an email to Vic scheduled to send later, that she could delete if she survived. But what if she didn't die? What if she was merely incapacitated in hospital, or with amnesia after a blast? She'd be alive to face the consequences. Admit nothing, she thought to herself, then there's a chance he will never find out.

You spend the whole affair trying to cover your tracks, ensuring no giveaways in diaries, no receipts, no gifts, no cards, no miniature toiletries given to your young daughter from hotels you shouldn't have been in. Write nothing down. Leave no trace. And yet now she had a sudden urge to write it down. If no one knows then it didn't happen. But that's what she wanted, wasn't it? No one to know.

Stop it Kate, you can't have it both ways. You want him to know or you don't. It's like 'Would you rather?' she thought. It was a game that had obsessed Lenny for a while. Would you rather be a cat or a dog? Would you rather not be able to stand up or not be able to sit down? Would you rather be too hot or too cold? Would you rather die but be remembered as a faithful wife or live and be known as a cheat? Live, of course, but what a choice. Or maybe it didn't matter anyway. Maybe there was another option. That everything might be true at once. That she was a faithful wife and also a cheat. That he might know and choose not to know. That as long as she loved him, and he loved her, none of it mattered.

You're always told that the world doesn't centre around you, Kate thought. But in a world of eight billion people, there are eight billion worlds each centred around one person. How many worlds in this hotel alone?

Sonder. It was a voice in her head. Vic's voice.

What?

No, it wasn't Vic's voice. It was like his though. Maybe Tom's. Certainly someone related to them. Maybe it was how Lenny would sound when he was grown up.

The voice continued. *Every room. Every holiday maker. Every business person. Every middle-aged wife and mother there fucking her lover. They all have their own complex lives that have led them to that room in this hotel on this day.*

When she was at school, aged about thirteen or fourteen, they'd been studying explorers and had been told to write a story as if they were on an expedition to the North Pole. Kate had loved it, embracing the diary-writing exercise with relish. *We were hungry but luckily an Arctic hare came by and we caught it and skinned it and made a stew. We were hungry again by morning but luckily another Arctic hare came by, so we did the same.*

She'd got a D. 'Too many coincidences,' her teacher had

Room 706

said. It had bothered Kate for years. Didn't it make sense that if there was one hare then there would be another, and if the first stew was delicious then they'd make it again? But more to the point, Kate thought now, isn't everything in life a coincidence, the random alignment of objects, events and feelings? Every meal, every smile, every baby conceived, every hare made into a stew? Another hotel or another day and she'd have been home in time to turn off the slow cooker and eat dinner with Vic and the kids.

She thought of the Arctic hare, and the stew. What would she write now, if this was an exercise in class? She could hear the teacher's voice. It was a soft voice, friendly, firm and kind. 'Write the end of a story where you are trapped in a hotel room with a lover who is not your husband, and the hotel is controlled by terrorists who may kill you if they find you, and may blow you up even if they don't find you.'

Could the fact they were both in this hotel be a coincidence?

At the end of the day everything was down to chance, wasn't it? A car not signalling. A cell dividing incorrectly. Choosing the wrong hotel on the wrong day. Her mum dying, Eve getting cancer, her hotel being taken over by terrorists. It was all just bad luck.

But chance happenings led to wonderful things too. Her and Vic both going to the cinema that day. That specific sperm meeting that specific egg not just once, but twice, making the two glorious children she was lucky enough to call her own.

KitKat, are you ok?

Vic was messaging again.

KitKat. He hadn't called her that for a long time.

Not really, she replied.

I know. What can I do?

She didn't know what he could do. She was the one having a crisis. Surely now was the time for him to work out how to help her.

No, that wasn't fair. There was nothing he could do. He should have chosen a wife who would be faithful, who wouldn't end up in this situation.

I'm scared, she wrote.

I know. I am too.

Of course, this wasn't just her crisis.

Selfish to the end, Kate thought, that's me.

God, she loved this man. She loved how he loved her, how he loved their children.

Remember the first time we met? At the cinema? Vic messaged.

Vic was typing more. She could tell by the flashing dots on her phone.

Yes, she typed.

The seat next to you, that genuinely was my seat. But when I came in the staff said to me I could sit anywhere. I knew it might be weird, sitting next to you in an otherwise empty cinema. But you looked around as I walked in and something drew me to you.

I bet you wish you hadn't now, Kate sent back.

Of course not. I couldn't believe my luck when you responded to my clumsy attempt at conversation. I still can't really believe it.

Room 706

Kate turned her phone over a few times in her hands. It felt heavy.

I need you, she sent him.

I am here, he sent back.

Kate tried to focus on her breathing. She took air in through her nose and out through her mouth. It wasn't working. She felt the panic rising.

I need distracting, she sent Vic.

Just a few breaths later, his next message came through.

You're sixty-eight. Where are you?

She thought about it. Sixty-eight. Grown-up children. Maybe grandchildren. Verging on the cusp of old age, Vic there already.

We're in Italy, at our beach. Tomorrow the kids are coming with their families to the villa we've rented, and we'll have prepared the nicest lunch to welcome them. But today it is just us, still laughing at people who have paid to watch the sunset.

Nice, Vic messaged back. *Your turn.*

Kate appreciated the distraction, even whilst knowing that's what it was.

Should she go older or younger? She suddenly felt the need to know more about young Vic.

Seventeen.

Vic's reply took a few moments for him to type. *I went to the party of a boy at school called Robert. His parents were the opposite of mine, very cool. They supplied the beer. And a girl, whose name I weirdly can't remember, Carrie or Coral or something like that, came over to me and asked for some of my beer and then leaned over and kissed me. It was my first kiss, it was nice. The week after, she started dating Robert.*

Kate had heard this before. What was Carrie or Coral doing now? She twisted her rings – Nonna's wedding ring, now hers, and her engagement ring that they had chosen together.

Forty-three, he sent her.

Forty-three, that would be in six years' time. Lenny would be fifteen. Annie would be thirteen. Dead, Kate thought. I'll be dead and forgotten, just one casualty from the Great Hotel Incident that preceded the Second War on Terror.

Play the game, Kate. If she wasn't dead, where would she be? She thought about it, then typed.

In our life, but everyone is a bit older than now. The kids are a bit easier. My hair is a bit greyer. You look exactly the same. Nothing much has changed except we're older. Your turn: six.

It took Vic a while to respond. Kate reread her previous answer. It was true, that was exactly where she wanted to be when she was forty-three. Vic had posted a heart emoji on the message.

Kate picked her fingernails while she waited for his reply. When it arrived it was a long one.

I'm in hospital. I tripped over at school and cut my chin on a table leg and now I am having to be stitched up while a teacher holds my hand and we wait for my mother to arrive. The doctor is very kind and she tells me I will have a scar but that they have made it as neat as possible, and that when I

Room 706

am a man my beard will cover it. My mother and Tom arrive and he hands me a square of chocolate krispie cake wrapped in a blue paper towel that he has procured for me from school lunch. It's our favourite and they only have it every few weeks. The doctor says I can eat it so I do, there and then. Even the bits of paper towel stuck to it are delicious.

Kate's nose felt heavy as she read the message. Her eyes brimmed with tears. She wanted to cuddle six-year-old Vic so much. She thought of nine-year-old Lenny and seven-year-old Annie. She wanted to cuddle them all, at every age. Six-year-old Vic. Seven-year-old Vic. Eight-year-old Vic. Every age Vic. She wanted to see his scar and touch it. She couldn't believe she had never heard this story before. She knew about the scar and the stitches, but not about the krispie cake, about the paper towel.

There was that noise again, the thud, louder this time. The sound was real, she was sure of it, coming from somewhere below them. She saw James hear it and every muscle in his body tense. There were voices as well, shouting, too muffled to even make out what language it was.

'Do you think it's Special Forces?' Kate whispered.

'I'm not sure,' James said, moving into a sitting position.

He silently got up and took the glass ashtray from the desk, before coming to sit next to her in the space between the bed and the wall. They wouldn't be hidden if anyone entered the room, but they wouldn't be seen from the doorway either. Kate scanned the room wondering whether they should have made it completely tidy and hidden all their belongings, moving the chair and stool from the door, so that it would look at first glance to be unoccupied. They probably should have done just that, she thought. But it was too late now.

The noises were definitely getting louder. It sounded like they were on the floor below. They had a rhythm to them. Bang bang, shout. Bang bang, shout. Like doors were being forced open with battering rams. There was a word they were saying each time. She listened hard. It was like hearing noises under water. Maybe they were talking through respirators. That would make sense if they were Special Forces. God, did that mean they were using gas? Bang bang, shout. They were getting closer. She heard it again. *Clear.* The word was *Clear.* That had to be rescuers, surely? But what if she was wrong? She put her hand in her bra and checked for the folded bit of paper telling Vic and the kids that she loved them. It was still there.

James was very still. His breathing was controlled. His eyes were shut. He held the ashtray tightly. It didn't seem like much of a weapon but it was all they had. This was it then, the end of their situation one way or another, no matter who was at the door when it was forced open. What would happen then? Hands up, she knew that much from films. Show your hands. Show you are unarmed. Stay on the floor. No sudden movements. She could do this, she just had to stay calm.

Her phone flashed in her lap and she picked it up. Vic. *Your turn. Ninety-two.* He was still playing their game, still trying to distract her.

Ninety-two. It was almost unimaginable. And yet also entirely imaginable. She pictured his face in her mind, remembering how it felt to touch her hand to his cheek, the

Room 706

bristles of his beard, the warmth of his skin. She thought about the smell of him when he pulled her in for a hug. The knocks were so close now. They'd reached the room next door. Bang bang. 'Clear.' Their room was next, any moment now. She took a deep breath and typed quickly.

I'm 92. You're 102. We're the happiest old couple in our retirement village.

Acknowledgements

The hugest thanks and admiration to Felicity Blunt, Flo Sandelson, Emma Walker, Sophie Baker, Katie Harrison and all at Curtis Brown, and to Sarah Fuentes at UTA. Without you there would be no book. Also to Jen Doyle, Jessie Goetzinger-Hall, Louise Swannell, Katrina Smedley, Isabel Martin and the team at Headline, and Lexy Cassola, Molly Stern, Sarah Jessica Parker and their teams at Zando. To work with so many clever and enthusiastic women has been a joy. Thank you also to Samantha Stewart, and to the translators and teams who have worked on international versions of this book.

Also to friends in books who have held my hand at various stages – Jenny Jacoby, Laura Shepherd-Robinson, Lisa India Baker and Sarah Ruddick, as well as Ruth Dugdall, who gave me invaluable advice in the early stages after I 'won' her at an auction, as did Sarah Simpson and Hilary Murray Hill. And all the editors and agents I did not end up working with but who gave such generous and thoughtful feedback along the way.

Thank you to all of my friends for being supportive when I talked yet again about how I was writing a novel, with extra thanks to my early readers for their comments on drafts – Anne Alexander, Ellen O'Donoghue, Emmanuelle Smith (who is also my endlessly patient grammar guru), Iain Hollingshead (who astutely pointed out that Christmas belongs to Bethlehem rather than the North Pole), Jane Clay, Sara Simpson (not the same one as above, the H matters) and Sarah Cousins. And also, for their particular help and encouragement, thank you to Claire Kober, Dan Fox, Julie Lovell, Kate Hilpern, Luce Brett, Lucy Openshaw, Matthew Carlile, Rebecca Bream and Thea Sherer. In addition, gratitude to others who hopefully know who they are but prefer not to be named.

To my book-club women – Gillian Duncan, Helen Nadin, Jane Clay, Jess Asato, Katy Smawfield, Rachel Miles, Sarah Cousins, Vicky Lacey and the much-missed Cath Dean – I wrote this for tired but clever women everywhere, but especially for us.

I'd also like to acknowledge all the articles, books, poems, conversations and activities that have inspired elements of this book. This includes a piece many years ago in which a columnist, whose name I now forget, suggested following a family across a city and being in the background of every one of their holiday snaps, and also my friend Sarah who agreed to play the 'people to talk about' game many years ago when we were backpacking. It also includes John Koenig, inventor of many words including the wonderful 'sonder'. And thank you to the excellent CoppaFeel! breast cancer awareness charity, whose monthly alerts inspired those my character Kate has signed up to receive.

Thank you also to my parents, Howard and Ros, for endless love and endless books.

And always, for everything, my husband Richard, and our three wonderful children who are, of course, greater than the sum of their parts.

Author's note

The idea for *Room 706* came to me when I was in the throes of parenting small children.

As truly grateful as I was to have them, I also yearned to have some time when no one made any demands on me, where I could take a moment to think, knowing I would not be interrupted, or even go to the toilet by myself with the door closed. I dreamed about going to a hotel, alone, just to enjoy the peace and quiet of my own room.

When I told people about this fantasy, mothers of young children would often confess to similar thoughts. However, other people asked if what I really meant was that I wanted time in a hotel with a lover. That's when I realised that for many the idea of a mother going to a hotel with a lover was almost more socially acceptable than going by herself.

I have also long been fascinated by the messages people

leave when they know they are going to die, including the notes and voicemails left by victims of the 2001 attacks on the US, such as those who were trapped in the World Trade Center towers, and those on United Airlines Flight 93 that crashed into a field in Pennsylvania. The notes that have been made public all boil down to one thing – telling people that they loved them.

And as a lecturer in journalism for many years, and an avid reader of magazines and newspaper features, I became struck by how many articles I would read along the lines of how to get your lover out of your mind, or how to make your lover leave their spouse. I taught feature writing to aspiring journalists, including how to come up with ideas for articles, and one of the things I always told students was to turn ideas around. If they read an article on how to get your lover to leave their spouse, then they should consider writing an article on how to ensure your lover does not leave their spouse.

These thoughts all came together in the idea of Kate and James, lovers who are both happily married to other people. They do not want each other to leave their partners, and know that any relationship beyond a sexual one would be a non-starter. Their affair has the potential to continue for years, with no one finding out and neither party attempting to make it anything more than what it is. Except that a *force majeure* happens – an event beyond their control. They have to contend with wondering whether to confess why they are caught up in this to their respective spouses, while their lives flash before their eyes, though the flashing is slow and the wait somewhat long.

Room 706

It was also important to me that Kate is a woman with few friends. Her best friend and her mum are dead. The person to whom she tells everything is her husband, who, for obvious reasons, she cannot tell about this. I wanted Kate to have no one to call, so that she turns inward instead, to examine her own life.

But although a major event is happening to Kate, one that may ruin her marriage and even end her life, when Kate reflects on all of the choices that got her to this point, she concludes that she would make all the same decisions again. In part this is her acceptance – or perhaps her way of absolving herself from responsibility for her affair – that whatever decisions she makes, the universe will do its thing anyway. This applies both to her, and to everyone else, whose lives are just as complex as her own – hence the word *sonder*, which grabbed me from the moment I first saw it as a meme, from John Koenig's word project, *The Dictionary of Obscure Sorrows*. The website version of this definition is reproduced at the beginning of *Room 706*, and later by Vic as a new word he has discovered.

I had been playing with these ideas for a while, but it's probably no coincidence that I actually wrote the first few lines of the manuscript on my laptop when I was on a weekend away with friends in late 2018, to visit one of our group who lives in Cyprus, and knowing that another of our party had terminal cancer and was nearing the end of her life. Our thoughts were focused on making the most of this time together, and what you do when you know you are going to die soon. It was also the first time I had been in a different country to my children, and I had my own anxieties about that, and how the universe may punish me for having fun without them.

My progress was slow and I told myself that I would wait until my youngest child had started school and then take a year to give writing a novel a go around my lecturing jobs. Except the pandemic happened. I spent a year stymied by that, and then a year working on another project. Finally, I told myself that it was time to do it seriously. That's when key parts of the book came into being, particularly the many games Kate likes to play, from the alphabet game with her daughter to the talking about friends when travelling with Eve (based on a version of this my friend Sarah and I played when backpacking together in 2000) and the describing scenes from the past and future with Vic. It was these games that helped me to work out what Kate ultimately wants to happen. It is only at the end of the book – and potentially the end of Kate's life, depending on whether it is terrorists or Special Forces that they are hearing at the end – that Kate has a clear vision of what her future should be. As such I think *Room 706* is as much a love story as anything else.